Praise for
KATHERINE HALL PAGE's
Agatha Award-winning
FAITH FAIRCHILD MYSTERIES

"Fun."
Denver Rocky Mountain News

"Fresh . . . distinctively different."
Ft. Lauderdale Sun-Sentinel

"Tightly written, with strong characterizations
and delightful descriptions
of its New England setting."
Publishers Weekly

"Page is known for leavening her work
with humor and warmth."
Boston Herald

"Satisfying and surprisingly delicious."
Los Angeles Times

"Enchanting . . . well-written. . . . Page's style
is entertaining and unpretentiously cultured."
Portland Press Herald

"Faith Fairchild . . . is a better detective than most . . .
and her plots actually have some
steak with the sizzle."
Toronto Globe & Mail

KATHERINE HALL PAGE

The BODY in the KELP

A FAITH FAIRCHILD MYSTERY

AVON BOOKS

An Imprint of HarperCollinsPublishers

AVON BOOKS
An Imprint of HarperCollins*Publishers*
10 East 53rd Street
New York, New York 10022-5299

"A Thomas Dunne book"
Copyright © 1991 by Katherine Hall Page
Excerpts copyright © 1990, 1991, 1991, 1992, 1993, 1994, 1996, 1997, 1998, 1999 by Katherine Hall Page
Published by arrangement with St. Martin's Press
ISBN: 0-380-71329-2
www.avonmystery.com

First Avon Books paperback printing: March 1992

Avon Trademark Reg. U.S. Pat. Off. and in Other Countries, Marca Registrada, Hecho en U.S.A.
HarperCollins® is a trademark of HarperCollins Publishers Inc.

Printed in the U.S.A.

20 19 18 17 16 15 14

For my mother and father, Alice and William Page,
who first brought me to the island

Acknowledgments

The author would like to acknowledge the advice and encouragement of the First Monday Quilters of Lexington, Massachusetts.

There is, one knows not what sweet mystery about this sea, whose gently awful stirrings seem to speak of some hidden soul beneath . . .

—HERMAN MELVILLE

Matilda Prescott's Quilt

One

Matilda Prescott was sitting up in bed piecing a quilt.

It was after midnight, but she wasn't sleepy. She never seemed to get really sleepy anymore and only tumbled in and out of fitful naps. Not what you'd call an honest-to-goodness night's sleep. Catnaps.

The cat, meanwhile, was snoring away at the foot of the pine four-poster that had been Matilda's grandmother's marriage bed. Matilda contemplated him with mingled affection and exasperation. Darn cat.

She put in the last stitches and cut the thread, then reached for a pencil from the nightstand. At the edge of the quilt top she lightly printed: "M. L. P." Matilda Louise Prescott. She'd always liked the way her name sounded. Solid. Then she added a few words. She'd embroider it in the morning.

The bedroom door opened a crack. Matilda glanced up brightly without surprise.

"Now what are you doing here at this hour? Oh, I know you're up and around. Don't think I don't know what's going on, but what do you have to come bothering me for? Just get out and leave me be. I'm sick to death of you. Sick to death of all of you."

The door closed. An hour later it noiselessly opened again. Matilda didn't look up. She thought she must be falling asleep, but this wasn't sleep. She needed some air.

1

She gasped for breath. Too many covers. She seemed to be tangled up in the quilt, but when she tried to pull it off, it wouldn't budge.

Sick to death.

Faith Fairchild and her husband, Tom, were sitting on the porch of the small Maine coastal farmhouse they had rented on Sanpere Island for the month of August. Tom was reading and Faith was doing nothing. The house was set high upon a granite ridge, and a broad meadow swept down to a cove. Across the water was a lobster pound, and Faith had grown accustomed to the putt-putt-putt of the lobster boats delivering their catch. When the wind was right, or wrong, they could smell the bait and fuel for the boats, a powerful combination; but somehow it seemed to go with the territory.

The farmhouse had long since been converted to summer occupancy and was filled with all the appropriate paraphernalia a rusticator might need: croquet and badminton sets, picnic gear, rain hats, sun hats, star charts, jigsaw puzzles, fishing poles, butterfly nets, board games, and bookcases crammed with slightly musty copies of Wodehouse, Jack London, Mary Roberts Rinehart, E. Phillips Oppenheim, plus all the paperbacks the family had ever acquired as well as those left behind by tenants and guests, everything from Jackie Collins to May Sarton. The adjacent barn hadn't seen a cow in more than fifty years, and it too was filled to the rafters with equipment for leisure-time activities: bikes, a Ping-Pong table, canoes, a kayak, gardening tools. Faith found it daunting even to look in there and unconsciously stood a little straighter whenever she entered the door. All this clean living—plunges into the arctic water at dawn followed by cold showers, no doubt—left her feeling vaguely uneasy. As if Teddy Roosevelt's ruddy, hearty ghost was spying on her from behind one of the archery targets. Her plan for August had been something less strenuous in the Hamptons.

Tom, however, was delighted. This was exactly the way he and his family had spent their summers, and the rest of the year, on Massachusetts's South Shore. When the weather had been too bad for messing about with boats, rafts, or anything else that would float—and it had to be gale-force winds to discourage the little Fairchilds—they had holed up inside the house to play Monopoly for hours. Faith's idea of a good time as a child had been to stroll over to the Metropolitan Museum of Art and play hide-and-seek in the Egyptian wing, followed by hot chocolate at Rumpelmayer's. She loathed all board games, and the only card games she knew how to play were go fish and poker.

Still, she liked the farmhouse and her native curiosity—"dangerous curiosity" according to Tom—had prompted her to snoop around trying to piece together a picture of the Thorpe family who owned it but no longer used it.

There was a photograph album in the attic that affirmed her conviction that their shoulders were broad, calves sturdy, and haircuts terrible. They also seemed to have a penchant for wearing each other's clothes, or maybe they just bought them in lots. In any case, most of the garments were tan, and to say that L. L. Bean would have been *haute couture* describes them sufficiently. Nevertheless Faith had grown fond of the family and given them names she thought they would like—good Yankee names like Elizabeth, John, and Marian.

That Faith was here, five hours north of Boston,

not two hours east of Manhattan, whiling away her time in this fashion, was due entirely to the blandishments of her neighbor and friend, Pix Miller, who had been coming to Sanpere since childhood. Pix painted such a vivid picture of deep-blue seas and murmuring pines that Faith agreed to try it. The fact that Pix also guaranteed a baby-sitter for two-year-old Benjamin Fairchild in the shape of her teenage daughter, Samantha, tipped the balance. At present Faith would have summered in Hoboken if someone had offered a baby-sitter along with it. They didn't call them "terrible twos" for nothing.

So, having made absolutely sure there was a bridge in good working order to the mainland, she packed her bug spray along with the Guerlain and prepared to "rough it." Pix was delighted. "You'll see. We'll have fun. There's always so much going on."

Staring at the absolutely calm water and flat horizon from the porch, Faith sincerely doubted that. Yet, although she wouldn't exactly say she was having fun, she was having something close to it. And Pix was right about one thing: Penobscot Bay was beautiful.

Plus there was the food—lobster, mussels, clams, fresh fish, and a small farmer's market on Saturdays with great vegetables and a goat cheese made by Mrs. Carlan that rivaled anything Zabar's stocked.

Faith's interest in food was personal and professional. She had risen to fame and fortune as the founder of a Manhattan catering firm, Have Faith, giving up the Big Apple for the bucolic orchards of New England when she fell head over heels in love with Tom Fairchild and married him soon afterward. Faith had a tendency to act precipitously. Tom, who was the village parson in Aleford, Massachusetts, did not. But this was a special case. A very special case.

Faith had managed to make life in the small town a bit more interesting by giving birth to Benjamin, finding a parishioner's corpse in Aleford's belfry, and getting locked in the killer's preserves cabinet—pretty much in that order.

Lately, when she was not chasing after Benjamin, conscientiously trying to help him reach his third birthday intact, she had been expanding the Have Faith product line—jams, jellies, chutneys, sauces. She was also thinking of starting up the catering business again in Boston, with the same name since Tom didn't seem to think it would rock the pews too much.

Faith was no stranger to the ministry. Her father and grandfather were both men of the cloth, and she had an insider's view of parish life from childhood. The last thing she had ever thought she would do was stretch her sojourn inside the goldfish bowl into adulthood. But in some cases the heart knows no reason.

Tom was naïvely insistent that it was possible to have a private life in a small parish and urged Faith to feel free to go her own way and voice her opinions. Although when Faith's remark to someone in the Stop and Save that she thought skinny-dipping was more wholesome than ogling the centerfold in *Playboy* came back to him as the minister's wife advocating mixed nude bathing, he was momentarily thrown.

At present, well out of the public eye, Tom was reading a Wodehouse and chuckling out loud. He was steadily working through all of them, and Faith had noticed some distinctly odd expressions in his speech lately, as well as an ever-so-faint British accent. She had become accustomed to his habit of sprinkling his conversation with his own versions of French expressions picked up in one blissful sophomore year in Paris, and it appeared these would soon be joined by those of France's hereditary enemies across the Channel. Faith both hoped and feared Tom was going to be eccentric in old age. They had both turned thirty in the spring, not thirtysomething, just plain thirty, and Faith was thinking a lot about age these days.

The wild roses that grew up over the porch filled the air with an intoxicating fragrance. A single gull flew across the sky, then dove straight in to the dark green water.

Faith had had enough scenery. She jumped up.

"What ho, Thomas, you old curmudgeon. How about a spot of footwook? It's absolutely ripping out and I must fetch the chip off the old escutcheon from Pix's abode."

Tom, deep in a fantasy of his own personal Jeeves, wrenched his attention away from the book and focused on his wife. She had cut her blond hair short for the summer, and it suited her. Some women have a tendency to look like fourteen-year-old boys when they do this, especially when dressed in jeans and a white T-shirt as Faith was; yet no one would ever mistake her for anything but what she was—a beautiful, sexy, healthy, and, at the moment, restless woman. He recognized the signs and abandoned his book with a tinge of regret. He was not above guilt induction.

"This *is* my only vacation, you know, Faith."

Tom was leaving Benjamin and Faith for three weeks while he went to work as one of the invited speakers at what Faith referred to as Spiritual Summer Camp. In fact, it was a series of retreats sponsored by the denomination. The Fairchilds had spent the long car trip from Boston thinking up workshop titles: "Job: Paranoid or Persecuted?"; "Muscular Christianity: Implants or Exercise?"; "Matthew and John: Who Really Told It Like It Was?" and so on. Tom would actually be speaking and leading discussions around the theme "When Good People Do Nothing," which covered everything from the plight of the homeless to the role of the church under Fascism. Faith thought it would be more interesting to speculate about good people doing bad things, but Tom pointed out it was often the same and this way he could fit in more topics. Since no forces on earth, or in heaven, would have dragged her to one of these noble gatherings, she felt she was not in a position to argue.

"Come on, Tom, don't tell me you won't have plenty of idle moments, and it's not as if a resort on a lake in New Hampshire is exactly a penal colony. Besides, you need the exercise. You're getting fat."

Tom hurled himself out of the wicker chair and grabbed Faith. "Take that back!" he cried, gently twisting her arm behind her back and trying to kiss her at the same time. "And if I am, which I'm not, it's your fault for cooking so well."

Having gotten him out of his chair, Faith went inside for a hat and some sun block. She had no intention of looking like tanned shoe leather by Labor Day.

"Shore or woods?" Tom asked, following her. You could reach the Millers' cottage either by a faint path through the pines or by scrambling over the rocks by the water.

"I don't care—which do you want?" Faith replied.

"Woods, my dear, every time." Tom smiled wickedly. Soon after they had been married, Faith had happily discovered Tom's love of the outdoors, or rather love in the outdoors. Fresh air and/or open spaces were an instant aphrodisiac for him, and they had happened upon a soft carpet of moss about halfway to Pix's that was definitely beginning to show signs of wear. They started off hand in hand and Faith imagined they must look something like an overgrown Hansel and Gretel. Tom was in cutoffs, not lederhosen, but she quickly glanced behind her anyway for the bread crumbs as they left the brilliant sunshine for the cool shadows of the forest. The path was visible and there were no birds in sight.

Faith hadn't thought much about what Maine would look like, except she knew there would be a lot of water, rocks, and picturesque fishing villages. She was a city girl and proud of it.

Yet these ancient trees, draped in veils of gray moss and growing so close together they almost blotted out the sky, filled her with awe. So did the quiet. The pine needles cushioned their steps, and a twig cracking far away was all they heard, aside from an occasional rustle as some creature passed by. It was like a church. The time-honored simile, a cathedral. Maybe that was why Tom enjoyed making love here so much: Everything came together, so to speak. She decided to tell him this great insight, but not now—they had reached the carpet. "With my body I thee worship," she murmured.

Later, looking over at his peaceful face, eyes half closed gazing up at the dusty motes in the shafts of sunlight streaming down, she decided not to break the mood. What eventually did break it was insects—ants and the whine of a mosquito. That was the trouble with nature. It looked so good, but once you were out in it, there were all these hidden drawbacks. It was so natural. Faith had never found that to be the case with Fifth Avenue for example, or Madison.

Tom slapped his arm. "*Merde!* These little buggers are eating me alive. Come on, Faith, let's get going."

They pulled on their clothes quickly and were soon approaching the cottage. Pix's family had been coming to the island for thousands of years and fortunately her husband, Sam, was a fervent convert. They had bought the land just after they got married, then built a small wooden summer house that sprawled out in several directions as various little Millers arrived. The oldest boy, Mark, was working as a sailing instructor farther up the coast, in a camp where ten-year-old Danny was currently a camper. Samantha, fifteen, preferred to stay on the island. Sam had taken off two weeks from his law practice in July and was returning at the end of the month.

Although the cottage was only about eighteen years old, it looked as if it had stood there for centuries. The clapboard was weathered gray, and Pix had planted delphinium, bleeding heart, phlox, and other old-fashioned flowers around the sides. There was a large vegetable garden in back and a substantial boathouse near the shore. This had recently been converted into a guest house, with a smaller shed nearby for Mark's sailboat and the dinghy the rest of them used to fish for mackerel, mostly in vain. Two potters, Roger Barnett and Eric Ashley, were currently renting the guest house, which the Millers still called the boathouse out of habit. Roger and Eric's own house, next to their studio and kiln, had burned down in May, and they had turned to Sam and Pix when they couldn't find a rental in the summer for love nor money.

As Tom and Faith approached, a giggling two-year-old traveling roughly at the speed of light zoomed around the corner, followed by two teenaged girls with outstretched arms, calling, "Benjamin! Stop!"

Faith could afford to look fondly on the scene. After all, she wasn't chasing him. His pudgy little legs were pumping away and his blond curls were plastered onto his forehead with the sweat of his exertion. He was laughing hysterically.

Samantha called out in explanation as she streaked past, "He thinks everything's a game!"

Faith and Tom nodded wisely, then went to find Pix.

She was in the kitchen making gin and tonics.

Tom gave her a big hug. "What a woman! You must be psychic. Even though I don't believe in all that, or at least not until Faith takes up table turning or Ouija boards."

Pix put everything on a tray and headed for the deck. Faith noticed that almost no one on the island ever stayed indoors when it was possible to be sitting out on a deck or in a field or on a rock. It probably had to do with the unpredictableness of the weather. It had been known to fog in for weeks on end, but Faith had a suspicion that Pix would go out anyway—in her sou'wester with a hot toddy.

Pix stretched out in an ancient canvas sling chair. That was another thing that made the house look old. It had been furnished with castoffs and permanent loans from Pix's relations, so everything looked as if it had been there forever. The wicker needed repainting and the Bar Harbor rockers new seats. All of which Pix and Sam planned to do as soon as they did everything else that needed doing. This was the only sure time of day to see Pix sitting.

Usually she was picking berries, or making bread, or instructing the children in the flora and fauna of the area, or walking the dogs, or weeding the garden, or . . .

She had started off life as a wee mite, and her whimsical parents had nicknamed her Pixie, which was abruptly shortened to Pix when she reached almost six feet at age fifteen. Faith had been trying to wean her away from the ubiquitous denim and khaki wraparound skirts and white blouses she favored, at least in the direction of Liz Claiborne and then who knows where? Today's outfit was one of the new ones, a bright blue-and-white-striped top with white shorts. Pix had fantastic legs, and heretofore Sam was probably the only one to know it. She stretched her long arms above her head and reached for the local paper from the table behind her chair.

"So who's having tea with whom this week?" Faith asked. She knew the first thing Pix read in *The Island Crier* was the social notes, "From The Crow's Nest."

Sanpere Island—the name was a corruption of the original French name bestowed by Champlain, St. Pierre—consisted of several towns, some of them no larger than a good-sized family. Each had a local correspondent who dutifully reported the news each week. Most of these ladies stuck straight to the facts. "The Weirs are at their cottage and entertained friends from Portsmouth, NH, over the weekend" and "Ruth Graham is out of the hospital and thanks all her friends for their cards and good wishes." However, the correspondent from Granville, the largest town on the island, kept not only her ear to the ground but her eye on the horizon. She always started her section with a brief weather report from her end of the island, then mentioned what birds

11

were around, animals she had noted in her yard, and what she was planting or harvesting, before getting to the more mundane activities of human beings.

"Well, let's see," said Pix, who had the paper sent to her in the winter so she wouldn't miss anything.

She approached the paper the same way she ate a boiled lobster, with meticulous dedication and an unvarying routine. First she'd suck out the sweet tender meat in the long thin legs most people threw away, then crack open the claws, and then the tail. Finally, she would open the body, spreading the tomalley inside on a saltine cracker and eating any roe before taking a pick to get every last morsel out of the cavity. Faith had never seen one person get so much meat from a lobster—or take so long to do it.

Settling down with *The Crier* on Friday when it came out, Pix had been known to make it last through Tuesday and once in a while longer if it was a special issue with a supplement—as for the Fourth of July, which increased the usual eight pages to ten. After "From the Crow's Nest" she turned, like most other people, to "Real Estate Transfers." The Fairchilds figured Pix could tell you the owner of every square foot of shore frontage and on back and how much the person had paid for it. At the moment the seller was usually the local Donald Trump, a man named Paul Edson, who had purchased land when it was relatively cheap in the Fifties and was now selling dear to the increasing number of Bostonians and New Yorkers willing to travel this far. Edson was an off-islander too. He'd married a local woman, a Hamilton, but that didn't change the way people felt about him, or now her. To say someone was "worse than Edson" on Sanpere was about as bad as you could get, not excluding mass murder, rape, and pillage. It was a rare day in town when he would return to his parked car and find air in all his tires. Although usually his wife sat guard, and nobody ever messed with Edith Edson.

"Come on, Pix, stop reading to yourself and share the goodies," Tom protested.

"I was just looking for Granville. Here she is:

" 'Perfect weather this week. Lots of sunshine during the day and rain for the gardens at night. Three great blue heron were spotted in the cove near Weed's Hill and we can be sure that they are beginning to return to this part of the island. Tomatoes are so good, we can't put them up fast enough and have been giving them away, but the carrots have not amounted to much. Old seed? I don't want to point a finger, but the packet was pretty dusty. A very big turtle stopped traffic outside Alice Goodhue's house last week. Fortunately the fella didn't grab onto anyone's finger or toe! Come out some night and watch the Fish Hawks play at the Old High School. You won't see a better team and they are 4-0 in the county softball league.' Oh, terrific!"

"What is it?" Faith asked. From the tone of Pix's voice, it was not old carrot seeds or the Fish Hawks' winning streak.

"There's a Baked Bean and Casserole Supper at the Odd Fellows Hall next Tuesday night. Too bad you'll miss it, Tom," she said with real regret in her voice. "I know you'd love it."

Faith rightly assumed that Pix intended her to attend—and what was worse, eat. The baked beans might be okay, but she knew what a casserole was— string beans (probably not from the garden, those had already been canned for next winter), mixed with cream of mushroom soup, water chestnuts if the chef was adventurous and had been to the big

13

supermarket off island in Bangor lately, topped with canned onion rings for crunch.

"The desserts alone are worth the price of admission. Now, Faith"—Pix leveled an admonitory glance at her—"don't turn up your pretty little gourmet nose. These ladies know how to cook."

Could the woman who sometimes served her family Kraft macaroni and cheese dinners and Dinty Moore stew be right? Faith doubted it, but she'd go. Blueberries were ripe, and that meant pie or maybe shortcake, the real kind of shortcake, on a biscuit, not store-bought sponge. New England was pretty reliable in the shortcake and other baked goods department, she had discovered. She cheered up about the dinner. Maybe there was a diamond in the rough out there who would do something delectable with lobster. Pix had given her a recipe for fiddlehead ferns clipped from *The Crier* last spring that had been delicious. Perhaps she was getting too critical. The thought was vetoed as quickly as it had come. The evening had tuna noodle written all over it.

"So what else is new?" If you had told her a week ago that she would be listening with not just pleasure but interest to a local gossip column, she would have shaken what was left of her locks in disbelief. Yet is was true. "And don't forget 'The Fisheries Log'—I want to know what those poor fishermen are getting compared to what Sonny Prescott is charging."

Pix continued, "Let's see, babies, birthdays, and family reunions. Gracious! Someone came all the way from Newfoundland for the Sanford gathering last weekend. They had a clam bake in Little Harbor. Oh, here's the card of thanks from Matilda Prescott's relatives: 'We would like to thank everyone for their kindness in this time of our bereave-

14

ment.' I guess they couldn't really put in what they thought, namely: 'She was a cranky old lady, it was about time, and now we can finally get the house.' "

"What do you mean, Pix? Who was she? Any relation to Sonny?" Tom was as interested in gossip as Faith, though a fraction of a hair slower to admit it.

"All the Prescotts in the universe and especially on this island are related. Matilda was his aunt, or great-aunt. The house they all want is that beautiful Victorian in Sanpere Village you can see from the causeway. The question on everybody's mind is which one of the thirty thousand Prescotts will inherit. Matilda never married, so there are no children. The way I always heard it was she went away to the normal school, and when she got back all her brothers and sisters were married, so she had to stay at home and take care of her parents. And they lived a long time. When her father died, he was the oldest resident on the island and had the *Boston Post* gold-headed cane. But she did teach, in the old schoolhouse by the crossroads, and I guess she didn't spare the rod much."

Faith had stopped listening after "beautiful Victorian."

"You mean the house with the gazebo?!" she exclaimed. A lifelong apartment dweller with an instinctive distrust of only two or three stories, she had been surprised to discover that she occasionally fell instantly in love with a certain house—a butter-yellow rambling Colonial in Aleford, a Bauhaus gem in nearby Lincoln; houses that seemed to be as rooted in the setting as the trees and bushes surrounding them. She'd seen the Prescott house the first morning they'd arrived when she'd gone to the IGA for supplies. A causeway separated a large mill pond from the small harbor, and the house was set

15

back in the woods across from the old mill with a spit of land projecting into the pond. The gazebo was at the tip of it, surrounded by slender white birches like girls in their summer dresses. The house, keeping watch a discreet distance away, was tall and stately, with the gingerbread, gables, and furbelows of the period kept firmly in check. Both the house and gazebo looked squarely out toward the western part of Penobscot Bay. Sunsets could be spectacular, streaks of deep rose and violet stretching across the sky, randomly broken by the dark shapes of islands that pushed up into the horizon line—islands with names like Crabapple, Little Hogg (and Big Hogg, which was smaller now), and Ragged Top.

"Yes, that's it." Faith was dazed for a moment by the sound of Pix's voice. She had been mentally dressed in voile and a picture hat, sipping some chilled chablis with Tom as they gazed at the setting sun and each other. Invisible hands were meanwhile feeding and putting her suddenly docile child to bed.

"That's one of the most beautiful houses I've ever seen." Faith spoke enviously. "I don't suppose you have any Prescott blood mixed up with all those New England strains, Tom?"

"Sorry to disappoint you, love, and I agree. It is a jewel. I wonder why houses like that never seem to end up as parsonages." He sounded a bit wistful. "Probably whoever inherits it will make it into condominiums or something."

Pix answered, "Oh, I doubt it. That's only farther down the coast so far. I think anyone who tried to introduce the idea of condominiums here would get quite a cold shoulder. Or worse. I'm not sure everyone here even understands what they are, but they sound bad—like Yuppies, and years ago Hippies."

"Which reminds me," said Tom, "I saw a flower child on the clam flats yesterday morning, quite early. Youngish with all the accoutrements—long hair, bandanna, granny sunglasses, tie-dyed mini dress around three inches long. And she had a baby or something in a pouch strapped to her back. Was I dreaming or is she a neighbor?"

"I saw her too, Tom, later. She was coming over the rocks, spied me, and fled instantly—before I had a chance to say anything."

"That's Bird, not her real name," Pix replied. "Although come to think of it there must be quite a few adults with similar names bequeathed to them by their letting-it-all-hang-out parents—I actually knew someone who named her daughter Emma Goldman Moonflower. Anyway, Bird lives with her significant other in that tiny shack you can see from your beach, directly across the water from the lobster pound. I don't think it even has indoor plumbing. They're into macrobiotics and she was probably gathering seaweed. The guy she lives with, Andy, is a rock musician and seems to spend most of his time in Camden playing with a group down there. I don't really know them, although they've been here all winter and I can't imagine how they survived in that house, especially with a baby." Pix paused for breath. There was nothing like fresh Maine air and a gin and tonic to loosen her tongue.

"Someone you don't know? Well, I, for one, am shocked," teased Tom. "You're slipping, Pix."

Pix clamped her mouth shut and returned to the paper.

"Come on, make up and read me 'Police Brief,'

you know it's my favorite. What kind of a week has crime had on the island?" Tom cajoled. With only one officer of the law and accordingly one police car, he hoped it hadn't been too unruly.

Pix acquiesced readily. "Well, the kids are stealing hubcaps again. Oh, and this is really funny—I'll read it: 'A pickup truck was found upside down in Lover's Lane last Tuesday evening. A search found a quantity of empty beer cans inside, but no driver. The truck, a 1967 Ford, was registered to Velma Hamilton, who reported it stolen the next day. The truck was totaled and the matter is under investigation.' "

Tom and Faith laughed. "You mean there really is a Lover's Lane on the island?" asked Tom.

"Yes, you follow Route 17 to Sanpere Village and it's the road before the lily pond. But what could they have been doing to turn the truck upside down?"

Tom and Faith laughed harder. Faith caught her breath and said, "Oh Pix, only you. Don't you think the truck just drove off the road? It couldn't have been stopped and flipped over no matter how frisky the couple were."

"You never know; one time I heard—" Pix started, when she was unfortunately interrupted by the appearance of a much-disheveled Samantha lugging a squirming Benjamin. She came up the stairs to the deck and deposited him on Faith's lap before he could take flight again.

"I hope it's all right, Mrs. Fairchild, but Arlene and I want to go swimming now while the tide is right." She motioned behind her. "Arlene, this is Mrs. Fairchild and Reverend Fairchild." Arlene giggled and said something in that Maine accent that Faith had not yet managed to decode.

"Of course, Samantha. We were coming to get him anyway, and after all this work you need a break. But don't tell me you actually swim in this stuff without turning into a solid block of ice."

Arlene giggled some more, and Samantha laughed. "This is the best time. The tide's come in over the rocks after the sun has been warming them all day, and the water isn't cold at all. You should try it."

Faith shuddered. "Not this lifetime."

Samantha turned to Tom. "How about you, Reverend?"

"You have a deal. Benjamin and I will go with you tomorrow. I don't want him to turn out like his mother. She doesn't know what she's missing." Tom had been swimming every day since they came.

Faith looked at Tom, planned to rake him over the coals later for suggesting in front of Benjamin that she might be an inadequate role model while Papa was simply too good to be true, and answered crisply, "Oh yes she does, thank you, and the only salt water I want to go near is in a pot waiting for a lobster or some mussels or clams."

Benjamin had had enough lap sitting and was ready for round two, so they said good-bye and started back through the woods. They had taken the shore route with Ben once, and it took so long to tear him away from the tidal pools and shells he found that they stuck to the wooded path now and tried to keep him from wandering off into the bracken. He insisted on walking these days and howled if either of them came near him with the stroller or backpack. He seemed to have developed a logic all his own—after all, these same people had wanted him to walk, coaxing and encouraging him to take those first steps. Now he could do it and they wanted him to stop. It was a very puzzling universe.

Tom reached for Faith's hand while he watched Benjamin career over the tree roots and pine needles in the path. "I know you're mad, Faith, and I'd adore Benjamin to grow up just like you. But a little like me. Besides, it wouldn't kill you to go swimming. You should try my method. You jump in all at once and swim like hell for a few seconds. Your blood gets going and it's really warm."

"Sounds like great fun, Tom," Faith said. "You knew I wasn't a Campfire Girl when you met me and I'm too old to change even if I wanted to, which I don't." Faith had always been suspicious of exercise conducted outside a health club, spa, or ski resort.

She took a few deliberately limber strides. "And I don't particularly care to have aspersions cast upon me." Umbrage tended to embellish Faith's vocabulary.

"I know, darling, don't worry. And I won't teach Benjamin to shoot, swear, and spit. He'll have to learn them on his own."

They looked fondly at said Benjamin for an instant before realizing he was no longer in front of them, but had abandoned the path for greater adventure and was in the act of climbing a huge rock. They lunged together. Faith might not be Gertrude Ederle, but she could run fast.

"Want wock!" Benjamin screamed. Faith sighed. Even with trusty Samantha, Tom's absence was going to be tough going. How did single parents cope? She made a mental note never to get divorced no matter how many touch football games Tom wheedled her into.

The phone was ringing as they entered the cottage. Faith picked it up. Pix was on the other end.

"Faith, fantastic news! They're going to auction off the contents of Matilda Prescott's house next Thursday. It's under 'Special Events' and there's so much listed I can't read it all over the phone, but there were some lovely things in the house and goodness knows what was in the attic! She only died a month ago, and I thought it would take them longer to go through things. I didn't even know the will had been probated."

It was good news. Faith loved auctions, although until she had come to New England they had been of quite a different nature and mood. Now she knew enough to bring her own chair and a thermos of coffee, and to arrive at the crack of dawn to inspect things.

She hung up and told Tom. He was crestfallen. House auctions were his favorites, and he told Faith to try to get him any old tools she saw, especially if there were box lots. You never knew what you'd turn up in one of those. He was still hoping to come across a daguerrotype of Lincoln at the bottom of one, as a friend of his parents allegedly had some years earlier.

Faith fed Benjamin and together they put him to bed, chanting *Goodnight Moon*, his current favorite, in unison. By the second bowlful of mush, he was asleep.

Afterward they sat on the porch again and ate steaming bowls of fish chowder. Tom was thinking how much better it was than mush, whatever that was, when Faith interrupted his train of thought just before he could speculate on what she had made for dessert.

"I'm going to miss you, Tom," Faith said solemnly. "This is the longest we'll have been separated since Ben was born."

"I know, sweetheart. I'm not looking forward to it much. I'd love to stay here. Pix is right. This place really is perfect. Anyway, the time will go fast. You'll have all these exciting things to keep you busy—auctions and potluck suppers."

" 'Exciting' is not the word we're searching for here. The last thing in the world these next couple of weeks are going to be is exciting. But that's all right with me. I'll get all those books and *New Yorker*s read that I've been putting aside all winter. And I have to work on some new recipes."

It was twilight and the tide was still high. A lone *Larus atricilla*, better known as a laughing gull, perched on a rock and slung his strident cry at the approaching dark: "Ha-ha-ha-haah-haah."

Two

The sun shone steadily on the ocean, creating island mirages and turning the real ones into silver silhouettes. Faith had closed her eyes against the brilliance and would soon have to move to a shadier spot, but for the moment it was delicious to bask in the warmth, listening to the steady thumping noise of the wheel as Eric Ashley transformed lumps of clay into graceful goblets. He had set up his kickwheel on the desk in front of the Millers' boathouse to take full advantage of the sun and the view.

Eric seemed to have no trouble talking and working at the same time, although his eyes never strayed from the cone shape he was pushing up and down. Faith had never watched anyone work on a wheel before, and she found herself irresistibly fascinated by the phallic shape that rose, fell, and rose higher again, before Eric plunged his fingers into the glistening shiny wet center, spreading it into the cup for his goblet. Her heart beat a little faster in time to the wheel. Tom had been away only since Saturday. Two days. Labor Day seemed further away than ever.

"Of course everyone is calling us 'fortune hunters' and worse, much worse," Eric was saying.

Faith didn't know Eric, or Roger, well enough to

have formed an opinion; but certainly Pix had been surprised along with the rest of Sanpere to find that Matilda Prescott had left her magnificent house not to flesh and blood, but to these two off-islanders. Pix had been in the IGA when she heard one bitter Prescott connection say, "Why didn't she just have the place town down? Same thing."

Matilda did leave the contents of the house to her relatives, and Sonny Prescott was the executor. It was his decision to auction the whole caboodle off at once rather than have endless arguments and life-time feuds over who was supposed to get which teapot and to whom Matilda had faithfully prom-ised the rosewood parlor furniture. This way, they'd split the money, and if someone was dying to have something, why he could just bid at the auction like everyone else. There was some grumbling over this, especially among those with the faithful promises, at least three of them for the parlor furniture; but in general the Prescotts thought Sonny had done the fair thing. However, first a bevy of them, including Sonny, was going through every chest, every drawer, every possible secret hiding place for the gold.

Darnell Prescott's gold that is.

Matilda's father, Darnell, had owned the lumber-yard, and it was widely known that he never trusted banks—even before the crash—nor did Matilda. He paid cash for everything, and there wasn't a Prescott on the island who didn't ardently believe in the existence of a well-worn leather pouch filled with gold coins. Others tended to clas-sify it with Captain Kidd's cave—the real one was on virtually every island within sight.

Even if some of the Prescotts were skeptical, they weren't taking any chances of seeing headlines in the *Ellsworth American*, "Vacationing Indiana Couple Buys Trunk Filled with Gold Coins at Local Auction." Or still more catastrophic, having Eric and Roger pull up a loose floorboard and discover the loot.

The kickwheel stopped, and Eric deftly sliced the goblet from the base of clay and set it in a row of others in the shade.

"It's not as if her family ever paid much attention to her. They couldn't stand her and she couldn't stand them. We lived next door to her for years, and they wouldn't even bother to plow her out in the wintertime. Roger and I did. Not that we ever thought she would do something like this. My God, I couldn't believe it when the lawyer told us, but now I realize she was dropping a lot of hints just before she died. I had made some lobster stew, which she loved, and brought it over. She was bed-ridden at the end, you know. She kept saying over and over how terrible it was about our house. It burned down in May, Pix probably told you. Then she went on saying we wouldn't have to worry long. I thought she meant because Pix and Sam had let us have this place and said something about the Millers being great people. Matilda kind of humphed, which meant she agreed, but she went right on talking about how far away it was from our studio and how were we going to meet our orders?"

Faith realized she was no doubt expected to make some comment about all this. She had been in a semicomatose state with the heat, drone of the wheel, and singsong cadences of Eric's seemingly guilt-ridden, seemingly self-righteous defense. She sat up, stretched, and looked at Eric, who was standing over her about to get back on the wheel.

"Well, I'm sure she knew what she was doing.

From all I've heard about Matilda, she was a very determined lady, and she must have wanted to give you a place to live. An incredible place to live."

Eric laughed. "It is, isn't it?" He paused. "It's the house of my dreams."

Faith moved back into the shadow from the boathouse. "It's the house of anybody's dreams. I wouldn't mind having it myself and I don't even like houses as a rule. You do things for a house you would never do for anyone or anything else, not even your husband, and what do you get back? You have to do the same things all over again in a while. So it has to be an extraordinary house to be worth it, and you've got one."

All's fair in love and real estate, Faith thought to herself, but just the same she would look behind her on dark nights for a while if she was Eric or Roger. If the two of them died without issue, the house reverted to the Prescotts. That was as good an invitation as any, and the Prescotts were certainly crying bloody murder all over the island. It was bad luck and lousy timing for them. If Matilda hadn't clung so tenaciously to what was left of her life, like one of the limpets on the granite ledges in the view from her windows, the Prescotts would have gotten everything. She had changed her will only after the fire had destroyed Roger and Eric's house.

But, Faith continued to reflect, then the Prescotts would have been at each other's throats instead of at Eric's and Roger's. They couldn't all have lived in the house. She stood up and stretched some more.

She could see Samantha and her faithful shadow, Arlene, valiantly trying to keep Benjamin from tearing himself to ribbons on the razor-sharp, barnacle-encrusted rocks near the shore. They were showing him the tiny crabs and other things that inhabited the tidal pools.

Samantha was a Pix in the making, or a Pix product, depending on whether you were looking at the apple or the tree. She had shell collections, rock collections, bird-feather collections, and fern collections, all carefully labeled, which would have put many a botanist, ornithologist, or whatever to shame.

Arlene seemed to know everything by osmosis. She didn't have Peterson's field guides, life lists, or Latin names, but she knew what would make you sick if you ate it, on which offshore islands the gulls nested, and the best places to dig for clams. What was even more important to Faith at the moment was that they were both the kind of adolescent girls who adored children.

Just as the adult world could be divided into cat lovers or haters, child worshippers or tolerators at best, there seemed to be a very clear distinction between those girls who baby-sat for the money and were perfectly adequate at keeping your child safe, even somewhat entertained and clean, and those girls who were happiest pushing a stroller, playing games, and marveling at the antics of small beings. Many of them seemed to move straight from horses to kids. Faith thought of suggesting this topic to a psychologist friend of hers for a scholarly monograph, "From My Friend Flicka to Rock-a-bye Baby."

She gazed out at the three tiny figures by the water's edge again. She had been thankful to have Samantha on the payroll and now it looked as though Arlene would join her. Not only was it close to an embarrassment of riches, but the girls seemed to be having fun.

27

It wasn't that she didn't have fun with Benjamin. She completely adored him. They were moving from the tactile, physical communication of babyhood to the tactile, physical, verbal, you-name-it relationship of the toddler. Somewhere along the line he had lost that sweet, milky baby fragrance and taken on a sweet, sweaty little-boy smell. It had happened before she realized it.

But talking to someone who referred to himself mainly in the third person, and who rarely achieved sentences longer than three words and these mostly self-involved, did pall occasionally, and it was then that she greeted Samantha with open arms. Arms that were opened to place Benjamin squarely in Samantha's.

Faith sat down again and leaned back against the boathouse. As long as they looked so content at the shore, she'd wait a bit longer before getting Ben for lunch.

From where she was sitting she could see Eric's profile. He was extremely good-looking. His normally blond hair was bleached almost white by the sun; he had blue eyes to match and a good body. He'd taken off his shirt, and she could see he was slim without being skinny. All that potting and loading and unloading the kiln had evidently been good exercise—nice muscles. She finished her inventory by looking down at his hands. They were large with long, tapering fingers. The kind of hands a statue has. In fact, it would not have been too adulatory to say he looked like a statue—Praxiteles, not Michelangelo.

Not my type though, Faith thought. Too much of a piece. Tom's slightly off-center nose and rusty-brown hair strayed across her mind. Benjamin might have the same hair. His strawberry-blond curls were beginning to darken. It was too soon to tell about the nose.

Faith hadn't asked, nor cared; but Pix had told her that Roger and Eric, contrary to public belief and often derision, were not gay. They were college friends, one from Iowa, one from Texas, who shared a common passion for clay. They became partners and built up a thriving business in New York, producing unique ceramic pieces as well as an elegant line of dinnerware, much of which appeared in at least one room in the Kips Bay Decorator Show House and went from there to penthouses, country homes, and favored dwellings on both sides of the Atlantic. Needing change and more space, they had come to the island on the recommendation of a printmaker friend who lived nearby on the mainland. They had been here for six years, going their separate ways for a month or two in the dreary winter months, but otherwise living and working together in what seemed like an easy harmony.

Eric was a master at glazes, although they both did everything. His current woman friend was Jill Merriwether, who operated a small gift shop in Sanpere Village. Jill didn't sell their work. Her line tended to run to objects with blueberries on them, clam-basket planters, lobster potholders, balsam pillows, books about Maine, and jam, usually strawberry and blueberry, made by a number of people on the island. The shop was, in fact, called The Blueberry Patch. Faith had bought Robert McCloskey's *Blueberries for Sal* there for Benjamin, and it was rapidly supplanting *Goodnight Moon* as the most-requested bedtime story. She figured she had read it about twenty times since buying it, and so far neither Ben nor she was tired of it.

Sanpere was an idyllic place, but still she imagined it must be pretty horrible in the off season. The population dropped drastically—from 3000 to 1200—although according to many islanders this was a blessing—and the cold weather forced an existence just ripe for cabin fever. She had met a friend of Pix's who had lived here one winter between jobs, and she had told Faith that by January she was going to every meeting on the island, even AA, just for the company.

"Don't you miss the city, Eric?" Faith wondered aloud.

"Of course I do, and when I can't stand it anymore I go down, and then after a week I miss Sanpere and can't wait to get back. That's how I know this is right for me. If you aren't satisfied in New York, then you must either be nuts or have found a spot that's better for you. Roger feels the same. He goes to the city even less often than I do, and it's usually for the business."

"But what about the opera, theater, bagels?"

She looked at his well-worn 501 jeans. Clothes were obviously not a problem.

"Our deep freeze is stocked with bagels, Jewish rye, decent steaks, and all those necessities, and we have Alistair and PBS for the finer things of life. We do miss our friends, but they love to come up here. It's a much better atmosphere for us to work in, less pressure, less distraction. We are happier as artists and happier as people than we've ever been in our lives. Saner." He gave the clay an emphatic slap, then started to kick the wheel.

Still Faith found it all very hard to understand. Aleford was bad enough, but at least Boston was not a cultural wasteland. There were all sorts of things to do that they seldom did. Sanpere didn't even have a movie theater. She'd heard that a group of residents did get up a little-theater production of *Cat on a Hot Tin Roof* a few years back. Then the week before the opening the Maggie ran off with the Big Daddy, and no one had tried since.

She stood up. "Well, I wish you good luck and much happiness in your new house, and if you have a housewarming, please invite me. I want to look in every corner and drink tea or something else in the gazebo."

Eric gave her a warm smile. "You don't have to wait for the party, Faith. As soon as we move in, you and the Millers will be our first guests, and anytime you want to sit in the gazebo, feel free."

Faith decided she liked him. She liked attractive people. They were nice to look at, but Eric had more than that—intelligence and the kind of good nature that charms, yet isn't revolting.

"Thank you," she replied. "That sounds wonderful and I'll try to dig up a parasol. Now I have to rescue Samantha and get Benjamin home for lunch and a nap. I never realized what a slave children are to routines. I always thought childhood was supposed to be a time of freedom, but if the same things don't happen at the same time every day, he gets totally crazy."

"I know; my sister's kids are such little conservatives. But with them it's food: 'I say it's spinach and I say to hell with it' type stuff."

Faith laughed, and her impression of him was reinforced—it was nice to share the same classics. She said good-bye and set off down the path to the beach.

Benjamin was right on schedule and started falling into his chowder at one o'clock. Faith scooped him up and put him to bed. She decided to take the new *Vogue* out to the hammock and have a rest herself. She'd drastically shortened most of her skirts a couple of years ago despite the prevailing fashion in Aleford, which had been mid-calf since the late twenties. Now it looked as if she would have to raise some of them an inch or two more. It was absorbing work coping with trends. Besides, all this lassitude was exhausting. And she needed her strength for clamming with Pix later in the afternoon when the tide was still low.

She had no sooner opened the magazine to an Issey Miyake quilted jacket that said "Faith, you need me" when a shadow fell across the page. She looked up. In this case, way up. It was Pix.

"Faith, how long have you been asleep? You were so peaceful I didn't want to disturb you, but you said you wanted clams."

"I don't even remember dropping off. What time is it?" Faith tried to avoid wearing a watch whenever possible.

Pix consulted her gigantic multipurpose timepiece, which did everything from simply reporting the hour to informing one of the current exchange rate in Addis Ababa and the exact date of the return of the male elephant seals to Año Nuevo.

"It's almost three o'clock."

"Oh, my God!" Faith leaped out of the hammock and started running to the house. "If Benjamin is up, there's no telling what he's into, and if he's not, he'll never sleep through the night."

He was up, but miraculously had stayed in his crib, diverted by one of the branches of FAO Schwartz Faith kept steadily rotating there in the vain hope of keeping him from climbing out. He had learned to climb out of his crib six months before, and for weeks Tom and Faith's life was a nightmare. Thrilled at the acquisition of this terrific skill,

Benjamin would repeat the maneuver seven or eight times a night. It was one of those things no one tells you before you have a baby, yet everybody mentions afterward: "Oh yes, Johnny climbed out forty times a night for eight months and we were regulars on the parental stress hotline." Leach, Spock, Brazelton, all the heavy hitters commiserated and said just put him firmly back. Of course they weren't the sleep-deprived zombies in question.

It was at three o'clock one morning, after lifting Benjamin back in and admittedly snarling at him, "It's time to go to sleep, you *must* stay in your bed," that Faith realized she had literally stumbled on the solution to the capital-punishment dilemma. It was fiendishly simple. Put the murderers, rapists, insider traders, what-have-you, in a cell with a two-year-old hardened crib evacuator and after a week tops, total rehabilitation or insanity would have occurred. Tom was not amused when she woke him up to tell him. "Faith, you're getting dangerously close to the edge," he had mumbled.

Although Benjamin had somewhat curbed his wanderlust and slept through the night now, Faith was haunted by fears of recidivism. She and Pix were discussing this as they walked through the aspen grove that separated the cottage from the nearest shoreline. The green-gray leaves were quivering in the slight breeze on stems that looked too fragile to hold them in place. Shortly after Faith and Tom had arrived in Sanpere, Pix had told her that legend had it that the reason the aspen always quivered was because the cross had been made of its wood and forever after it mourned. Faith had been amazed that she had missed this tidbit of ecclesiastical folklore in her clerical upbringing and resolved to work it into the conversation at the next meeting of the church's ladies' alliance. She had found herself woefully lacking in such bona fides as a minister's wife. Pix would have been far abler, she reflected—not for the first time.

Samantha followed behind with Ben in a Gerry backpack. For some typical two-year-old reason he would let Samantha and no one else carry him this way.

All three of them were armed with clam hoes and wooden clam baskets lined with wire mesh. Faith was intrigued and a bit wary. Her wariness had increased when Pix had handed her a pair of olive-green rubber boots, size sixteen and encrusted with the vestiges of ancient mudflats. Flapping along in these, wearing a bathing suit (Pix had said an old one, but then she didn't understand about updating a wardrobe), and beginning to feel uncomfortably warm, Faith found herself thinking that the victory might not be worth the price. However, she wanted clams and Pix said there was nothing in the world like absolutely fresh ones.

Faith decided to concentrate on dinner and hoped that would give her the sticking power. She had invited Pix, Roger, and Eric to taste something new she had been working on. She'd been invited to St. Louis last winter as one of the judges of a barbecue-sauce competition and while there had had a local specialty, toasted ravioli—ravioli rolled in bread crumbs and quickly deep fried. It was tasty, but she realized it could be even tastier with more interesting fillings and sauces, different bread crumbs, better oil. Since then she'd been trying all sorts of combinations. For tonight she had prepared some with chèvre and red pepper and wanted to stuff the rest with these sweet whole clams, a hint of garlic, and fresh-tomato-and-basil coulis for dipping. This primo piatto was to be followed by grilled lobsters brushed with pastis and fennel butter. Pix was bringing new potatoes and salad ingredients from her garden. The thought of what awaited took Faith over the rocks, and she stepped off, firm of purpose, into the mud, ready to rake. She instantly sank down to her boot tops and couldn't move an inch. It was like quicksand, and she felt like a mighty Hoover was sucking her into the bowels of the earth. No clam was worth this.

"Pix!" she screamed. "Save me!"

"Oh, Faith, you have to walk carefully. Now just turn your foot to the side to break the suction and pull."

Faith turned and with a truly disgusting noise freed each captive leg.

"Okay, now we're ready." Pix had barely paused. Faith was incredulous, but she didn't see how she could get much muddier even at Georgette Klinger's, so she assumed an attentive air and thought about a long soak in the cottage's giant lion-pawed bathtub.

"You see all these little holes on the surface? Each one is a clam breathing. You don't want to put the tines of your hoe into the holes or you'll break the shells. You dig in just above and turn over the mud, like this." Pix swiftly uncovered a cache of clams, all busily taking their last breaths and squirting streams of water as they tried desperately to escape. She bent down quickly and put the larger ones into her basket. "They have to be at least two inches. People don't seem to understand that if they strip away all the clams, there won't be any. They used to be so plentiful and so cheap. Now they're almost as much as lobster." Pix was waving her clam hoe for emphasis, and Faith knew she would not hesitate to use it on anyone who dared to dig an undersized clam. She instantly resolved to pick only elderly-looking ones, even if the babies were sweeter.

"I'll start over here and you can keep working this stretch. It should be good, judging by the number of holes."

Faith could see the holes. They were opening and closing in the mud with a faint popping noise. Samantha had taken Ben out of the backpack, and the two of them were farther up near the high-tide mark playing in the sand. There was nothing to do except dig. Pix had given her a pair of Sam's work gloves, disdaining them for herself. They were too big, of course, and scratchy, but Faith did not intend to stick her fingers into the unknown, especially when it could well mean the loss of a nail. She put her hoe exactly as Pix had shown her and pulled. Nothing happened except for a slight soreness in her upper arms. She tried again. The clams might get scared and find another spot. The third time she succeeded in turning over two or three cupsful of the stuff with nary a clam in sight. A mosquito whined near her face. She was covered from head to boot toe with Cutter's, but she didn't relish the company. Her sun visor was making her forehead sweaty.

After an hour or so she had developed some expertise, been squirted in the face a surprising number of times by recalcitrant clams, and actually had what was going to have to be enough for dinner. Her arms, legs, and back ached, and she slid gingerly across the surface of the flat toward the tiny speck in the distance that was Pix. As she moved, she could see the overturned dark-gray mud, which looked as if someone had been able to move a backhoe in but actually marked Pix's progress. When Faith got closer, she could see Pix's basket was brimming. Maybe she would share.

"Pix, I think I'm going to call it a day."

Pix looked up smiling. "I just love clamming. All this delicious food, just waiting for us here."

"You are truly amazing. I hardly think the back-breaking labor it takes means the food is exactly 'waiting.' "

"We'll get mussels next. That really is easy, Faith. It's cleaning them that takes time."

"Yes, I know, except I don't believe any of this gathering stuff is easy. But by the next time I'll forget how sore my shoulder blades are and go musseling or whatever else you have in mind."

"How about berry picking? The cranberries should be ripe, and I know a secret spot on the Point where there are millions of them."

The Point was a forty-acre finger extending in a curve from the end of the Millers' property. The far side faced east straight out to sea, and the views were magnificent. They often walked over at sunset. No one knew who owned it, not even Pix. Many records had been lost in a fire at the town hall in the early fifties, and people had come to regard the Point as community property, going to its long, sheltered sandy beach, a rarity on Sanpere, to picnic and swim. There were the remains of a large Indian shell heap at the tip, a reminder that the Abenakis were the first summer people.

"Berry picking I can do. Unless there is something peculiar to Maine berries so they cling to the branch and require brute force or anecdotes from 'Bert and I' to get them off."

"No, I promise you. Although I'd like to hear you imitate a Down East accent. I'll give you half my clams if you tell the one about the guy in the balloon asking the farmer for directions."

For clams Faith would do anything, she discovered, and the two of them became convulsed with laughter as they plodded off to the water's edge to rinse the clams. Samantha, watching them from the shore, couldn't figure out what they were doing to make them weave and pitch, but then she wasn't close enough to hear Faith say, "You're up in a balloon, you darn fool."

As they were walking back to the cottage, Faith asked Pix if she ought to invite Jill Merriwether.

"I know Eric and she are an item, yet I don't like to assume that couples go everywhere together."

"Well, they do seem to be serious. Though I've been to lots of things where only one or the other has been invited. I'd say do what you want. She's very shy, but once you got to know her, I think you'd like her."

"Then I'll invite her and make the 'Crow's Nest' notes with our daring girl-boy-girl-boy-girl table."

Later that evening, as Faith surveyed the group over the toasted ravioli, she realized she needn't have worried about an unbalanced table, because one of the girls might just as well have been a china doll. Jill didn't look like a china doll, except for her tiny size. They hadn't made bisque in quite that shade of deep tan, nor straight brown hair that fell to her shoulders after traveling in an unequivocal line across her brow. She was pleasant. She smiled. She sat down and ate. She just didn't talk.

Faith made a few attempts to draw her out, which yielded the information that Jill was native to the island but had lived most of her adult life off, returning only for visits to the grandparents who had raised her and managed to put her through college.

She had come back four summers ago to start the store. In the winter she lived in Portland and did something in the schools. Probably a speech therapist, Faith reflected.

Eric and Roger were teasing Pix, one of their favorite pastimes, and after two glasses of a full, slightly tart Montrachet Pix was rising to the bait. At the moment it was Pix's penchant for sweeping generalizations that coincidentally served her purposes. "Everyone knows that developers are going up and down the coast convincing families to sell their land for what seems like a fortune, and then they turn around and make millions while the poor family has to move the trailer they bought with the money, a trailer that falls apart instantly when the warranty expires, inland on a tiny piece of land nobody wants and they never even get to see the ocean hardly."

"I suppose you mean it's common knowledge, Pix?" Roger smiled.

Roger was even taller than Eric. He looked like a basketball player of the Kevin McHale variety, big hands, long arms, and slightly pigeon breasted. But basketball players didn't have full beards and hair past their earlobes as Roger did. It was all very tidy and he was an attractive man, yet he didn't seem to generate the energy Eric did. He had gentle, large brown eyes the same color as his hair and beard. His face was tanned, and the whole effect resembled an underpainting waiting for the definitions of color. His voice matched—calm, slow, and, Faith was pretty sure, slightly stoned. Pix's voice, in contrast, was like a circus barker's, one who had made a stop at the Winsor School and Pembroke.

"Yes I do, and you and Eric know it as well as I do. Could you afford to buy anything on this island? I know Sam and I couldn't, at least not something with frontage."

Eric broke in, playing devil's advocate. "It hasn't been my impression that people on this island are easily talked into anything, Pix, let alone swindled out of their birthrights."

He stopped suddenly at the thought in everyone's mind, then recovered gracefully. "Case in point. Do you think it likely that Matilda Prescott could have been talked into leaving her house to the two of us, delightful as we are, if she hadn't wanted to? Forget for a minute what the whole island is saying."

"Well," Pix grudgingly admitted, "Matilda might have been an exception. Besides, she really could have sold the property for a fortune. Paul Edson would have killed to get it and years ago told her to name her price. Her answer was to tell him if he ever raised the matter again or set foot on her land, she'd shoot him. No, Matilda couldn't have been sweet-talked into anything."

"Exactly," Eric said. "And the Prescotts know it too. Otherwise they would be contesting the will. This is a very litigious island, remember. People love to have the excuse to go up to the county courthouse and maybe take in a movie or eat at McDonald's while they're suing."

Everyone, including Jill, laughed.

Pix doggedly returned to her point. "But everybody is not Matilda, and I think a lot of people have been cheated out of their land, or at least have not gotten the fair market value for it. It's all these wealthy summer people with their big yachts."

"But Pix, you're a summer person," Faith reminded her.

"Yes, but a different kind. We respect the island and the people who live here."

"How do you know the new people don't? Just because they live in big houses and need five bathrooms, eight bedrooms, hot tubs, big-screen TVs for one double-income-no-kids couple?" Roger asked.

"Dinks! Exactly my point, Roger—I knew you agreed with me," Pix cried out. "And so does Eric, only he's too stubborn to admit it."

"Oh, I do admit it, Pix, and I don't think it's just that developers are offering large sums for shore lots. It's that the economy, basically the fishing industry, is in such trouble that people have to sell to support themselves. Plus the new people build houses, which means more jobs."

"So we're going to end up with a gentrification of the whole coast. Lots of snazzy planned communities with a view," Roger added. It was obviously something they both felt strongly about.

"And the first thing they'll do is go back to the original spelling, 'St. Pierre', because it looks more elegant on stationery," Pix fumed.

Faith rose. "Let's have dessert outside. I put some citronella candles on the porch, and if we douse ourselves in repellent we may be able to survive. Although the mosquitoes could be your first line of defense. And the black flies. Maybe we should be grateful and let them have a nibble."

She realized as she spoke that she found any thought of change on the island as distasteful as the rest of the group. The place was certainly getting to her.

Jill started to pick up a plate, but Faith stopped her. "And please just leave everything. We have some fromage blanc—and strawberries from the

Miller garden—that needs to be eaten immediately."

"Is it true, Pix, that Sam is having the road widened so the trucks from Birdseye can make it down to your place?" Roger asked.

"Very funny, but I must say we are having a pretty terrific yield this year."

"Then by all means say it." Eric opened the door for her and bowed.

Everyone left early, as island custom seemed to dictate. All those energetic things to do at dawn, like weeding.

Jill had thanked Faith and hoped they would see each other again soon. Faith watched them drive away, noting that Eric had joined Jill in her car. Maybe he liked a good listener, and she was certainly a striking woman. Faith would call her beautiful—probably most other women would. Tom would say no. They never agreed on female pulchritude, so she automatically said "striking" instead of "gorgeous" in her mind. Jill had worn a gauzy white-linen shirt, full skirt of the same material, a wide dark-brown leather belt, and matching flats. She was willing to bet Jill didn't do her shopping at JC Penney, not even in the Stephanie Powers Collection.

She saw Jill again the following night at the Baked Bean and Casserole Supper with Eric and Roger. She was wearing jeans and a huge gray Champion sweatshirt, probably Eric's, and she still looked striking. They had managed to save seats for the Miller-Fairchild contingent at one of the long trestle tables set up in the IOOF Hall. It was covered with white butcher paper and someone had placed an arrangement of wildflowers in a spray-painted coffee can exactly in the center. Faith imprisoned Benjamin in his Sassy Seat with Samantha on guard while she and Pix went to load their plates with food that even from afar seemed to fulfill Faith's prophecy. There was a good warm food smell in the air, like bread baking with a freshly brewed pot of coffee on the back burner, but it seemed to bear no relationship to what Faith could actually see in front of her.

The hall was full, and outside in the increasingly cool evening a patient crowd waited their turn for three-bean salad and watermelon pickles. When Faith returned with as little of the mystery casseroles and as much of the fresh crabmeat salad, homemade bread, beans, and what she knew was Pix's black-seeded Simpson lettuce possible, the table was full too. She recognized Elliot and Louise Frazier, long-time friends of the whole Miller family, who lived in one of the old ship's-captain houses in Sanpere Village. The others were new to her.

Pix hastened to make introductions. "Faith, these are our friends Bill Fox and John Eggleston. Bill writes books and lives not too far from us, toward South Beach. John is a wood sculptor and another man of the cloth. He lives in Little Harbor."

A booming voice cut her off. "*Used* to be, Pix. Whatever sermonizing I do now is to the gulls and myself."

The voice matched his size and general appearance. He was well over six feet, with startling bright-red hair shooting out in flames all over his head. A few gray strands were beginning to ameliorate the effect, and Faith judged him to be in his mid-forties. He was wearing a Welsh fisherman's smock and a Greek fisherman's hat, which created an ecumenically nautical effect or vice versa. He must have been something to see in the pulpit. She wondered about the "used to be" part. Who left whom?

Bill Fox was a neat, dapper little man with a crisply pressed Brooks Brothers striped oxford-cloth button-down shirt. It was open at the neck, but Faith knew there were bow ties at home, just as she was willing to bet that when he stood up, he'd prove to be wearing chinos and Topsiders. He was the kind of person who has looked the same for most of his adult life, appearing middle-aged in his twenties, then when everyone else caught up looking perennially youthful. Slightly balding, horn-rimmed glasses, and anywhere from thirty to fifty. Faith was struck by a sudden thought and asked, "Bill Fox. Not William H. H. Fox!"

He smiled. "I admit to such, yes."

"Pix, 'He writes books.' That has to be one of your greatest understatements of all time." Faith turned to Fox. "I love your work and have reread all of it constantly throughout my life. I've never thought of them as children's books."

"I don't either," he confessed. "But children seem to approach them most readily."

Faith knew that Pix's reading, when she had the time, was limited to breeding manuals for Golden Retrievers and Rodale Press best-sellers, but she couldn't believe that she had been on the island all this time in close proximity to William H. H. Fox and Pix hadn't mentioned it.

He had written a series considered modern classics in which two children discovered that they had the power to make themselves as tiny as field mice and explore the natural world in exquisite detail. One day in the forest they ventured down a hole and came upon an enchanted land, Selega, ruled by

Prince Herodias and Princess Ardea. Further books related their travels in Selega and followed them through childhood in both worlds. The last book ended with their discovery that they couldn't make themselves small anymore. Faith always cried whenever she got to that final page. It was hard to pinpoint the appeal of the stories—they were a mixture of real and surreal, fantasy and adventure, with a lot of nursery tea-type coziness thrown in whenever the children were in the big world. And Selega was perfect. There had been many a day, Faith remembered, when she longed to be transported there as Princess Ardea of the flowing dark hair and the eyes like violets. Not to mention all the handmaidens and silken gowns.

"Would you mind telling me what the two 'H's stand for? I've always wondered."

"Not at all. I'd put the whole thing in, but it might not fit on the cover. My full name is William Henry Harrison Fox. With a short last name, my mother figured she could have free rein with the rest. My brother is Ulysses Grant Garfield Fox. Mom liked double initials and famous men."

Faith had read that Fox was a shy recluse, but it was hard to attach that image to the genial man sitting across from her heartily enjoying what appeared to be canned corn mixed with sliced hot dogs and elbow macaroni.

By dessert Faith had decided Pix was right. Baked Bean and Casserole Suppers and their like were not to be missed. It wasn't the food so much, though the baked beans had been delicious, but the ambience. Everybody seemed to be having such a good time. The hall was full of happy noise, and there was a constant change of scenery as contented diners relinquished their places to newcomers. Faith sat with

45

a thick white china mug of the coffee she had smelled earlier, a huge slab of blueberry pie, and a couple of chewy oatmeal cookies to fill in the corners and watched. John Eggleston had departed, after delivering a lengthy and learned answer to Eric's query about who were the Odd Fellows anyway? (Roots in medieval England, the first lodge in the U.S. chartered in the early 1800's and dedicated to educational assistance.) Faith wasn't surprised. Ministers always seemed to know things like this. Samantha was also gone, joining Arlene in the kitchen, where she was helping out. Everyone else was lingering over the desserts with slightly guilty glances at the line that still remained. Ben had plunged two fists into a plate of pie and was now singing softly to himself as he licked his fingers.

"I don't think I can eat another thing," sighed Pix blissfully as she finished her second piece of pie. "Of course I said that after the main courses."

Faith started to invite everyone back to the cottage for brandy or whatever one had after such an event, when she realized that the line had shifted again and the two people who had just edged through the door were attracting a few surreptitious glances. (She had already learned that no one in Maine actually displayed overt curiosity.)

It was Bird with her rock musician. He looked quite ordinary, or at least for the Hard Rock Café or some other place where adolescents and post-adolescents dressed the part. He was wearing tight black leather pants and a vest with no shirt, which had to be pretty nippy Down East, and his hair was carefully arranged in careless spikes. Faith had never seen Bird up close. She was certainly dressed like a flower child, and a rather pale baby was tied in a sling on her back, but no one was noticing her dress or the baby.

Bird was beautiful. Not striking. There would be no argument. Long shining deep black hair and luminous eyes that seemed to change from blue to purple as the light caught them. Cheeks flushed from the cold and rosy lips that were slightly parted. Absolutely beautiful.

Faith looked across the table. Bill Fox was gazing at the door with a sudden look of intense longing on his face. Roger was looking too, a slightly blurred duplicate. They wouldn't want to go anywhere for a while.

Princess Ardea had just walked into the room.

Three

"Going, going, gone." The auctioneer brought his gavel down with a bang on the crate he had set on top of a chest of drawers. Another quilt had been bid up by the dealers and off-islanders. But Faith felt confident that she would get one eventually. There were so many. It seemed that generations of Prescott women had done nothing but cut up their old clothes and piece them into quilts. During the viewing in the barn, the choicest ones had been hung on the walls and suspended from the rafters like glowing pennants for a tournament. And in a way an auction was like a tournament as knight jousted with knight for the prize—a fair damsel, splinter of the true cross, or walnut five-shelf corner whatnot.

They were holding up another quilt now, a particularly beautiful one with a huge Mariner's Compass in the center in shades of blue, surrounded by smaller ones quilted in white on white. Faith raised her card hopefully when the bidding started, then sighed, sat back, and watched.

It was fascinating. The auctioneer spoke so rapidly she could scarcely follow, and as he rattled off the bids—"Two hundred dollars, do I heayre two fifty?"—his partner, an elderly man who looked like he'd be more at home in a dory on Eggemoggin Reach checking his traps, reached toward the crowd and grabbed the bids out of thin air, keeping up a constant accompaniment—"Yep, yep, you have it. You have it."

It was all over at five hundred dollars.

"Remember, it was one of the older ones, Faith," Pix comforted her.

They had arrived at seven o'clock, laden with chairs, a thermos of coffee, another of cold lemonade, sandwiches, tape measures, and a firm resolve not to get carried away; if one showed signs of it, the other had solemnly sworn to push her companion's chair over. Faith could afford to bid high for what she wanted, since she had a tidy little trust fund started by her perspicacious great-grandfather. The next egg had shrunk to plover size after she had begun her catering business, but her success had let her replace what she had taken out and a good deal more. Tom looked upon it as a golden egg—insurance for old age, and also back-up college tuition for Benjamin and whoever might follow. Faith agreed, with one exception: She would pay for her clothes. She supposed that loosely defined, that could include a quilt, but she was at the auction for bargains, unless she fell head over heels in love with something. And then there was always Pix the watchdog; if she started to bid wildly, Pix would see to it that she was literally head over heels.

Pix could afford the high bids, too, but she had an ingrained Yankee frugality that continued to astound Faith—the kind that cut off the one leg in her pantyhose that had a run, matched the good leg with a similar survivor, and suffered two elastic waistbands and goodness only knew what kind of discomfort in the crotch. Faith had given her a pair of thigh highs, and Pix was initially enthusiastic until she went to Filene's to get more and found out the price.

They were both dressed in layers today. The morning had started out foggy and cool, but Pix had predicted they would be down to their tank tops before noon, and she was right.

Despite a good-sized crowd, they were able to set up camp under the tent in a prime spot—close enough to the front to follow the action there and slightly off to the side to follow any action in the crowd. They didn't have to wait long.

The first skirmish of the day broke out between Eric and Sonny Prescott before the auction started. Eric claimed that the weather vane, an old copper one in the shape of a three-masted schooner, was part of the house and not the contents thereof. Sonny said it was like the pictures, mirrors, and other detachable things. It could be taken off, so it was auctionable. Eric pointed out with increasing heat that the ship had raced against the wind on top of the barn since it was built and was as much a part of the house as the gazebo. Sonny replied that he didn't wonder but the gazebo could be auctioned too. One of the onlookers, a spoil-sport or good Samaritan depending on how one viewed these matters, had gone to get the lawyer.

Mr. Foster was quite explicit, armed with foresight, experience, and a list. The gazebo stayed. The weather vane went. Eric angrily told the auction-house workers not to touch it, he was going to buy it, and the lawyer told the auctioneer he thought it could be bid upon from the ground. An uneasy peace reigned.

Roger arrived shortly after and went with Eric into the house, possibly to make sure the Prescotts weren't removing the wainscotting in the dining room or linoleum in the kitchen.

Now it was almost ten o'clock and it seemed that Stanley Gardiner, the auctioneer, had scarcely made a dent in the lots, even at the breakneck speed he and his runners steadily maintained. Faith sat transfixed, her index card with the number on it clutched in her hand. On the back were some sketchy notes to remind her what she wanted.

"Lot 56—Carnival glass—a beautiful grape-and-cable compote in perfect condition, with a small flake at the base. We don't often see them this size. What am I bid for this lovely piece? Do I heayre fifty, fifty, seventy-five? All done at seventy-five? Are we buying or renting today? Fair word and fair warning—sold for seventy-five."

Faith glanced down at her card. Lot 58 was a cherry cradle. After all, Benjamin was getting up there and it might be time to start thinking about another baby. Her mind instantly recoiled from the memory of all those sleepless nights and the fact that "easy childbirth" was an oxymoron.

She thought instead about little toes and a satiny-smooth bottom, those milky smiles and gurgles. Meanwhile the cradle could hold Ben's stuffed-animal menagerie.

"Now here's a pretty piece," the auctioneer was saying. "Lot fifty-eight, a cherry cradle. Not a scratch on it. Do I heayre twenty-five to start us off?"

Faith raised her card fast, and the old man whom the auctioneer addressed as Walter and occasionally Wally snatched the bid in his gnarled grip. "You've got it."

Faith didn't look behind her, but apparently only one other person was interested in the cradle judging from Walter's movements.

"Nobody having babies on this island anymore? I have fifty-five. Use it for a planter—look swell with petunias in it. I have seventy-five and ninety-five. Ninety-five, ninety-five. Going, going, gone at ninety-five dollars." Faith grabbed Pix's arm ecstatically. It could have been a can full of rusty nails. The point was, *she* was the high bidder.

"Have cradle, will reproduce," Pix said, laughing.

The tent was full and people had set up chairs on the lawn. Earlier, Pix had used the occasion to give Faith a rapid overview of the island population: four basic groups with numerous subdivisions. There were the year-round native islanders, an inordinate number of whom were named Prescott, Hamilton, or Sanford, and the year-round off-islanders, many like Eric and Roger—artists or writers—others wanting to get away to what they thought was a simpler life. There had been a big influx of this group in the late sixties and many had stayed, but to the Prescotts et al they might have arrived a week ago. The summer people were also divided into two main groups: what Pix called the "rusticators," families who had been coming to the island for generations and marched in the annual Fourth of July parade with banners that said "Fiftieth Summer," and the newcomers, people like Faith who rented cottages for short periods of time. People who might never return to Sanpere, impossible as that was to imagine.

Faith looked around. Once you had the labels, it was easy to stick them on. A group of rusticators sat on sturdy canvas folding stools not far away with grandmother's fitted wicker picnic basket, "the one we always take to auctions," filled with egg-salad and watercress sandwiches, the thermoses with fresh-minted iced tea at their feet. Some of the women were knitting Fair Isle sweaters, and the men strolled purposefully down to the water to check the tide from time to time. The new people had the equipment, but their baskets lacked the patina and validation of old age. The local people were eating the hot dogs being sold, and most of the artistic group had gone home after noting Matilda's taste—a Wallace Nutting or two, Granville Fuel Oil calendars—and searching fruitlessly in the boxes from the attic for a Hiroshige.

There were a large number of day visitors too—dealers from up and down the coast and summer people of both varieties from the mainland. Pix had spoken in a disparaging way about them—people who needed a movie theater within twenty miles.

The next couple of hours went by quickly. It got hotter under the tent, but it was worse outside in the sunshine. They ate their sandwiches and drank the lemonade. Pix had to supplement her lunch with one of the hot dogs after she smelled the one the person next to her had, heaped with sauerkraut.

"It goes with an auction," she told Faith, who refused.

"Funny, I don't remember seeing them at Christie's," Faith remarked, and Pix jabbed her.

"When in Rome, Faith . . ."

"I know, I know. If they were selling clam rolls I might be interested, but hot dogs, no, not even for you and Sanpere."

Pix was the successful bidder on a mixed lot of Heisey glass and almost got a repulsive Roseville jardiniere and pedestal. After that episode Faith asked her if it was permissible to overturn her chair if she bid on something hideous.

"Faith, Roseville is highly collectible, and besides

it would have looked beautiful with that asparagus fern I have. I thought you liked that period."

Before Faith could reply that there was such a thing as selectivity, their attention was drawn away by another quilt, and again it went high. Some had been sold for lower, even bargain bids, but they did not appeal to Faith. She wanted a very special one for their bed in Aleford. The parsonage was in constant danger of slipping into New England country, and she had met the threat by bringing in modern pieces of her own; so far they coexisted happily. She thought she could safely add a quilt without fear of heart-shaped baskets, wreaths, stenciled herds of cows, and pigs in all forms following.

"Faith," Pix whispered excitedly, "the weather vane is next."

It had been a relatively calm auction with only one minor altercation, when a lady wearing red heart-shaped sunglasses who was definitely not Lolita claimed she, and not the couple in front of her, had been the high bidder on a Limoges fish service. The auctioneer had backed up and started the bidding again. She got the fish service and left. The young couple found solace in a Nipon dessert set.

Now the crowd under the tent grew still, and people who had wandered off to the shade under the big oak trees came to stand on the sidelines.

Eric and Roger had been sitting in the front row, with the Prescotts filling in the chairs to either side and the rear. It was like a wedding where the bride or groom had only two friends. Eric's arms were folded across his chest, and Roger's eyes assumed a steely glint quite unlike their everyday softness. Faith saw Jill standing to one side of the auction worker's table. She must have closed the store. Eric saw her too and raised a hand in greeting. Jill smiled encouragingly.

Walter had taken over for a while, but now Stanley Gardiner returned, took the microphone, and placed it around his neck. Walter moved to the side, his eyes darting around the tent, gearing up. You could hear a fly's wings flutter.

"Lot two twenty-five. Copper weather vane. As trim a vessel as ever set sail—thirty-six inches long. You've all seen it, ladies and gentlemen. Right on top of the barn. I can tell you there are no patched-up bullet holes in this one. It is in the original condition. A beauty. Fifty to open."

Eric raised his card high, and immediately one of the Prescotts countered with a bid of seventy-five dollars. There was a lot of interest in the vane, and the bidding went high. At nine hundred dollars everyone had dropped out except the Prescotts and Eric and Roger. Eric bid nine hundred and fifty. The Prescotts looked grim and bid a thousand. The crowd was gasping. Eric bid twelve hundred and the Prescotts seemed to waver. Then Joe Prescott jumped up and rushed at Eric and Roger. Stanley Gardiner stood in his way, and Joe began shouting around him, "It's the gold! Why do you think they're bidding so high! You bastards! She told you, didn't she!? It's got to be gold underneath or something."

"Are you out of your mind!?" Roger yelled at him. He and Eric were on their feet. Sonny Prescott stepped next to the beleaguered auctioneer. "Now Joe might have an ideah here. I'd say we better have a closer look at the hull of that boat."

"If you touch that weather vane, I'll kill you." Eric spoke in a flat measured voice, but his words reached all the way to the back rows. Jill moved away from the table and came up quietly behind him. Nobody else moved. Then the lawyer came and spoke to the auctioneer.

"Now everybody sit down and calm down. Gorry, I've never seen anything like an auction to get people riled up." Mr. Gardiner took out a big white handkerchief and mopped his forehead. Faith felt a thin trickle of sweat make its way down her cleavage. It was hot. And it was tense.

"What we're going to do is withdraw Lot two twenty-five for the time being until the heirs can have it appraised to everyone's satisfaction, and whether it will be done up there on the blasted roof or down on the lawn is something you can work out with Mr. Foster here." He motioned to the lawyer, who looked as cool and collected as he had at seven o'clock. "Now there's plenty left for everybody. Lot two twenty-six—Well, what do you know? An Atwater Kent in a Gothic box. Have to be a few of us here who remember this baby. Now what am I bid? Who will start the music at twenty-five?"

The music stopped at two hundred dollars and an oak chest of drawers, a tray of spongeware, and a Seth Thomas Westminster chimes clock rapidly followed. The parlor set was put up and created some excited bidding among the Prescotts. It might have a nick or two, and the rosewood needed some elbow grease, but it had stood in splendor in the front parlor since Darnell had brought it home from Pain's in Boston as a wedding present for his bride. Nora Prescott from Granville was the high bidder at $850. Just as Matilda had promised her, only she hadn't thought she would have to buy it to get it. Nora's sister, Irene, to whom it had also been promised, decided not to bid at the last moment. Blood was thicker than Old English polish, and Nora had always been there when she needed her, taking the kids when she was up at Blue Hill having her appendix out, telling her she was well rid of him when her husband took off with a hairdresser from Belfast. Irene's noble sacrifice did not go unnoticed, and Nora decided to give her the little marble-topped table, which really wasn't going to fit in her living room anyway.

Pix bid quickly and got a pretty spool bed for Samantha's room and a dry sink before Faith even knew she was bidding.

And so the auction unfolded, assuming a character distinct from all the other auctions Gardiner and Company had run or the crowd attended. You never knew what was going to happen. The Warhol cookie jars turned out to be wooden lobster pots that had been in the barn. Few lobstermen used them anymore, and as the tourists and dealers bid them up, all the locals resolved to go clean out their sheds.

Pix and Faith were determined to wait until the bitter end for all the real bargains, and at about four o'clock the box lots started. Faith quickly snared one with tools she had noted for three dollars and Pix bought two mystery boxes of china for four dollars each, which upon inspection proved to contain a lovely Wedgewood ironstone teapot, lots of saucers without cups, something that could possibly be a piece of Imari, some Tupperware, and other treasures. Faith grabbed another box, one filled with board games of varying vintages, which she had seen at the viewing. Tom's family was addicted to board games, and she knew they would be happy to have more, especially for a dollar fifty. She bought two more boxes of china on speculation for two dollars each and figured she was done. After the cradle she had successfully bid on an odd lot of plate serving pieces for thirty-five dollars, elegant Victoriana with elaborate scrolls etched on the knife blades and ladles and repoussé flowers on the handles. It had been a productive day.

Just as she and Pix were packing up and getting ready to settle their accounts, the runners brought out another quilt, or actually a quilt top. It had been pieced, but not quilted to the batting and underside. Faith paused to watch as they unfolded it. It was a sampler quilt. Every square was different, connected with lattice stripping. The colors were repeated in each design, strong blues, greens, and touches of the same pink as the granite rocks by the shore.

It was a Maine quilt. Maine colors. And Faith had to have it. She sat down and pulled Pix into her chair.

"A beautiful quilt top here. All it needs is a back, and I'm sure a lot of you ladies out there could put this together in no time. What am I bid? Do I heayre ten dollars?" Faith raised her card. She was so excited she felt slightly lightheaded. There was something about this quilt. It was ridiculous, really. She hadn't the slightest idea how to quilt; it was not one of her accomplishments. In fact any sewing more complicated than buttons or a running stitch went to the tailor and always had. But she'd solve that problem once she had it. And she got it. Apparently there weren't any quilters in the audience and it was hers for forty dollars.

"Faith, it's gorgeous, and I can show you how to quilt. It's not difficult at all," Pix said.

"I think it would be easier if you quilted it, Pix, but as you have seen with the clamming, I'm willing to try anything." And with that they went home to gloat over their finds and bemoan all the ones that got away.

They passed Eric and Jill on the way out. Eric was tight-lipped and Jill was talking to him in a low voice. They stopped and Pix asked if they wanted to come to the cottage for a drink, but Jill said they were going to the mainland to get some dinner and distance. Eric smiled wryly. "Can you believe they actually think the mythical gold is in that weather vane? And how is it supposed to have gotten there? Did Darnell climb up one night and ballast it with doubloons, in which case it would have toppled off the barn long ago? Or maybe he took it down and replaced it with one cast of solid gold and no one ever heard anything about how he got it made? Well, at least we got the wicker porch furniture and some of the bedroom sets. I'm just glad it's over and we can move in."

Pix patted his arm. "Situations like this are always horrible. You should hear some of the stories Sam tells about settling estates."

"Did you get some nice things?" Jill asked as they turned to leave.

"Oh yes, nothing earth-shattering, but you have to go home with something from an auction, especially a historic one like this. Faith got a cradle, a quilt top, and who knows what in the boxes, and I got my usual—china, glass. Sam says *we're* going to have to have an auction soon."

"Thanks for the invitation, Pix. We'll see you soon," Eric said. "Good-bye, Faith—I haven't forgotten about our gazebo party. You and Pix and whatever husbands are around can come sometime next week."

"That would be lovely, but husbands are not arriving until close to Labor Day, so you'll have to put up with the company of women."

"Never a chore." Eric smiled. His mood seemed to have lifted, and Faith was sure it was not just her imagination that Jill gave them a look filled with gratitude as she said good-bye.

The events of the auction had been unsettling, and Faith found it hard to sleep that night. It had been after six when she finally got back, and she was exhausted. She left the boxes in the barn to go through later and brought the quilt top into the house. It was even more beautiful than she had thought when they had held it up. She spread it on the bed in the spare room. It seemed at home.

After a hasty supper she read to Benjamin and settled him into his crib, then got an Angela Thirkell out of the bookcase and went to bed herself. She must have slept, because when she looked at the clock several hours had passed, but now she felt wide awake. She opened the book again and tried to lose herself in Barsetshire, but the comings and goings of the Brandons did not distract her.

There also seemed to be a lot of comings and goings in the cove and on the shore road opposite the cottage. She remembered that she had heard the same boat and truck noises a week ago Thursday night, because Tom had been lying next to her and thought it might be night fishing. The next day they had seen herring nets, so the fishermen must have been catching a run, then unloading at Prescott's straight into the trucks.

She got up, turned out the light, and went to the window. She couldn't see much, just pinpoints of light and the occasional long sweep of headlights. She didn't hear any talking—just the boat engines and the trucks. Well, it was after two o'clock and they, of all people, would know how voices carried on the water. Still, it surprised her a little that they should be so considerate. From what she had seen at the auction, Sonny Prescott didn't seem like a man who would whisper if he had something to say. If it *was* Sonny out there in the dark, that is.

Benjamin would be up in a few, very few hours. Faith crawled back into her bed, thought wistfully about Tom, and wondered if she would feel better or weird if she piled some pillows in his approximate shape next to her. Weird. She fell asleep.

Faith spent most of Friday in the hammock watching Benjamin chase croquet balls on the lawn. The owners of the cottage maintained a large, carefully manicured lawn in the back of the house, bordered on three sides by the meadow filled now with Indian paintbrush, Queen Anne's lace and other wildflowers. The lawn looked a bit odd there, as if someone had spread a piece of felt over the meadow, but it provided a place to sit and play all those games stored in the barn.

She did rouse herself to get lunch, which the two of them ate on the grass. Faith found feeding Benjamin al fresco made life much simpler. Anything he dropped would be picked up by the gulls later. At four o'clock Tom called. They had decided he would call her, since he wasn't as sure of his schedule as she was of hers. No schedule.

It was a case of two people who are very close to each other with not much to say. Or rather a lot to say, but nothing to say of common interest. Faith started to tell him about the Casserole Supper and Bird's entrance and the auction and the trouble between the Prescotts and Roger and Eric, then she realized he didn't really know these people and it all meant nothing to him. Tom started to tell Faith about the difficulty he was having keeping his Ecclesiastes study section on the path; the incipient power struggle between this year's conference chairman and the recently named next year's; and the distracting presence of a certain lady from Minneapolis—distracting of course not to *moi*, Tom protested a bit too much to himself, but some of the other men—when he also realized how boring it all was when you weren't there. Of course, Faith would have been even more bored if she had been there. And so they talked at cross purposes for a while, tried to explain, then Faith said, "Tom, I love you. Is that it? I mean isn't that why you called?"

"In a word, yes. And I love you. And I miss you. You do sound like you're having more fun. And getting better things to eat."

"Think of it as food for the soul, and I'll make it up to you when you get back. The things to eat and especially the fun."

"I hope you're thinking of the same kind of fun I'm thinking of," Tom commented.

"Absolutely, brisk swims in the ocean followed by volleyball and ten-mile hikes. Isn't that what you Fairchilds call 'fun'?" Faith teased.

"Watch out, sweetheart, or I'll hold you to it."

"Oh, Tom, I almost forgot. I had a letter from Hope on Friday. She and Quentin are going to be visiting friends in Bar Harbor and wondered if we wanted company over Labor Day weekend. What do you think?"

"I think I don't want any company but yours, but you know I love your sister dearly, and if there were the slightest chance that our example of connubial bliss would nudge the two of them toward the altar, I'd take it."

"Good. I already said they could come."

"Dammit, Faith! What did you ask me for if you had the whole thing decided?"

"I wanted to hear what you would say and it was what I thought, so there's no problem. Besides, you always like Quentin after the first shock of the new wears off and he forgets he's flawless."

"That's beside the point."

"Are we quarreling?" Faith asked. "I hope not, because it's horrible enough on the phone."

"No, not quarreling. It's just necessary that I occasionally try to cling to what's left of my independence."

"Oh, Tom, this is silly. All right. It was a little high-handed of me." She paused. Tom didn't say anything. "Okay, even very high-handed and I promise faithfully, don't laugh, to consult you first in the future about house guests. And when you see the wonderful box lots I got at the auction, you'll let me do anything I want."

"I do anyway, but promise me that you'll leave at least one box for me to go through myself."

"Better, I'll give you two. I bought four, so that's fair. You can have the tools and one that looks like old games. I thought your family might like them."

"That's terrific, Faith. Now I have to go, honey. A group of us are going to Portsmouth for dinner at The Blue Strawberry."

"Sounds tough, Tom."

"Believe me, Faith, after a week of this food, we deserve it."

"I'm sure you do. Just make sure any legs you encounter under the table belong to it."

After some more of this nonsense, they hung up and Faith went back to the yard. Ben was still napping. Must be all the sea air, she thought. She had noticed that the locals touted it as either invigorating or soporific depending on what the situation called for. Just another one of those charming contradictions that seemed to crop up on Sanpere.

No sooner was she outside than she decided to go in. She felt at loose ends. Pix had invited them for supper, but Faith had wanted to go to bed early after her wakefulness the night before and declined. She sat down at the big rolltop desk by the window facing the cove and got out her recipe notebook to jot down a few ideas. The phone rang. Of course.

"Hello, Pix," she said.

"How did you know it was me?"

"You and Tom are the only people who call me, and Tom just called, so that leaves you, Watson, my good fellow."

"Oh, I see. I called to see if you wanted to change your mind. John Eggleston is bringing over some lobster from his traps—he just has a few in front of his house—and the Fraziers are dropping by. Oh, and Jill is coming, though she wasn't sure when. She's taking inventory or something. Eric went up to some friends on Drake's Island for a couple of days, so she's at loose ends. I asked Roger too, but he's up to his elbows in new glazes, he told me this morning."

"You people seem to exist in a frantic whirl of gaiety here. One party after another. How are we going to settle down to life in Aleford? And think how bored I'll be next time I go home to the City for a visit," Faith said, reflecting on the difference between Pix the hostess as hostage of Aleford and Pix the Perle Mesta of Sanpere. Several times a year she had to give dinner parties for Sam's law partners or clients, and she would start worrying a month before. The night of the dinner something disastrous always occurred. Either with the food—one time she had forgotten to remove the plastic bag with the innards from her roast chicken—or with her person—a zipper stuck halfway up on the dress she was attempting to put on—and Faith had to rush over to save her. But on Sanpere Pix thought nothing of inviting large groups on the spur of the moment. If she didn't have enough plates, she switched to paper with casual aplomb.

"I do want to get to bed early, Pix, but I'd like to see the Fraziers and especially your renegade priest again. Could Ben and I come for the aperitif?"

"Of course, and Faith, you'll never guess! The Prescotts took turns watching the weather vane all night until they got some expert down from Orono this morning. And Eric was right. There was no way the gold could have been hidden in it. Too heavy. Anyway, the man didn't mind climbing on the roof, so he went up, poked around, and took scrapings. It's copper through and through. So now it goes in the next auction Gardiner has, and they'll all go to bid against Eric and Roger out of spite and disappointment. Since the weather vane was part of the contents of the house, if it had been gold, it would have been the Prescott clan's. That's a lot of trips to Florida for the winter."

"From everything I hear about her, Matilda would have enjoyed all this," Faith commented.

"Definitely. Fortunately, she liked me—or didn't dislike me, I should say. I used to take her some of my strawberry preserves every once in a while. Oh, and Louise Frazier told me that your quilt top is probably the last one Matilda made. She was piecing one with those colors when Louise visited her just before she died."

"Thanks, Pix. It's nice to know who made it. If she

appreciated your delectable jam, she couldn't have been too horrible."

"Oh, she wasn't horrible at all—just lonely and unappreciated, I think. Sam used to enjoy talking with her, sparring really. He thought she should have gone into politics. She was bright and totally honest, and had so much drive. Too much for her family. She liked to be in charge, and when she got old and couldn't be, they were used to keeping their distance."

"I want to hear more about all this, Pix, but Ben's awake. He's starting to hurl things violently out of the crib, always a bad sign, so I'd better go. When do you want us?"

"Around five?"

"Fine. I'll see you soon."

Faith hung up and raced upstairs before one of Benjamin's missiles found the window as a target. Everything was on the floor, and Ben, having taken all his clothes off, was just climbing out of the crib. She carried him into the bathroom and sat him on the potty seat. Unpredictable in all things, he had virtually toilet trained himself. Just as she was culling information from all the experts and getting ready to start, he had announced, "No diapers," and had scarcely looked back. It was big-boy underpants—BBUs, as Tom called them—from here on in.

An hour later Faith was sipping a glass of wine and eating cold mussels and the remoulade sauce she had taught Pix how to make. She was enjoying herself. Samantha was reading to Ben, which she appeared to be able to do for hours on end without going crazy and/or speaking like Mr. Rogers.

John Eggleston was regaling them with tales of the island during Prohibition, which he had heard mostly from his neighbor and good friend, Elwell Sanford.

"Of course Elwell swears he himself wasn't involved in any of this illegal activity, although his constant references to a 'friend of mine' leave me a mite skeptical. Maine was a rum runner's dream, with this convoluted coastline—twenty-seven hundred miles of small coves, harbors, and inlets sandwiched into a four-hundred-mile loaf. And all the islands off shore. People tell me there are still cases buried on the Point, but I haven't heard of anyone finding one recently, Elwell's classic story, which I must admit I have heard up and down the coast, is about one of the Marshalls who was feuding with his neighbor. They were both selling hootch. One stormy night a revenuer came to Amos Marshall's house, desperate for a drink, he said. Well, Amos looked at him. His slicker was weatherbeaten and he needed a shave, but his boots were brand-new; so Amos sent him up the road saying he had taken the pledge himself, but his neighbor could oblige. The neighbor, unfortunately, wasn't so observant."

Everyone laughed, and Pix said, "Maybe you have heard it elsewhere, but I'm sure it started here."

After the laughter died down, Elliot Frazier remarked, "Of course we have the modern-day version with the illegal drug traffic. You're right about the coastline, John—it is virtually impossible to police it, and boats are landing the stuff all the time."

"When I first came to Sanpere in the late sixties, it had just started, or people had just become aware of it, and every newcomer to this island was thought to be either a drug peddler or an undercover agent. They certainly didn't know what to make of me,"

John said, laughing. "I used to fill in during the summer for a preacher over in Cherryfield, and when that got back to the island, they were even more confused."

"But John," Louise interrupted in her soft, faintly Southern voice, "you were doing so much good work with the teenagers here." She turned to Faith. "There was, and is, a big problem with alcohol on the island, and some drugs. There is really nothing for these kids to do here. John was the one who started the community center."

A different kind of ministry, Faith thought. John Eggleston was certainly a compelling figure, and she could imagine he had quite an effect on kids once he got going. She liked his stories and certainly he was to be admired for whatever he'd done for Sanpere, yet there was still a suggestion of fire and brimstone lurking just behind the pupils of his eyes and the clarion surety of his voice made her uneasy. A man who thinks he is absolutely right in everything he says and does. She had the feeling that if you ever got in his way, he'd roll implacably over you. No turning the other cheek here. Maybe that was why he had left the ministry. Tom wasn't a doormat, but he had a sense of his own limitations, humility in the presence of imponderables. Faith slid in somewhere between the two. She hoped she'd go around, and not over, but knew too that humble was not her best pie.

"Faith, whatever are you thinking about? You have the most peculiar expression on your face—sort of like the two corners of your mouth can't decide whether to go up or down," Pix commented.

"That's about it, Pix. I was thinking about good and evil," Faith replied, not realizing until she said it that that was what she had actually been considering.

There was silence for a moment as they all looked at her. Then Elliot Frazier asked, "Is this in light of the auction? I ask that because the day triggered many thoughts for me, starting with the whole event. Was it good or evil of Matilda to separate things that way? We knew her well, and I am still puzzled that she wanted to have the house dismantled after she died. The things in it were as much a part of the house as the structure itself for her."

"I hadn't connected my thoughts to the auction, but you may be right. I certainly have been restless since yesterday. There seemed to be so much tension, and I don't even know all these people." Faith looked at him with a feeling of respect. An insightful man.

The Fraziers had moved to Sanpere almost forty years ago. They were in their early thirties then, with two small children. Elliot had had a serious heart attack and they had wanted to get away from the stress of life in Washington, where he had built up a thriving accounting firm. At about the same time, Louise had inherited enough money from her family to enable them to buy their lovely old house on Sanpere. Elliot never had another heart attack. He had retired years before from the job he got the first year they were here—postmaster of Sanpere Village. They were the exception to the rule—most people on the island had forgotten the Fraziers weren't born on Sanpere. They moved comfortably among all the groups on the island. Sanpere had few secrets the postmaster and his wife hadn't heard—and kept.

"I think I know why Matilda divided things,"

Louise offered. "She might have felt slightly guilty about leaving the house to Roger and Eric, but more likely she wanted to get everything cleaned out. Have someone start fresh, which I'm sure she wanted to do herself at times, much as she worshipped those ancestors of hers."

"You could be right," Pix said. "The end of an era."

"Exactly." John closed the gate on the conversation, and Faith realized it was getting late. She resisted their attempts to convince her to stay for dinner and set off through the woods with Benjamin in tow. The path led close to the shore at times, and Faith could glimpse the sunset through the trees. The sun was a fiery-red rubber ball making a straight path across the water, the clouds streaming out along the horizon like purple and scarlet kite tails. Life with Ben was reducing her to kindergarten imagery.

The rocks that sloped down to the water were already in darkness, and on the other side of the cove she could see a few lights at Prescott's lobster pound and the houses to either side. Bird's tiny cabin stood out against the sky. There were no lights on, and Faith wasn't sure Bird even had electricity. She had seen her with the baby on the shore again and this time had received a brief nod and slight smile in answer to her greeting. The baby, who appeared to be under a year old, still looked pale, and whether this was from the macrobiotics or lack of sunshine penetrating the sling Bird carried it in Faith didn't know.

The porch light at her own cottage blinked a welcome as she emerged from the woods carrying Benjamin, who had suddenly decided he wanted to be picked up and was now sound asleep.

She had no trouble sleeping that night either. Her last semiconscious thought was that she had never realized Nature was quite so noisy—crickets, owls, bullfrogs, and always the sea, just close enough so she could make out the faint rhythmical lappings of the waves on the rocks.

The next morning Faith was up virtuously early. If she was a jogger, she'd go jogging, she thought. It was that kind of day. Newborn and sparkling. She packed a lunch in one of the two or three hundred knapsacks hanging from nails in the barn and set off with Benjamin for the beach at the Point. She had her bathing suit on under her shorts and shirt and thought they might even go wading, which would be something to tell Tom when he called next.

By the time they got to the beach, she was worn out. It wasn't that Benjamin didn't keep up. He could match her pace for pace, but he was stubbornly determined to forge his own trails, and it took all her energy and patience to keep him on the track. Now he could roam at will over the beach and had already found a little stick with which he was furiously digging his way to China or whatever was directly below. Faith opened the knapsack and spread out a towel next to him. She sat down and looked at the water. The tide was out and had left a wavy line of seaweed, shells, odd pieces of wood, rope from traps and buoys, and other assorted flotsam—bleach bottles, which people cut to use as bailers, a waterlogged shoe, a sardine tin. The beach itself was arranged in layers. Farthest from the sea, near the wild roses, sea lavender, and spreading junipers, the sand was covered with stones and broken shells, pushed up by the waves. A line of dried, blackened seaweed separated this layer from the sand that had recently been underwater and still glistened in the sun. When it dried, it would be soft and almost white. Down near the water's edge the rocks started again.

One of the big schooners sailed by, and Ben jumped up and down waving excitedly. "Wanna ride! Wanna ride!" He was actually beginning to make sense these days, and the next step might be conversation. In a way it was nice to concentrate on Ben, although a few days would have more than sufficed. Before he was born, she hadn't realized that there would be times when husband and child would pull at her from different directions. Like that poem of Robert Frost's that compared a woman to a silken tent with "ties of love and thought" binding her to the earth. They were either holding her up or pulling her down, depending on the day, or as Frost pointed out, the movement of the wind.

Faith and Ben ate their sandwiches and wandered out to the receding water. This wasn't a clam flat and there was no mud. Faith held tight to Benjamin's chubby little paw. He was racing toward the water crying, "Swim! Swim!" Faith stuck her big toe in and promptly lost all feeling. She decided her shoes would fit better if she did not get frostbite and managed to steer Ben away from the beckoning deep, over to the tidal pools that had been left behind in the warm sun.

"Sweetheart, we'll go look for little fishes and shells in the pools, okay? We'll swim another day." And in another place, Faith added to herself.

She helped Ben climb up onto the flat ledges that stretched around the Point, and they began to explore the endlessly fascinating pools. At first Ben wanted to jump in or at least stick his hand in right away, but Faith was able to get him to pause and look first—to see the busy world of tiny fish darting among the sea anemones and starfish, small crabs making their way across the mussels and limpets clinging to the pink and orange algae that lined the bottoms of the pools. They went farther away from the beach, carefully avoiding the sharp remains of the sea urchins the gulls had dropped on the rocks and the lacelike barnacles that covered the granite.

"What's that, Ben?" Faith looked up from the life in the pool she had been studying. It looked so arranged, so deliberate, like the pine cones she had found in the woods placed on a mat of gray moss in a star shape with a feather in the middle.

"Wait, honey, I'm coming." She made her way across the flat rock and stood next to Ben, who was crouched and gazing intently at something in a lower pool.

"Man swimming," he said. "Ben wanna swim."

"What man?" Faith started to say before she looked and the question was answered for her.

It was Roger Barnett, draped over the rocks and secured with thick ropes of brown kelp. Small waves were systematically covering and uncovering his head, filling his slackly opened mouth with sea water, fanning his long brown hair against the rockweed. His shirt was gone, and the dark kelp stood out against the unnatural whiteness of his bare arms and chest. His eyes were open and staring straight into the sun. Roger wasn't swimming.

Roger was dead.

Four

Faith opened her mouth to scream, remembered Benjamin, and swallowed hard. Then she grabbed him and started to walk quickly back to the beach. Her legs felt as rubbery as the kelp that lashed Roger to the rocks, and she had trouble focusing. She stepped on a sea urchin, the sharp tines puncturing her heel, and for a moment the pain was a welcome distraction.

There had been no point in investigating closer. Roger was beyond any resuscitation attempts. She felt extremely nauseated thinking about trying.

In with the good air, out with the bad.

And she knew she wouldn't be able to move the body herself. She had to get help before the tide came in and carried him away. Faith didn't read the charts, but she could tell when it was out and when it was in. It was out now, so that meant it would start to come in sometime. Maybe soon.

They had reached the beach and she stared to run. Ben laughed delightedly and raced after her. She paused to stuff their things into the knapsack, put their sandals on, and kept going. At the end of the beach she stopped. Where *were* they going? Roger's face kept blotting out any reasonable thoughts. She sat down suddenly on the sand and pulled Benjamin onto her lap. She had to get herself together and think. Her heart was pounding.

The Millers' cottage was closer than hers, but Pix and Samantha had gone up the coast to visit Mark and Danny at camp. Faith doubted that Pix would lock up, but she couldn't take the chance. She looked across the beach and saw the gulls hovering over the tidal pools. A sudden image of the birds walking impersonally over Roger's body, pecking at him with their sharp beaks, made her shudder uncontrollably, and she held Benjamin tight.

There was a fisherman's house on the other side of the Point, and she'd have to try there. If they didn't have a phone, at least someone might be able to move the body.

The body. This was Roger. Roger, who less than a week ago had been at her house, smiling and joking, enjoying the wine and the food. Soft-spoken, easy-going Roger, who created beautiful things. How could this have happened?

She found the path that led across the Point to Long Cove and, half carrying, half dragging a suddenly weary Benjamin, felt the tears start down her face. What a terrible, terrible tragedy. Eric would be distraught—all of Roger's friends would be.

The fisherman's house emerged in front of her. She had been looking down, picking her way through some blackberry brambles, when she realized she was walking on lawn. Thank God! There was an elderly woman hanging up clothes in the back.

"Please, I need your help. A man has drowned and his body is back on the Point," Faith blurted out.

The woman looked at her in amazement, and

Faith realized the whole situation was like your worst nightmare. Does she believe me? Does she think I'm a lunatic? Benjamin started to howl.

"Well now." The woman stuck the clothespin she had been holding poised over a sheet back in her apron pocket and took Ben by the hand. She put an arm around Faith's shoulders. "You'd better come inside, deah, and sit down while I try to get someone on the CB. Freeman, that's my husband, will be home for his dinner soon anyway. Could you tell who the man was?"

"It was Roger Barnett—do you know him?" Faith was having trouble with tenses.

"One of those pottery boys, wasn't he? And so young." She sighed. "This is the second one this summer. A woman thought her little girl was in trouble, went in to fetch her, and drowned herself."

They walked in the back door into the kitchen. It was crammed with foul-weather gear, a lobster trap that was being repaired, firewood, and furniture, and all as neat as a pin. The aromas from a large coffeepot and some thick slices of ham in an iron skillet keeping warm on top of the wood stove mingled not unpleasantly with a faint smell of bait. Faith realized she'd better sit down before she fell down.

"You come over here in this rocker by the stove. I started it up today; it was so cool this morning. And here's a cookie for your little boy."

Whoever this woman was, she was managing to do everything at once. Faith didn't see her pour the cup of coffee that was placed firmly in Faith's limp hand, and it was only when the CB began crackling back that she realized a message had already been transmitted. A man's voice gave some call numbers and asked what the problem was. It was the island's only police officer.

"Earl, it's Nan Hamilton. Roger Barnett has drowned and one of the summer people found the body over on the other side of the Point."

Nan paused to listen and turned toward Faith in case she had missed it. "Earl wants to know if you can tell him where it is and I never did get your name."

Well, it hadn't exactly been a time for Miss Manners, Faith thought, and quickly made amends. "The body is at the end of the big beach in a tidal pool, and I'm Faith Fairchild—we're friends of the Millers."

Nan nodded and conveyed the information to Earl. "It's Faith Fairchild, you know, that minister from Massachusetts, friends of the Millers. She says the body is at the end of the big beach, up on the ledges it sounds like. Shouldn't be hard to find, and when Freeman comes we'll go over."

There was more crackling and she signed off.

"Well, that's all over the island now," she said. "Half the population will be there waiting for him."

"Do you think the police will want me to stay here to show them where he is or could I go home?" Faith asked, hoping she could go.

"If Earl needs you, he'll be able to find you, I'm sure, but I think you ought to sit a bit longer before you go racing off. You've had quite an experience, I'd say," Nan answered. "And let me cut you a piece of pie to go with that coffee."

"You've been so kind," Faith replied. Nan was right. She didn't feel like sprinting off just yet, and it was a long walk back.

Benjamin had finished his cookie and was busy

exploring the kitchen. Faith started to get up to stop him from opening the cupboards, but Nan laughed and said she had seven grandchildren and the cupboards were turned out regularly.

"That's some of them," she said, proudly pointing to a row of school pictures tacked to the wall. "We've got better ones in the parlor."

Faith knew there must be a mantel crammed with photos—the wedding poses and then the kids. Her own parents' mantel had a pair of cloisonné candlesticks and a few pieces of antique Chinese porcelain. For a fleeting moment she wanted to stand on someone's mantel hemmed in by Sears portraits. I must still be in shock, she told herself. Ming was Ming, after all.

The door opened and a large man who must be Freeman came in. He had white hair cut close to his head and a fisherman's tan—face, neck, hands, and forearms. You could see where it ended when he took off the top layer of several shirts. He had left his boots outside and padded around in a couple of pairs of heavy socks. If he was surprised to see Faith and Ben there, he didn't show it.

"Hello, Nan, what's for supper?" He grinned at Faith. "And who's this pretty young thing sitting in my rocker?"

"Now Freeman, behave yourself. This is Mrs. Fairchild. They're renting the Thorpes' cottage. She just found poor Roger Barnett drowned over on the big beach."

"Drowned! Why in tarnation people think they can swim here beats me. I've lived here all my life and then some and I've never been in this water on purpose. Too darned cold."

"I couldn't agree more," said Faith. "But do you mean you can't swim?"

Nan answered. "More fool he is, deah. Many of the fishermen here can't swim, and if they'd taken the trouble to learn, a lot would be here who aren't."

Freeman was all for changing the subject. "Roger Barnett. Well, I do call that a shame. He was a nice enough feller." He chuckled and turned to Nan. "Won't those Prescotts be steamed? Of course there's still the other one, and knowing Matilda, she would have left the house to him anyway."

"Freeman, hush up now, Mrs. Fairchild doesn't want to hear about all this dirty linen."

Mrs. Fairchild did, but evidently Freeman thought Nan was right and he veered off on another tack.

"Did I hear you were from Massachusetts? I went there once. To Boston. They wanted eight dollars for a lobster dinner, so I come home." He laughed and Nan joined him. "Course lobster isn't as common as it used to be. When I was a boy, we'd get tired of it and beg my mother to make something else for a change."

Benjamin was banging on pots, and Faith decided it was time to go. But first she asked Nan for a piece of paper and a pencil to write a note to leave at Pix's when they went past the house. Freeman had finished two enormous pieces of ham, several biscuits, a couple of helpings of mashed potatoes, beets, and applesauce, all washed down with coffee that his wife kept steadily pouring into his cup. Then he allowed as he'd go over to see if he could help. He'd have his pie later. Nan said she'd go with him, so the four of them set off across the Point.

As they left the porch, Freeman placed Benjamin on his shoulders. Benjamin laughed and all of them smiled up at the little boy, brown from the sun, his blond curls bobbing in the breeze. It should have been a nice day.

They parted where the path forked toward the beach one way and back to the Millers' the other.

Faith offered her hand to Nan and thanked her warmly. She hoped they'd meet again under more pleasant circumstances.

"Come over anytime. I love to have company. And I hear you like to cook. So do I. We'll go mushrooming someday. The Point is full of them."

"You go with Nan," Freeman advised, "and you won't need a silver coin to boil with them. She knows which ones can be et."

"Freeman! You know that coin business is just an old wives' tale. Now, we'd better get going."

Benjamin gave her a kiss and Freeman said he wouldn't mind one too and one from Mrs. Fairchild for that matter. Nan pushed him toward the path. "Don't mind him. He just never growed up."

"That's all right," Faith said. "I'm flattered." And she was.

She walked as quickly as possible to Pix's house. She had decided that she ought to drive into the village and see Jill. Faith didn't know any of these people well, but for the short time she had been on Sanpere, she felt she had been caught up in their lives with a swiftness that surprised her. She knew Jill would be trying to get in touch with Eric, and she wasn't sure what she could say about finding the body, but maybe they'd want to ask her something. It also seemed impossible to pick up a magazine and sit on the lawn after all this. She wanted to be with people.

Pix wasn't back—which Faith had expected. It was over an hour's drive to the camp, and they'd stay awhile. The door *was* open and Faith went in to find some tape. If she left the note on the table, it was probable no one would find it until evening. Pix and Samantha would rush in, pee if they had to, and then rush out to attack the weeds, chop firewood, or cut alders—whatever beckoned most furiously.

She couldn't find tape, but there were Band-Aids in the medicine cabinet, and with one of these Faith attached the sad missive to the door. Benjamin was happily pulling Pix's yarn out of a basket next to the fireplace, and Faith managed to get to him just before he unraveled a few weeks' worth of an Irish fisherman's sweater for Danny.

Back at her own cottage she was struck by the unreality of it all. They had just gone for a picnic. Had they really found a body in the kelp? She knew it was unfortunately true, but it was like one of those "What's Wrong with This Picture?" puzzles. An incredible day—bright-blue skies, white puffy clouds, sailboats moving gracefully in the wind, the long stretch of gleaming sand, and the tidal pools filled with jewellike mysteries and Roger's dead body.

She grabbed Benjamin and headed for the car.

Tom had taken their own car to New Hampshire, since a car came with the house. It was an old wooden station wagon—a 1949 Plymouth Suburban in "mint condition," Tom had gloated as he stroked the side panels. While Faith had not arrived at the point where she felt the need to caress the car, she loved driving it. To her the romance of the Woody was a solid, dependable one, based on mutual trust and shared interests. The gears shifted smoothly and she sat up high, as if she were in a truck, with a clear view of the road. Today she didn't pause to appreciate the car, backed out quickly, and set off down the long dirt road to the macadam that circled the island and led to Sanpere Village—the long way if you turned left, the short way if right. Faith turned right.

She pulled up in front of Jill's shop. Benjamin had fallen asleep in his car seat, waking drowsily when the car stopped. The shop was closed, but Faith knew Jill lived in the apartment over it and decided to go around back and knock. Jill came almost immediately. Her eyes were swollen and she was still crying. She was tucking a shirt into her jeans and was obviously getting ready to go someplace.

"Oh, Faith, I'm so glad you came. I've been calling you since I heard. I just can't believe it. Roger was such a strong swimmer." She began to sob, and Faith stepped into the back of the store and put her arms around her—quite a feat, since she was carrying Benjamin.

"I don't know anything about these waters, Jill. It may have been some kind of undertow." She had no idea what an undertow was, but people usually said that in these situations, Faith recalled, and it was reassuring to blame Nature.

Jill wasn't really listening to Faith, which was understandable. She had stepped back and kept talking.

"I've got to go to Eric. There's no phone where he is, and anyway I don't want him to hear the news from a stranger." She turned to face Faith suddenly, fully taking in her presence for the first time. "Faith, tell me honestly, was the body in bad shape?"

"I can tell you the truth, and it may help Eric too. There were no marks or cuts of any kind. Benjamin saw him first and he thought a man was swimming, and it would have been easy to think that." Except for the expression on his face and the fact that he seemed to have no bones, Faith thought.

"That's a relief. And Eric will be happy to hear at least that. I don't know what he'll do. They've known each other so long and are closer to each other than to anyone else on earth. You couldn't be friends with one and not the other, not that that was likely in any case." She was moving around the back of the store, closing the windows and putting things into a large purse.

"What about Roger's family? Will the police notify them?" Faith asked, suddenly curious as usual.

"Roger has been estranged from his family for years. It was a source of great bitterness to him. He came from Iowa, and they never understood his way of life or approved it. I don't know what Eric will say, but I'm pretty sure Roger will stay right here, in the place he loved most." That started the tears again. "Faith, he was so wonderful to me—you can't imagine how many times I've cried on his shoulder, especially when I was starting the store and didn't know what I was doing. It's the weirdest thing. I keep thinking, 'I've got to go see Roger, he'll comfort me'; then I remember."

It suddenly occurred to Faith that taciturn Jill was talking and, what's more, as if they were old friends. She sat down in a chair by the cluttered desk. Benjamin was all but asleep and rapidly becoming a dead weight in her arms.

"Please tell Eric if there's anything I can do, let me know. Or if he wants to talk to me about finding the body, although there isn't much to tell. We walked up on the rocks at the end of the long beach at the Point, and Roger was lying in one of the pools."

Which was a pretty calm way to describe finding

a body, she thought. She wanted to take some of the horror out of it for Jill. There was enough in the event itself without the details. The details that were running through Faith's mind like a video—the water in and out of Roger's mouth, his fingers clutching the rockweed.

No, it certainly wasn't necessary to recount that.

Jill was ready. Faith noticed she paused long enough to put on some lipstick and run a comb through her hair.

"Are you all right to drive? Ben and I could come with you if you want?" Faith offered, suddenly concerned at the possibility of another accident.

"Thank you, Faith, but the worst is over now and I have to be strong for Eric. He's going to need all my help."

And, Faith realized, that might not be such a bad thing for Jill.

They left the store, and Faith waved good-bye to Jill before lowering Ben into his car seat. It looked as though he would be having his nap in several locations today. She stopped at the post office, dashed in, and found a letter from Hope and a circular from True Value Hardware in her box. She dropped the junk mail in the trash and sat in the car to read what Hope had to say.

Her sister was writing to confirm that she and Quentin were definitely coming at the end of the month, and after that she chattered on about what they had been doing. Faith felt a swift pang of longing as she read about their weekend at the house of friends in Oyster Bay, the great meal they had had at Le Bernardin, and the terrific Armani suit Hope had found at Barney's. Faith looked through the windshield at the harbor in front of her with the quaint wooden houses sloping up from either side. There was such a thing as too much charm.

But this was good news. A welcome distraction after the tragedy of Roger's death. She was glad they were coming. Now that she no longer had to live with her, she was always happy to see her sister, and Quentin was growing on her. He was so intense and well organized under a carefully composed surface calm that he made her feel incurably frivolous—suspecting, no doubt, she hadn't firmed up her plans for the next twenty years or so. He was the only person Faith knew whose Plan To Do Today list was the same as his Did Today one. She was sure they weren't getting married yet because Quentin hadn't planned to until he was thirty and had made X amount of money. And Hope loved it. Faith folded the letter, put it in her pocket, and resolved firmly that this visit she would finally tell her sister she hated being called Fay.

Pix didn't get back until after five o'clock, and she rushed straight over to Faith's. Faith and Benjamin were eating spaghetti alla carbonara in the kitchen. Pix had paled under the color the summer sun had given her and slumped into a chair. Faith made her a drink, and after a few sips she started to cry.

"I can't understand it, Faith! How could he have drowned? He was in great shape, and I think I heard he swam in college. It was wonderful having them this summer. We had all become so close. Samantha doesn't even want to talk about it. She's up in her room and I can't reach Sam."

Faith had called Tom earlier and had been lucky enough to catch him between events. He offered to come up the next weekend, but she said she was fine. She just wanted to hear his voice.

Pix finished her drink and ate some spaghetti. Faith had discovered earlier that she was starving, and Pix seemed to be too.

"I'm sure he'll be buried here. He wasn't close to his family."

"That's what Jill said."

"I don't know what Eric will do without him. Roger was like the rudder. He kept the business, and actually their lives, on course. He was the one who pushed to move up here. Jill told me once that Eric had been close to a breakdown and had to get away."

Bright lights, big city, Faith thought, and remembered her conversation with Eric. It sounded like he not only wanted to be away from the city, but needed to be. An artist friend of hers had once shown her his engagement book. It was crammed with openings, cocktail parties, private showings. She had wondered how he ever found the time, or energy, to paint.

"Eric had been afraid that they would lose their customers and contacts up here, but Roger convinced him that they had built up a solid-enough reputation to make a move. And if anything, they have become more well known in the last years. Living on an island gave a certain aura of inaccessibility to their work, having to be tracked down and persuaded, although of course it is all much more businesslike than that."

"Maybe Eric will marry Jill now," Faith mused out loud.

"I wouldn't be surprised. It's going to be terribly lonely for him without Roger. And the island is no place to be alone." Tears were running down Pix's face, and Faith knew she was mentally getting her guest room ready for a long visit from Eric.

"I've got to get back to Samantha and try Sam some more," Pix continued as she got up and brought her plate to the sink.

"Leave that, Pix, and call me if I can do anything," Faith said, thinking that she had already done enough. In some perverse form of logic she reasoned if she hadn't found the body, Roger would still be alive. Or it would be yesterday and she could tell him not to go for a swim.

"Thanks, Faith. I keep forgetting what an awful time you've had. Do you want to spend the night?"

"No, but if I change my mind I'll come knocking at your door. It's funny, but I'm beginning to think of this as my house and my own little bed. It feels very comforting."

Ben had been miraculously quiet, playing with a wooden train Faith had bought at H.O.M.E. in Orland. She resolved to go back to the store and get cars, trucks, whatever they had. He looked up with one of those surprisingly adult expressions children sometimes assume. This one was slightly careworn, a little *weltschmerz*, a "Why do these things have to happen?" look.

Faith felt the same way and, despite her assurances to Pix, had trouble blotting out the images of Roger's body, which kept floating across her eyes every time she closed them to go to sleep. It wasn't just a reminder of the fragility and transitoriness of life; it was a dreadful reminder.

The next day brought the real horror.

Freeman Hamilton was setting traps off the Point when he spotted a dinghy washed up on the shore. It was Roger's, and when Sgt. Dickinson and Freeman went over it, they found a number of recently drilled holes. Since it was unlikely that Roger would drill holes in his boat and then put to sea, there was only one conclusion.

Murder.

Faith heard the news in the market after church and once more found herself with the grim task of bearing bad tidings to Pix. As she steered the old Woody over the hills and dips on Route 17, she kept repeating the same question over and over to herself: "Who on earth would want to kill Roger Barnett?"

And this was Pix's second response. Her first was that there had to have been some mistake.

But there was no mistake. The boat was definitely Roger's. He had painted it bright turquoise with a broad white stripe around at the waterline. Apparently the holes under the seats had been filled with corks and painted over. It wasn't a spur-of-the-moment job.

"And it was in our boathouse! Whoever did it had to have done it there!" Pix cried.

Roger didn't use the boat much. Mostly for picnics on one of the small islands nearby. He had been planning to replace it with something larger and more seaworthy. In fact, they had joked about it the night of the dinner party at Faith's. "I have to bail so much, I never get to see where I'm going," he had said. He would probably not have noticed anything unusual about water in the bottom of the boat until he got a ways out and it was too late.

"But why Roger? He didn't have an enemy in the world. I just can't understand it, Faith."

Faith was picturing the phalanx of Prescotts surrounding Roger and Eric at the auction and thought they might aptly be described as enemies. Still, you didn't go around killing someone just because he inherited the house you wanted. Or did you? On reflection, it was a pretty good motive.

Pix evidently thought so too.

"The only thing I can think of is that one of the Prescotts trashed the boat to give him a scare or whatever and had no idea it would turn out this way."

Which seemed to be the prevailing opinion on the island, fueled by Eric's angry accusations. He had arrived back late in the morning and headed straight for the police station, or rather the police room in the combined town hall, office of the law, and post office in Granville. He wanted Sgt. Dickinson to bring in Sonny Prescott and any other Prescotts around for questioning. The sergeant had already decided to do this, but he didn't want Eric or anybody else telling him what to do. Instead, according to Eric's incensed account to Pix and Faith later, he ordered him to sit down and grilled *him* on his whereabouts and relationship with Roger.

Eric looked terrible. He had obviously not slept and his eyes were red. He had started to cry when he saw Pix.

"What am I going to do without him? I'm nothing without Roger. Why didn't they kill me?"

Pix made a pot of strong tea and Eric began to calm down.

"I called his mother, and do you know what she said? 'The world is full of sin. He is in a better place now.' Can you imagine that? That's what you say when you hear your son is dead!"

"Maybe it was the shock, Eric. Roger always said she had become very religious after his father died."

"Well, she doesn't want to have anything to do with his burial, and that doesn't seem very Christian. She said to do what I wanted. That it was no concern of hers. Roger had made his choices. All that old stuff. No wonder she made him crazy." He laughed bitterly. "The last thing she said was 'Did he leave a will?' I just hung up. I couldn't believe it."

Well, did he? Faith wondered.

"I asked young Dick Tracy down at the police station when we could have the service, and he said as soon as they finished the autopsy, probably Tuesday. Roger wouldn't have liked a big production, so I thought I would just ask John to say a few words at the cemetery." Eric's voice was cracking. Pix put her arms around him.

"Do you think you could sleep a little? Maybe that tea was a mistake."

"No, it was good, and I couldn't sleep anyway. But I guess I'll lie down. Jill said she'd come by later, so would you tell her where I am?"

"Of course," Pix assured him.

Eric left and they watched him walk slowly down the path to the little house he and Roger had shared all summer. Faith imagined how shattering it must be to walk into a room and see all the everyday possessions left so casually and so recently by someone you loved. She thought of Tom's old bathrobe hanging on the hook in the closet, the coffee mug that said, "I love you, Dad," that Benjamin had given him for Father's Day, the books he was reading. That would be the worst part. The things. They'd never be used again. The owner wasn't coming back.

Pix was saying something.

"He did make a will, though. He asked Sam to make one for him when we were here in May opening the cottage. I'm sure Eric knows about it."

"He wouldn't have had much to leave then,

would he? I mean that was before he inherited the house."

"Well, he couldn't have left that in any case, because of the provisions in Matilda's will. But I imagine he did have quite a bit saved. The business was very profitable, and I've heard both of them talk about their broker, so he must have had investments. He might have left something to his mother, and I think there are some brothers and sisters, but I'm sure the bulk of it has gone to Eric."

The tragedy was compounded by the news on Monday that the autopsy showed a significant amount of marijuana in Roger's body at the time of death. This time Pix brought the news. Faith and Ben were in the kitchen. Faith was experimenting with zucchini chutney recipes to help stem the squash invasion in the Millers' garden, and Ben was banging on pots as usual. Faith looked at him sternly. "Get it out of your system now, Buddy Rich, because you're not getting drums." She was startled by the knock on the door and Pix's serious face.

"Oh, Pix, tell me quickly. It's more bad news, isn't it?"

"Sad news. The autopsy showed that Roger had been using drugs just before he died. Oh Faith, that was why he couldn't swim. He was too stoned!"

Somehow Faith wasn't surprised. The few times she had seen Roger, he had seemed to be slightly more relaxed than the rest of the group. But it was sad. Terribly sad. He had probably taken a few hits in the boat, and it was enough to disorient him when it sank.

"I never knew he used drugs, or Eric either."

"Now, Pix, you don't know that either of them

were habitual drug takers. I wouldn't leap to any conclusions."

But there was a conclusion. If Roger hadn't taken anything, he'd probably be alive.

The coroner thought so too. Roger had never been too far offshore and was a strong swimmer. The water was cold, but not killing cold as in the wintertime.

It was Jill who reassured Pix that she had not unwittingly been landlady to an opium den all summer. Eric didn't use any drugs at all, and Roger only occasionally rolled a joint with some home-grown, pretty mild marijuana a friend on the mainland grew mixed in with his herbs and vegetables.

The state police had virtually concluded that the whole thing was a tragic accident. The holes were drilled by persons unknown and the investigation would continue, but it was clear that whoever had done it had not known it would lead to Roger's death. Roger's reputation as a swimmer was well known, and the boat would have filled with water before he was away from the shoreline of the Point. Death by misadventure, possibly second-degree murder. Sgt. Dickinson was not having much luck questioning the Prescotts. To a man, and woman, they denied any tampering and were indignant that the question was raised. Everyone on the island had a drill, and it was easy to approach the Millers' boathouse undetected from the shore, so it looked like one of those island mysteries where eventually everyone would know who had done it, but no one would tell.

Roger's body was released and Eric made the arrangements to have him buried in the Northview cemetery. He bought a plot and told Pix there would be plenty of room for him and anyone else who cared to be there. Pix thanked him, but explained that she and Sam had purchased a plot in the King Row cemetery years ago. The Fraziers were on one side and some cousins of Pix's on the other, so she figured she'd have plenty of company and conversation should that turn out to be what awaited.

Tuesday arrived. A foggy Tuesday and humid. The kind of day that made some people's hair curl and some people's go limp. Faith's was curling damply as she searched through her summer wardrobe for something vaguely appropriate to wear. She hadn't planned on this kind of occasion when she packed, but she did have a black dress—an indispensable Anne Klein that she'd rolled up and tucked in at the last moment in case something came up off island at Bar Harbor. It would do very well for the funeral. She slipped into it, and it immediately stuck to her like a second skin. Maybe there would be a breeze at the cemetery.

Samantha was happy to watch Benjamin. She didn't want to go to the funeral and Pix didn't see why she should. Samantha prefered to remember Roger the way he had been when she had seen him last. He had been teaching her how to use the kick-wheel, and she had been making steady progress under his guidance. They'd had a long session on Friday before he left for his row. It occurred to Faith that Samantha might well have been the last person to see Roger alive.

She was pretty sure Samantha had had a crush on Roger, and it was making life very difficult for her now. When she'd mentioned it to Pix, her reply had been, "Why, Faith, he was old enough to be her father! I'm sure not. Besides, she would have told me. She hasn't gotten to the stage yet where she keeps things back."

Faith was under the impression that that stage went all through childhood for most children, but she didn't disabuse Pix of her conviction and instead kept Benjamin away from Samantha and let her have her grief to herself. When Samantha came to get him on Tuesday, she looked more like her old self and picked Ben up, tossing him high. "I've missed you! Have you guys been busy?" Ben went into paroxysms of joy at the sight of her, and Faith murmured something in explanation, then went into the house to get her purse and the car keys.

"I'm sure this won't be long, Samantha," she said.

"That's all right, Mrs. Fairchild, we'll have fun, don't hurry."

Which is more than I'll have, Faith thought as she drove to the cemetery. Pix had gone with Eric earlier.

After today the summer can return to normal and we can pick up where we left off, she told herself. There was still so much of the island to explore and so many precious hours of idleness to leave unfilled.

When she got to the cemetery, she had to park quite far down the road. It looked as if the entire island had turned out for the service, and she might have known that Roger would have made so many friends in his own quiet way. She walked over to where Pix was standing with Eric and Jill next to John Eggleston, who had donned a robe for the service and was perspiring profusely.

Looking around at the crowd, she recognized a few faces. The Fraziers, Bill Fox, Freeman and Nan Hamilton, who gave her a slight smile. The rest seemed to be a combination of all the different groups on the island and a few off-islanders standing in an uneasy group together. Faith had heard some New York friends were coming, and there could be no doubt that these were they standing uneasily in well-cut dark suits and sober black-linen sheaths. One woman wore a large black cartwheel hat that would be long remembered.

It was a beautiful cemetery, and Faith suddenly realized it mattered to her where she ended up. She didn't believe she would notice her surroundings after death, but she liked the idea of selecting the spot. It was a little like choosing a house or apartment, and you would certainly be there a lot longer. She wouldn't mind a final resting place like this one. The cemetery was surrounded by tall pines and clumps of white birches. The neatly mown plots were bordered by the ferns and mosses of the woods that circled them. Wildflowers were everywhere, along the paths and even mixing with the plastic flowers and VFW flags placed in memory by the headstones. Some of the stones were old, the white marble covered with green lichen. There were a few large memorials, including one with a schooner in full sail carved at the base of the obelisk. Most of the headstones were granite, highly polished pink, gray, and black, glistening in the sun.

John Eggleston stepped forward and looked around. He seemed satisfied that everyone was there and started to intone the service. The fullness and beauty of his voice startled Faith. She had placed him in the pulpit-thumping category. He started quietly. The air was still, the crowd of mourners silent.

"I am the resurrection and the life, saith the Lord: he that believeth in me, though he were dead, yet shall he live: and whosoever liveth and believeth in me shall never die."

There was a long pause, and Faith, who had been looking down at the soft green grass feeling unutterably sad, wondered why he had stopped.

It was Bird. She was at the entrance to the cemetery walking quickly. When she got near the group, she slowed down and appeared to be searching for someone. Bill Fox stepped toward her and she went to him. She was wearing a long purple gown apparently fashioned from one of those Indian print bedspreads. There was no rosy hue to her cheeks despite the heat and long walk she had had from her house. Her hair was loose and shone in the sunlight. She looked noble and tragic and beautiful. Tennyson, Shakespeare, a Beatles lyric—there were any number of lines that would have described her perfectly. The baby was hanging from a sling at her hip, as silent as its mother. Faith realized she had never heard either of them make a sound.

John Eggleston gave a nod of welcome, acknowledgment or something, and continued.

It was a long service, and Faith began to tune out. She heard the familiar lines from Ecclesiastes without really listening: "A time to be born and a time to die," until John reached the lines about wickedness. "That iniquity was there." The voice was no longer lyrical, but harsh—and he was right. There had been wickedness and iniquity, evil had been done to this man. It was not his time to die.

At the end of the chapter, Eric stepped forward, pulled a card out of his pocket, and started to read: "Roger Barnett was the closest friend I ever had or will have. Many of you know how we have worked together over the years, but may not have known how much was due to Roger. He brought us to this beautiful island, which I cannot think of as the cause of his death but rather the place he would have wanted to be for eternity.

"As potters we knew that the clay was alive and our task to fashion it into the objects our imaginations saw. In the same way, I was Roger's clay and he shaped me with as sure and steady a hand as he did a bowl or vase. In Japan when the potter is very pleased with a piece he has taken from the fire, he bows to the kiln in thanks. I would like to do the same."

He walked slowly to the open grave and bowed. "Thank you, Roger."

When he got back to Jill, the tears were running down his cheeks. He was not the only one.

John Eggleston finished the service with a reading from *The Prophet*, which seemed quite appropriate for the forever-youthful feeling generated by the day. Faith's own copy of the book had been a junior high graduation present from Hope and was reverentially inscribed, "To my sister, Faith. I hope you gain understanding and knowledge from this book. Love forever, Hope."

Gibran's words and Eggleston's voice were a good match.

> For what is it to die but to stand naked in the wind
>   and to melt into the sun?
> And what is it to cease breathing, but to free the
>   breath from its restless tides, that it may rise and
>   expand and seek God unencumbered?

Faith often got a lump in her throat when she heard Gibran quoted—the memory of Hope's words and of the time when these phrases had seemed to supply all the answers. The answers weren't quite so simple anymore, but today's lines had been well chosen. She swallowed hard and blinked away the tears that had started.

Then it was the Lord's Prayer, ashes to ashes, and the final benediction. The service seemed to pick up speed, impelled by its own "restless tide," just as Roger had been engulfed by them. A few gulls screamed raucously; then it was quiet again. And still.

John picked up a handful of dirt from the mound next to the grave and threw it in, Eric followed him with Jill, and the three walked slowly toward the road. Faith and Pix fell in behind Bill Fox and Bird patiently waiting to make this final gesture. Bill dropped his handful on the simple wooden casket and stood aside for Bird.

She was taking the baby out of the sling. Her eyes darted about and settled on Pix. Placing the baby firmly in Pix's surprised grasp, she crouched down next to the grave and jumped in without a word. Her long hair streamed out behind her and disappeared as she hit the coffin with a resounding thump.

The crowd gave a collective gasp and people started running. Aware that something out of the ordinary was occurring, John, Eric, and Jill stopped and turned back.

Faith was stunned. She had seen the way Roger had looked at Bird, but that it had been reciprocated, and to such an extent, was a total surprise.

Clearly, no one knew what to do.

The baby was quite content to be in Pix's arms and gave her a smile that revealed several pearly teeth, happily oblivious of the fact that its mother was trying to get herself buried alive two feet away.

Eric arrived at the edge of the grave and looked down.

Bird was lying stretched out on top of the coffin with her eyes closed and her arms crossed at her breast, waiting for the earth to cover her. If it had been a funeral pyre, her task would have been more easily accomplished.

"Bird," Eric implored, "this won't bring Roger back. Please stand up and we'll help you out."

She didn't move.

He continued. Was there an edge of irritation to his voice? Faith thought there was and with good reason. It wasn't exactly the tribute to Roger that Eric had envisioned.

"Bird, Roger would definitely not have wanted this. Now please get up and come back to the house with me."

Bill Fox moved next to Eric. "I'll stay with her and get her out. Don't worry. It's hit her very hard, and this is her way of showing it. I should have held on to her, but it didn't occur to me that she would really do it."

"You mean you knew?" Eric clearly didn't like it.

"I knew how upset she was, and given that, this was the natural gesture."

"That's an odd choice of words, Bill, but you know her better than I do." Eric shrugged. "This is the worst day of my life, or rather Saturday was, and it's just going on and on. Compared to what's already happened, this just doesn't matter at all. If you think it will help to bring her back to the house and talk with people who knew Roger, please do so."

"I don't think she'll want to do that, but thank you."

"No, thank you, for taking care of this."

Eric gave one last helpless look at the motionless figure in the grave, trembled slightly, and left.

Everyone else was leaving too, many after a curious peep at Bird first. The Fraziers offered to stay with Bill, but he said it would probably be better if no one was around. Jim Sanford, the gravedigger, mumbled something about his dinner and coming back later before throwing his shovel in the back of his old pickup and bumping down the road.

Finally only Bill, Pix, Faith, and the baby were left. At Faith's suggestion she, Pix, and the baby had moved away to sit under the trees. The baby proved to be older than they had thought and a girl—a sturdy one-year-old on the point of walking, despite her unhealthy pallor. She was happy and sat playing with some pine cones, cooing and burbling softly. She was also soaked, but they couldn't do anything about it. Bird apparently didn't carry a diaper bag, but relied instead on the absorbency of several layers of cloth. They were on the point of telling Bill that they would take the baby home for the day when they saw him kneel down and pull Bird out of her untimely grave. She didn't bother to brush the dirt out of her hair or off her dress, but walked over and took the baby as calmly as she had relinquished her. Then she reached for the hand Bill offered, and they started off down the road. Halfway to the cemetery's entrance, she sat down abruptly on one of the stones in the Sanford plot and exploded.

"It's not true! It's not Roger!" she screamed over and over, through violent tears. She clutched her child to her breast. Bill held her tightly.

Feeling like voyeurs, Pix and Faith crept away, leaving Bird to the realization of the enormity of her grief, and the patient consoler ready beside her.

Always beside her.

Five

Faith swept her hand over the thick carpet of shiny green leaves emerging from the stiff gray lichen and quickly began to pick the tiny ripe wild cranberries that appeared.

That morning Pix had arrived at her door bright and early with Samantha and berry-picking containers in tow. "After yesterday I decided we desperately needed a return to normalcy, and picking berries is about the most soothing thing I can think of," she had announced.

Faith had to agree. Short of a day at Elizabeth Arden.

Unlike Tuesday, Wednesday was sunny with a cool breeze. The sky was brilliant blue with the kind of Rorschach clouds that assume shapes—an elephant, a dog running, the sixth-grade teacher you hated.

They were picking far out along the Point, on rocky outcroppings at the edge of a meadow that, judging from the old cellar hole and ancient fruit trees, must have been part of someone's farm in the past. In the large open field there were still some blueberries the birds had missed, and Samantha was concentrating on them, picking a handful, then feeding them to Ben, who was beginning to resemble one of the Picts from the juice.

The berries weren't making that satisfying ping as they hit the pail, and Faith saw she had already picked several pints. She began to think about recipes. Of course cranberries and game, but a scallop-and-cranberry dish began to take shape. She also wanted to continue her quest for new and different chutneys to please what seemed an insatiable market. It would not have surprised her to see Charred Seaweed Chutney or Cherry Pit Butter the next time she was at Dean and Deluca. Wild cranberries and caramelized onions? That was a possibility. And what about shrub? It suggested long-ago childhood lunches with her grandmother at Altman's Charleston Gardens or The Bird Cage at Lord & Taylor, a tiny frosted glass of pulverized fruit. Refreshing in summer. Shrub instead of sorbet as a palate cleanser?

Her hands picked automatically as her mind stirred the pots. When Pix started talking, it took a moment to turn down the flame.

"I had to tell her. She would have heard from Arlene, and I was afraid she'd be terribly upset."

"Sorry, Pix, I haven't been listening. You mean you told Samantha about Bird?"

"Yes, and I needn't have worried. She made a face and said, 'That's the grossest thing I've ever heard! What did she look like, Mom? Ugh, think of all that dirt in your mouth and hair!' "

Faith laughed. It was good to find something in all this to laugh about.

"But Faith, you know what was interesting? She wasn't a bit surprised to hear about Bird and Roger. It seems he had been talking to Samantha about her all summer, how beautiful Bird is and what a rotten time she has with Andy. He takes off whenever he wants and she never knows when he's coming back."

"Then why didn't you ever see Roger and Bird together?"

"Samantha says that Bird feels she has to be loyal to Andy. I guess she really loves him, and after all he is the baby's father. Also I gather he can be violent, and she was afraid to have him find out. Lately she has been trying to decide whether to leave him for Roger, and judging from her behavior yesterday I guess she did. Thinking back, I do recall seeing them in the boat together, and Samantha said Bird was supposed to go with him on Friday. They were going to have a picnic somewhere, but the baby was sick."

"Somewhere in the boat or on the island?"

"I don't know. Samantha didn't say."

"If she had been in the boat, she might have been able to save him. No wonder she's so upset. She must be blaming herself."

Faith thought for a moment about Bird and the men in her life before speaking. "Aren't you glad you're married, Pix? I can't imagine going through all that emotional turmoil. Not that marriage is totally without turmoil, but at least it's the turmoil you know."

"Exactly."

They continued to talk about the funeral. It was destined to go down in the annuals of island history as the most talked-about funeral of all time, just edging out Virgil Baldwin's, where the bereaved widow wore a bright-red dress to show how happy she was that the old tyrant was finally gone.

Those who had attended yesterday's obsequies

had gained a sudden popularity and found themselves besieged by sidelong invitations to come around for a cup of coffee or some tomatoes from the garden or whatever from those who were kicking themselves for missing it all.

Pix and Faith picked steadily, well satisfied with themselves and their labors, until it was time to stop and eat lunch. They went down to the rocks by the water, where Samantha was trying to show Ben the harbor seals sunning themselves on the rocks offshore. Every time she placed the binoculars against his eyes he tried to grab them, and eventually she gave up.

Faith had piled anything she could find in the fridge on her sandwich—fresh tomatoes, red onion, sprouts, lettuce, and Boursin—and was having a hard time controlling the drips, which were running down her fingers stained bright pink from the berries. Samantha was trying to keep from laughing. "I'm sorry, Mrs. Fairchild, it's just that I never see you like this. A mess!"

"Mess, mess!" Ben chortled.

"Sharper than a serpent's tooth," Faith said to Pix.

"Just wait," Pix replied.

"Hey, watch what you're saying, Mom. You should count yourself lucky. It's not like we're delinquents or druggies or anything."

"Indeed. I am thrice blessed." Pix smiled.

"You know, it's really sad about a lot of the kids on the island. Arlene has been telling me. There is nothing to do here. Absolutely nothing. Especially in the winter. Can you imagine, the nearest mall is up in Bangor? So there are quite a few druggies. A kid Arlene really liked this year got really messed up and totaled his car, and her parents won't let her see him anymore, but she thinks she can help him."

The Joan of Arc syndrome, recalled Faith, as several pathetic, needy, albeit handsome faces in her own past marched past.

"But where could kids on this island get drugs?" Pix asked.

"Oh, Mom, kids can get drugs anywhere if they want them enough, and anyway mostly they drink. But it's the same thing."

They sat contemplating the cove. The breeze had stirred up the water, and several sailboats were skimming across the top, white sails and whitecaps. The schooner *The Victory Chimes* sedately made her way across the horizon.

There are so many layers to life here, Faith thought. Or rather it's like life anywhere, but we are so seldom visitors to the places we live. On the island she had a sense of being only at the surface of things as a summer person, and a transient one at that. Finding Roger's body and the funeral had been dips below, and the auction, too, with its undercurrents of tension; but she really had no idea what life on Sanpere was like for most of its residents.

"Bird is staying at Bill Fox's for a while." Pix brought her up to date after Samantha and Ben went down to the tiny beach being created by the ebbing tide. "And Eric is still at our boathouse. He and Roger had planned to start moving into the new house this week, but I don't think Eric wants to be alone there."

"You mean he's afraid?"

"Possibly, but it may be more a question of loneliness, although Jill would stay with him, I'm sure. He was at her place last night. I thought he might go back to New York with some of his friends, but he decided to stay. He came by this morning to change his clothes and told me he honestly doesn't know what to do. He seems totally lost."

"Judging from all we've heard, I think it would be a mistake for him to move back to the city. He has so many friends in Maine, and he'd just be caught up in the stress they were escaping."

"I agree, but he's even saying he's not sure he wants to continue the business without Roger. I thought what he said yesterday was beautiful and perhaps true. Without Roger he might not be able to be the artist he was. He's thinking of teaching, and of course any of those places would be happy to have him—the Rhode Island School of Design offered both of them jobs years ago and has wanted them, even temporarily, since."

"I haven't thought about it, but it looks like he has lost not only his dearest friend but, for the moment anyway, his livelihood. Teaching might be a good idea." Faith paused. "I wonder where Jill will fit into his future?"

After some further discussion the two women had settled Eric happily ever after with Jill and several children in a big old house in Providence for the school year, returning to the island for the summers until it was time to retire. At which point Eric and Jill, gray haired but nimble still, would move to the island year round and await visits from their devoted children and grandchildren. Eric would surmount his depression and make more beautiful pots than ever. Jill would get him to dress better.

Satisfied, they returned to the berry picking for an hour, then went their separate ways—Faith to her hammock and magazines, Ben to a nap, Samantha to Arlene's, and Pix to the turnout of her drawers and closets that she had been trying to get to all summer.

As Faith flipped the pages, her eyes barely skimming Lacroix's new direction—inspiration or desperation—she thought instead about Eric and Roger. One of the things under the surface that they hadn't talked about during the morning was the scuttling of the boat. She didn't blame Eric for not wanting to stay alone in that huge house, no matter how beautiful. If the Prescotts had drilled holes in Roger's boat, there was no telling what they would do to Eric, whom they appeared to dislike even more. Then again maybe they were frightened by the unanticipated outcome of their prank.

If it was a prank and if it was unanticipated. There was the unavoidable fact that Roger had died because of it. And the Prescotts might have known of his penchant for grass. They couldn't have been sure he would smoke that day, but maybe they had hoped to get lucky.

That made it murder.

And with one gone, it might be more than some varieties of human nature could bear not to have a shot at the other. Or if not literally a shot, something else deadly. Faith hoped Eric was being careful about what he ate. No mushroom casseroles left by a kindly friend at his door, for instance.

She wondered why Pix hadn't brought the subject up, or why she hadn't herself. Maybe it was that talking about it made it more real, more dangerous. And they were trying to keep Eric safe.

They were both invited to the Fraziers' for dinner that night, and Pix called Faith at four o'clock to remind her to bring the quilt top with her. Louise was an ardent quilter and had asked to see it. She had left the auction before the quilt was put up and regretted it, although she told Pix she was glad Faith got it. Faith was secretly hoping that she might prevail upon those itchy quilting fingers to do the job for her, but she was not too optimistic. In her experience, quilters were second only to the Jehovah's Witnesses in their proselytizing. She could hear Louise and Pix chorus now: "It will be so much fun to quilt. I'd love to do it, but wouldn't want to take it away from you. It's like eating peanuts!" Pix had actually said this to her once. Faith had never had any particular difficulty stopping herself when eating peanuts, and she knew that the quilt would be one of those things she would forsake for anything from cleaning her bathroom bowl to perusing Addison's *Essays*.

Samantha and Arlene appeared for tandem babysitting. Faith had left food for them, but they came armed with their own Pringles. She sighed at the foibles of youth and told them there was plenty of Diet Coke, their preferred beverage, in the refrigerator.

She stopped to pick up Pix, and it didn't take long to reach the Fraziers' house, set high on a knoll overlooking the harbor at Sanpere Village.

Louise Frazier opened the door. She was wearing a long Marimekko dress with large windowpane checks in white on black. Around her neck was a heavy silver necklace made by an artist on the island. She was tall, with gleaming white hair, and the total effect was stunning. Never one to hold back, Faith told her how lovely she looked.

"Thank you. This is one of my favorite gowns. I bought it many years ago in Finland and never get tired of wearing it. Now let's see that quilt before the others get here."

Elliot Frazier walked into the room. He had dressed up too, in a well-worn brown velvet jacket with a slightly equestrian look to it and an Oscar

Wilde bow tie. Not the at-home garb of most retired Maine postmasters, Faith reflected, but then you never knew with Maine.

"Now Louise, let this poor young woman have a drink first before you start in with all that quilt talk. We have a nice Chardonnay, from the Bonny Doon winery in California, that you might like to try. We visited the winery last spring. Beautiful country. There's also gin and tonic, vermouth, whatever you want."

Faith asked for some wine. She had heard good things about this small vineyard near Santa Cruz, but hadn't sampled the wine.

Glasses in hand, they spread the quilt over the sofa. It looked almost alive, the colors were so intense. Yet at the same time they blended well together; the effect was perfectly harmonious, and in the end calming. Faith thought again that it was a Maine quilt. She could point to the fabrics and remember just where she had seen the colors duplicated in nature—the tall pine by the cottage, the silver-gray of the ancient apple trees on the Point, the pink granite with sparkling flecks of black and white lining the shore, the jade-green hues the water sometimes assumed.

Louise was silent, then drew an audible breath.

"It's magnificent, Faith, and I won't deny being terribly, terribly jealous. Oh, you're going to have so much fun quilting it!"

There it was. No hope at all, Faith thought gloomily.

"Now let's see what we have here." Louise pointed to a square. "That, of course, is Mariner's Compass." She was starting to name another when Jill, Eric, and John all arrived at the front door at once.

Eric looked a little shaky, but he was clearly trying to deal with his grief. The first thing he said upon entering the room was, "Yes, Elliot, I'd love a very large gin and tonic and I'm doing okay."

Elliot put a drink in his hand, and he sat down in one of the comfortable overstuffed armchairs that filled the room. John, with a glass of wine, followed suit.

Rooms seemed to get filled quite often in New England, Faith noted. Maybe because people didn't want to throw anything out. You never knew when something might come in handy. In the case of the Fraziers' living room the result was not chaos but comfort. The bookshelves were lined with all the books a person could ever want to read, especially curled up in one of the chairs on a foggy day with a fire in the fireplace. There were large pitchers of wildflowers mixed with a few garden civilians set on the pine tables scattered around the room. A huge glass-fronted china closet stood in the corner, too large for the dining room, Faith suspected, and it was filled not only with majolica and French pottery gathered on trips, but with shells and rocks collected closer to home. At Faith's side a polished slab of deep russet granite rested on top of the wrought-iron base from an old Singer sewing machine. The quilt was spread over a slightly faded chintz sofa, which provided a soft background for the brilliant squares. There were twenty of them connected by pale serpentine-green lattice strips.

"Oh Faith, is this what you got at the auction?" Jill asked. "It's beautiful."

"The same, and I feel very lucky. It's exactly what I wanted. Only I do wish Matilda Prescott had been able to quilt it too. I think it may take me until the next century."

"Now don't be discouraged. I'd be glad to help you baste it and get you started," Louise offered.

"Me too," Pix said. "Besides, if it had been quilted, you probably wouldn't have gotten it. I've never seen one like this. Once you start, you'll love it. We could go up to Ellsworth and get batting and fabric for the backing tomorrow or Friday if you want."

"Leave the island?" Faith teased. "I didn't think anything would get you to cross the bridge before Sam dragged you kicking and screaming home after Labor Day."

"This is a special case," Pix replied.

"I remember seeing Matilda working on these squares last Spring," Eric said. "She was having a lot of fun with them. She subscribed to all the quilters' magazines and was constantly ordering books on quilting. She'd finish one square, then go through her collection to decide which one she'd do next."

"I was able to get some of her books at the auction, Faith, and you're welcome to borrow them and my magazines. As I said, I know this is Mariner's Compass"—Louise placed her finger on the square, then moved it to another—"and this is Shady Pine, I'm sure, and Fern Berry. I wonder if she picked them for their association with Maine? Perhaps not. This is Old Maid's Puzzle, and I don't think that is particular to the state."

They were all standing over the quilt now.

"It's interesting to know the names. I always think a sampler quilt is very special, choosing different squares instead of repeating the same one," Pix said.

Jill was looking closely at the squares.

"Her stitches were exquisite—just look at how even they are." She bent down to count them. "Oh, here are her initials in the corner. She must have planned to embroider them. And the date, but I can't read what's next to it; the pencil got smudged."

"Let me see," Louise said. "No, we need the magnifying glass." She went over to the reduced Oxford English Dictionary and took a large magnifying glass from the top. "Here, Faith, it's your quilt. You look."

"This is exciting," said Faith. "Like a secret message." She read slowly, " 'Seek and Ye Shall Find.' I'm sure that's what it says, but what does it mean?"

They took turns looking and agreed on the words. Elliot offered an opinion: "Remember, Matilda was a very religious woman. It may not be cryptic at all, just simply what it says, Seek and Ye Shall Find—God, peace, salvation."

"I think Elliot's probably right," John added. "She had a big bowl next to her bed filled with tiny slips of paper with the chapter and verse of parts of the Bible printed on them, and she'd pick one every morning and every night, then read whatever passage it told her. I wouldn't be surprised if all her quilts had quotations from the scriptures on them."

"Aunt Matilda *was* a God-fearing woman," chided a voice from the doorway, a voice that more than hinted that few in the room would be counted in that number. Faith turned around, startled. It was Margery Prescott, Sonny's wife, and she was putting on a sweater. She was a substantial woman in her late thirties. Her hair was the same snuff brown as her sweater, and standing with her back to the door, she looked like a greatly enlarged doorstop. One of the old cast-iron ones guaranteed to keep the door from slamming shut in any wind.

"So that's what she was working on at the end,"

Margery said as she strode toward the group clustered around the quilt. "She made beautiful quilts. We all got one when we got married. Kept her busy, I suppose."

"Margery brought the mussels for our supper and was kind enough to stay and clean them for me," Louise explained. Margery was moving toward the door.

"I'll be going then. Enjoy your meal." She was gone, but was it Faith's imagination or did Margery cast a glance of malicious amusement toward Eric? A glance that suggested that his mussels might have something other than pearls in them?

"And now it's my turn," Louise said. "It won't take long. I hope you all like Billi Bi?"

Faith was slightly reassured to hear that Margery had not prepared dinner too.

Louise wasn't gone long, returning faintly flushed. "Please come and sit down. It's a simple summer meal, but it does have to be eaten hot."

Besides the delectable creamy mussel soup, the simple summer meal included lots of crusty bread; corn from their garden, picked as the water reached a boil; juicy slabs of tomatoes; and rhubarb compote with heavy cream for dessert. Afterward they took their coffee out to the back porch.

The sky looked like an overturned bowl of stars. It was the time of year for shooting stars, and they fell in trails of light across the darkness. Eric was sitting on a lower step leaning against Jill. John was sitting alone off to the side. Eric spoke in a low voice.

"You know, I can't believe Roger is really dead. Here we all are sitting on the porch as always, but he's not here. I just haven't been able to take it in somehow."

"Early days yet—don't try," Elliot advised.

"I believe he is here, Eric," Pix spoke softly. "Because we're here, he's here—and always will be."

Nobody said anything for a while; then Eric said, "Thank you, Pix."

It was almost the same group who had been together at the covered-dish supper just over a week ago. They must have done a lot of things together. But now one of them would always be missing. Bill Fox was missing too, but Faith was sure he would have been invited if Bird hadn't been his house guest. It was not likely that Eric would want to see her just yet. Faith wondered if Bill had prevailed upon her to change her dress.

They didn't stay much longer. Faith thanked the Fraziers and realized she wanted to get to know them better. She had a feeling Tom would like them too.

Tom. It was a stabbing thought as she drove home. She missed him so keenly these days, it was easier not to think about him too much. She'd spoken with him last night after the funeral. He had called to see how she was, but she didn't want to tell him about Bird. He'd just worry, and it wasn't as if there was any danger. But Tom didn't like unpredictability, except in his wife, and if he thought people were jumping into graves on the island, he would assume it was only a small step to other forms of aberrance. Like pushing Faith into a grave. She knew how his mind worked.

Samantha and Arlene left after telling Faith what an angel Benjamin was, and Faith once again questioned the order of the universe that had determined that a child will always behave better for anyone, even a perfect stranger, than a parent.

After she closed the door and turned off the

lights, Faith sat on her porch for a while, reluctant to go in. It was too beautiful. The air was warm and the world was full of stars—in the sky and reflected back by the water, lapping the rocks at high tide.

She thought some more about the evening at the Fraziers'. Jill had been warm and friendly; apparently recent events had penetrated her shyness and she had let down her guard. Faith was sure she was deeply upset about Roger, but there was also the way she looked at Eric, slightly maternal, certainly in love. She was needed. John Eggleston had been restless and uncharacteristically silent. Was it likely that he was still troubled by the funeral? Somehow Faith thought not. He was a cipher to her and she wasn't sure she liked him. He didn't seem to fit the circle of friends. Someone who had forced his way in and stayed? She'd forgotten to ask Pix why he had left the church and made a mental note to do so.

She lay back on the rough porch boards and tried to find the Big Dipper. Tom knew all the names of the constellations. She smiled. He would be here soon and she'd try to learn one or two. That was a good thought. She saw the flash of a shooting star and made a wish. She knew it would come true. Faith had primitive beliefs when it came to stars and fortune cookies, believing in their infallibility more than the average minister's wife was wont to do. She found the Big Dipper and something that might be Orion's belt. Tom would tell her.

The next afternoon Faith brought the quilt over to Pix's and they spread it out on the dining-room floor. Pix had some books, and Faith had borrowed a couple from Louise. They hoped they would be able to identify the squares. Samantha had gone off to Arlene's house to lend moral support while her mother gave her a perm, and for the moment Benjamin was happily playing with his little cars and some blocks Pix had dug out. He sat sputtering away at their feet, and Faith realized it wouldn't be long before her car keys, at present an instant baby calmer, would exert a different fascination. She had always been a strong proponent of environment versus heredity, but faced with objective reality, she had to admit there might be something to inborn preferences. As a truly liberated woman, she had presented Ben with balanced choices since birth—a sweet Corolle baby doll, a tea set, a truck—and it was wheels every time.

They decided to have lunch before getting down to work and had moved into the kitchen when they heard a car pull up. Pix looked out the window. "It's Bill Fox and he's alone," she said, drying her hands hurriedly on her shirttail and walking toward the door. Faith followed her after locating a dish towel.

"Oh, Pix," he said, "there you are. I came by earlier and no one was home. I wanted to leave you a note, but I couldn't find any paper without rifling your drawers. It was an enticing notion, though perhaps a bit familiar."

"Bill, you can rifle my drawers any time," Pix offered.

This was Pix? Faith thought in amusement—our Pix who dropped her drink at Aleford gatherings if a man so much as admired her canapés?

Bill walked into the house and set a large paper bag on the dining-room table.

"I was wondering if you could follow me into Granville tomorrow and bring me home. I have to leave my car at the garage to have the brakes checked, and they're going to get rid of all this grime for me. I don't think it's been washed since last year."

"I have to go tomorrow anyway, so I'd be happy to help you out. Morning or afternoon?"

"Let's be optimists and say morning, around nine o'clock? Maybe it will be done sooner that way. Oh, and this is for you. Some things from my garden that I don't think you're growing."

"Or if we are, they're nowhere as good as yours. Thank you and I hope you tucked some of that white eggplant in." Faith had learned that Bill Fox's garden was famous on the island. It was beautiful to look at. Flowers, fruits and vegetables were planted together in seeming disarray. Scarlet runner beans on tepee trellising were bordered by beds of white phlox and deep-blue bachelor buttons. But the garden was not only a feast for the eye. Bill delighted in producing new and unusual varieties—all the things that were not supposed to grow in this climate. Radicchio, arugula, and baby vegetables had all been in his patch of earth long before they had inhabited Balducci's bins and Manhattan's menus.

"Faith and I were just about to have lunch, Bill. Would you care to join us?"

"Delighted." Faith studied him as they entered the kitchen. He really did look delighted. Surely his glowing expression could not simply be due to the prospect of a ride and a roast beef sandwich?

It wasn't.

They were sitting on the deck in the back of the house. Benjamin had eaten two bites of his sandwich, thereby covering himself from head to toe with peanut butter and jelly, then had promptly fallen asleep.

Two great blue heron were slowly flying across the cove, long legs streaming straight behind them, and enormous wings moving gracefully through the air, like an early flying machine. Their shadows rippled the water, until they landed on the top of an ancient black oak along the shore.

" 'A dusky blue wave undulating over our meadows' is how Thoreau saw them, and I've never read a better description," Bill told them. "They're favorites of mine. I could watch them for hours. Ardea Herodias, the tallest bird in New England, the royalty of the shores and marshes."

He took a big gulp of lemonade as if to fortify himself and abruptly changed the subject. "Nothing official yet and I know I can rely on you both to keep this under your bonnets, but I'm getting married."

"Married!" gasped Pix as Faith quickly covered her over-abundant surprise with congratulations and best wishes.

"That's wonderful, Bill. Whoever she is, she's a very lucky person. It was my childhood dream to marry Prince Herodias, and in a way she is."

He smiled. It was such a happy, calm smile. The smile of someone who feels completely fulfilled, who lets out that anxious breath he's been holding for thirty years and knows he's going to live happily ever after. After all.

"Is it someone we know?" Pix asked.

He appeared to find the question irrelevant. "It's Bird, of course."

"Bird!" Pix gasped again, and again Faith covered her confusion with happy noises about how lovely she was and how her baby would have a good home. She would have burbled on further, but Bill interrupted. He was obviously eager to share his news and tell his tale.

"I met her last winter, and it was the proverbial falling in love at first sight. I knew I didn't have a chance, but I was happy to be her friend and she enjoyed coming to the house. She's a very bright woman, you know."

Since they had never heard her open her mouth except for that anguished outcry in the cemetery, Faith and Pix did not know.

"She has been desperately unhappy with Andy, but felt she had to try to stay with him since he was the father of her child, and they also shared a commitment to living in the natural, or rather primitive, way they did. And they are both macrobiotics. Although I have been able to get her to eat chicken and fish on occasion. What I do is put lots of sprouts on everything, and she thinks she's eating salad."

Faith was appalled. What a way to start a marriage. This must be what was meant by living on love alone.

"I don't pretend to think I'm Bird's first or only choice. I'm quite certain that had he lived, she would have married Roger. She's marrying me because she wants some stability in her life and she wants to stay on the island." He paused and colored slightly. "Of course, she does have some affection for me too."

"Of course she does, Bill. If she didn't, she'd be out of her mind. She's the lucky one here." Pix was getting a bit irritated at all the self-deprecation. Trading life in a fisherman's bait shack with no amenities and a quixotic, perhaps abusive, would-be rock star for Bill's beautifully designed modern house and unswerving love and devotion wasn't exactly a step down.

"We're both lucky, Pix," Bill smiled as he put his hand over hers. "One of those serendipitous blinks where two people find themselves in the right place at the right time. And Zoë makes it even more perfect," he added.

"Zoë?" asked Pix. "Oh, the baby, of course. I never knew her name."

"Well, her name has actually undergone several transformations that are too embarrassing to reveal, but it's Zoë now for keeps. Zoë Fox."

"I like Zoë. I think it means 'life,' doesn't it?"

While Pix was musing on Zoë's name, Faith was concentrating on Bird's. Bird Fox? Better than Bird Dog, but still ludicrous. If Bill could get her to eat meat and change the baby's name, maybe he could convince her to go back to her original name, whatever that was. More important, maybe he could get her to stop tie-dyeing her clothes.

A lobster boat returning from a long morning of hauling made its way across the inlet. The herons rose up and flapped off in the opposite direction.

"I have to be going," Bill said. "Bird and Zoë had fallen asleep when I left, and they must be up by now." And he didn't want to miss a single waking moment, Faith surmised.

They walked him to his car and returned to the job of identifying the quilt squares.

Pix took a sheet of paper and was making a list.

"Why don't we give them numbers starting at the upper left-hand corner and going across each row. So far we know number one, Old Maid's Puzzle, number five, Mariner's Compass, and this one, number seven, is Crossroads or something like that."

"And Louise said this was Fern Berry, number sixteen. I remember, because it was an interesting name."

"Right, and in the next row, number eighteen is Shady Pine."

Pix stood back, regarding the quilt intently. "Number thirteen is obviously Schoolhouse, or Little Red Schoolhouse, I think it's called. And number fourteen is Jacob's Ladder."

"Pix, this is great. We've already named seven, almost half."

"Make that eight, because number ten has to be some kind of tree design. See the trunk and the leaf pattern?"

"I've been stupid about this. Of course the squares are pictures. Look at number nineteen. It looks like a chest or a trunk."

"I know what you're thinking and it may be crazy, but I think you're right. The quilt does have some kind of message."

"Matilda may have been religious, but I'm sure 'Seek and Ye Shall Find' meant something else. Something like 'God helps those who help themselves.' And what else is there to seek but the gold?" Faith was definitely getting excited.

"Naming the first block Old Maid's Puzzle is too much of a coincidence to be one, together with the quotation and that square at the bottom with the chest or whatever on it."

"Exactly. Now all we have to do is solve the puzzle."

"And to do that, we have to find the names of all the squares. Not an easy job. But we can start by figuring out if the squares are four-patch, nine-patch, appliqué, what have you."

"And what have you? What's all this patch business?"

"Many blocks are made up of four, six, or nine, etc. smaller squares sewn together, and the books list the patterns this way, so we don't have to go

122

through every category searching. We can narrow it down a little."

"Wonderful. Appliqué is in my vocabulary, but I don't see any here, except maybe this schoolhouse." Faith was down on her hands and knees, looking closely at each square. "No, it's your little nine, ten, whatever blocks too."

Pix had started to open a book. "Ickis's *Quilt Making and Collecting* is a Bible for quilt makers, and Matilda is sure to have had it. Let's see. . . ."

"Pix!" Faith interrupted. "There's something peculiar about some of these squares. Look—on Mariner's Compass she only embroidered one point, and E for East. And in this one, number three, the top triangle is red and all the others are blue. It's not a code. Pix—the quilt is some kind of map!"

Pix knelt down next to Faith. "You're right! Look at Crossroads. The calico for the one on the left is different from the rest."

"And number nine has the same thing—the fabric in the upper right is different from the rest. She's telling us which way to turn. What a smart lady. I'm really sorry I never knew her," Faith said with regret in her voice.

"I have a feeling you're going to be a whole lot better acquainted with Matilda by the time we ever figure this out," Pix commented.

They pored over the books, taking turns at amusing Ben, who awoke and vociferously demanded some entertainment. After an hour and a half, they had identified four more squares: Harbor View, number two, Weather Vane, number three, Odd Fellows Chain, number six, and North Star, number eleven.

"Harbor View is the name of the Prescott house. It's painted on a board over the barn door. So that means the map must start there and we must read across the rows, not down."

"Then Weather Vane refers to the ship weather vane. Which way is north?"

"Toward this side of the island, but we don't know what the square in between is—before Mariner's Compass."

Faith had been scanning the designs in one of the books. "It looks like this one, Pullman Puzzle, but that doesn't make sense. There aren't any train tracks on the island."

"I should have told you," Pix said apologetically. "Many of the same squares have different names depending on what part of the country you're in."

"Wonderful. All right, we'll put a question mark next to that one. And in any case we may not have to identify all the squares to figure it out. The most important ones have to be the last few. Why don't we concentrate on those, now that we know the starting point?"

Another forty minutes yielded only two squares: number nine, Winding Ways, and number twenty, Prosperity, which Faith noted assured them they were on the right track, but gave no clues. Ben had had more than enough of sitting indoors. Eager as she was to figure out the quilt, Faith was glad to take a break.

"I think I'll take Ben home the shore way, and he can explore to his heart's content."

"Leave the quilt and I'll keep trying. It's addictive. Besides, I'm dying of curiosity." Pix was standing on the floor with a stack of *Quilter's Newsletter Magazines* to her side. "Look at this quilt. Can you imagine the work that went into it?" she asked Faith.

Faith took a look at the magazine. "It's gorgeous and could not possibly have been accomplished by human hands." She paused, then added, "You know we could be at this until Christmas, especially if we get sidetracked like this."

"Don't worry, I'm working. That was just a momentary aberration."

"Speaking of which, was Matilda the type to go to all this trouble for an empty box? Some kind of joke from the other side?"

"I don't know. It's an awful lot of work to do for a joke."

"On all our parts," Faith agreed.

Before she left, she jotted down the names of the quilt squares they had identified. They were assuming the clues were in sequence from left to right across, but they could be wrong. She wanted to look at it all again when her mind was clearer and see if she could figure anything out.

"Call me if you find any more names," she said as they left.

Faith and Ben took their time following the shoreline between the two cottages, stopping to watch some eider ducks bob about in the water. Faith's pockets were heavy with all Ben's treasures: assorted shells, sea urchins emptied of their contents by the gulls, and rocks. She had finally pried him away from a boulder almost as big as he was that he seemed to want to add to the collection, and they climbed up into the meadow in front of the cottage. The landscape had that peculiar flat, intense light it sometimes assumes in the late afternoon, or just before a storm. Everything was absolutely still and light flooded into every corner. It was like a stage set. Ben and Faith stopped for an instant.

"I'm going to get you!" Faith cried and reached out for him. He squealed in happy terror and ran for the house. It worked every time.

The door was open. Faith thought she had closed it. When she walked into the living room, she was sure she had.

But the person or persons unknown who had been in the house since and torn it apart hadn't bothered.

She didn't linger to see if Goldilocks was sleeping in Ben's bed, but grabbed her car keys and child, drove straight to Pix's, and called the police.

Faith hung up and turned to Pix. "He's going to check it out and then come by here. It's very strange. There's absolutely nothing of value in the house that people know about. Not even a TV set. What could someone have wanted?"

Which was Sgt. Dickinson's question as well. The house was empty, and he asked Faith to come back with him to try to figure out what was missing. Pix jumped in next to Faith.

They stood and surveyed the living room in silence. It wasn't as bad as Faith had first thought. Drawers were pulled out and cushions from the couch strewn around, but nothing had been smashed or broken, thank goodness. Short of haunting every yard sale on the Maine Coast for the rest of her life, she would have had no idea how to replace the vintage noncollectible cottage furnishings. The other rooms showed the same regard for property, but not order. Things were messed up, particularly the beds, but intact. Sgt. Dickinson showed special interest in the beds, examining the sheets with care. He was a medium-sized, well-built man with aspirations toward a Burt Reynolds mustache, the whole effect only slightly marred by a persistent cowlick.

"They might have done a little rolling around in here, but nothing else," he reported to Faith and Pix. "If you catch my meaning," he added solemnly. They nodded vigorously in unison and Faith felt slightly relieved. The sanctity of the cottage beds had been preserved. It had been plain to her from the start that all those hours of exercise and masochistic dips in the ocean by the previous inhabitants had been to quell certain urges. And as for the current inhabitants—well, they *were* married.

Ben had sensed something was amiss and had clung to Faith since they had entered the house, refusing even Pix's familiar arms. Trying to remember whether she had brought her Hermès scarf with the boat design or not was made more difficult by Ben's anguished cries whenever she tried to set him down for a moment. Pix had told her life was simple on the island, and Faith hadn't brought any good jewelry Nor, she finally recalled, the scarf. But Pix was wrong. Life on the island was certainly not simple. Yet it wasn't something for which one dressed. She'd been right about that.

An hour's careful inventory revealed only a few items missing: some bottles of scotch, gin, vermouth, and wine Faith kept in the pantry; and a cuff bracelet Tom had bought for her from a silversmith on the island when they had first arrived. The wine in the basement had not been touched. Possibly, the fear of Faith and Ben's arrival had driven the miscreants away before they had had a chance to get to it.

They assembled on the porch to hear Sgt. Dickinson's parting words.

"Looks like kids, Mrs. Fairchild. No tire marks, except yours going out. I expect they were out in a skiff, saw you leave, and decided to have a party. Or at least get the makings of one. This happens a lot in the winter. But they're getting pretty foolish lately. I have an idea or two who they might be, and I'll keep an eye out for that bracelet of yours."

"It wasn't worth that much, but my husband gave it to me."

He took a small memo pad out of his pocket and made a note, as he had been doing every time Faith opened her mouth. He was nothing if not thorough.

"I don't think they'll be back to bother you, but I'll make it a point to check by here for the next couple of days."

"I think you're right, Sergeant. There's really nothing for them to steal. But thank you all the same. It's reassuring to know you're around." Faith gave him one of her more radiant smiles and he was properly impressed. He blushed and left.

"Do you think this is some sort of record, Pix? For summer people, especially?"

"What are you talking about, Faith?"

"Making the 'Police Brief' two weeks in a row, of course."

Pix patted her on the shoulder and they went in to start cleaning up. Ben had fallen asleep—he hadn't slept long enough earlier—and Faith had put him in his crib. His room was untouched. Evidently these were not teenagers who collected stuffed animals.

"Faith, why don't you come and stay with me until your sister gets here? There's plenty of room and we'd love to have you," Pix offered.

"That's very sweet and thank you, but I'm not

nervous. Whoever it was has had a look around and won't be back, and I know how to make sure of it."

They were stripping the sheets off the bed.

"What do you mean? They'll probably watch you the next time you go to the state liquor store. You know there's always that line of teenagers sitting on the stone wall next to it."

"Oh Pix, don't tell me you think it was kids who broke in here! It wasn't booze and bangles our thief wanted. It was the quilt."

"The quilt!"

"Of course. Look at the way the beds are messed up and which drawers are open. No small ones, only those big enough to hold the quilt." Faith stood for a moment, her arms filled with bedding.

"And we have to do something about it as soon as possible, because if we don't he, she, or they will try again."

Six

Despite her brave words to Pix, Faith spent a sleepless night. She was jolted to full consciousness by each noise outside and inside the cottage.

And it was an extremely noisy night.

Prescott's was loading lobsters, and the trucks seemed to grind every gear. Every floorboard in the house creaked in turn; the glass in every window rattled; and every diurnal creature decided to join his nocturnal cousin for a night of raucous fun. On top of all this, Bird's little chick wailed most of the night on and off. From the sound Faith was convinced that their cabin had suddenly located itself in her yard instead of on the next point of land.

Bird must have gone back to pack things up, Faith thought. She realized they had forgotten to ask Bill when the nuptials were going to be celebrated, but she had the impression it would be soon. But not soon enough. She yawned and turned over to punch her pillow.

Still, Faith didn't hear the dog bark, and that was something.

Pix had insisted that she keep one of the Millers' three golden retrievers and swore that he would bark if anything human approached. He would not attack—more likely run forward in friendly greeting—but he would sound an alert. He was sleeping on the hooked rug at the foot of the stairs and added a steady adenoidal snoring and occasional doggy nightmare snarl to the cacophony of sound. His name was Dusty; the other two were Henry and Arthur, aka Hanky and Arty. The next generation had fortunately limited to dogs Pix's parents' penchant for whimsy in names, although Samantha, after her father, was getting dangerously close.

Ben was up at the crack of dawn, and for once Faith was glad to get up with him. He came running gleefully into her room, his soaked nighttime diaper swaying between his legs. He had taken his sleeper off. It was probably wet too.

"Mommee, Mommee," he cried, and stretched out his little arms for Faith to pull him into her warm bed for a cuddle.

"Not a prayer," she answered as she got up and swooped him into her arms and off for a bath. He laughed in delight. She could do no wrong. At least not for many years to come. She was his own "Mommee" and he loved her passionately. This is why women have sons, Faith reminded herself as she turned on the taps.

It was a brief detour from the all-important task of the morning. She had outlined the plan to Pix the night before and lost no time, once Ben was dressed and fed, in executing it. As she came downstairs with Ben and his Brio Spool Wagon to keep him occupied, she heard the other baby crying again. Faith was a little hazy on when babies were supposed to have things, but she thought Zoë was too old for colic. It could be teething. That was a reasonable answer for a few years when anyone asked why your child was screaming. It sounded better than "bad temper" or "horrible personality." She turned to the matter at hand, happy she wasn't the one futilely pacing the floor or rocking in a chair.

First she spread the quilt on the floor in the living room and carefully photographed each square with Samantha's Polaroid Impulse, which Pix had brought over when she had delivered Dusty and the quilt top. Then Faith numbered the pictures, put them in an envelope, and stuffed the envelope in the folds of one of the diapers in Benjamin's diaper bag.

Afterward she wrote a short note to her friend Charley MacIsaac. He also happened to be the chief of police in Aleford, the place she was still startled to call home.

Dear Charley,

Please put the enclosed in a safe place. Don't give it or show it to anyone. I'll explain when I get home.
It's nice here and everyone is fine. See you soon.

Love, Faith

The good thing about Charley was that he would do it and not feel he had to call her up and ask a lot of questions. Like Tom.

Next she opened one of the desk drawers, which she had discovered earlier contained enough brown paper and string to send the Queen Mary by parcel post, and took out what she needed. She wrapped the quilt and tied it, taped the letter to it, and wrapped the whole thing again. If Charley didn't know what was in it, it was all the better. She addressed it to "C. MacIsaac, 1776 Revere Street, Aleford, Massachusetts." Then she called Pix, who she figured should be back after taking Bill Fox home from the garage in Granville.

"Everything's ready. Can you come with me now?"

"No problem, and Samantha wants to take Ben for a walk."

"Perfect. We wouldn't want to cut things short because of a restless child, and if he's behaving well, he might upstage us."

A half hour later Pix and Faith were standing in line at the IGA in Sanpere Village. Pix had filled a basket with things she didn't need and Faith was holding the unwieldy package. Pix went first.

"Faith," she said, managing to sound genuinely reproachful, "you know Louise and I would have been happy to help you get started. There is really no need to have someone else quilt your top."

"Oh, Pix, I am very grateful, but you know that I'm hopeless with a needle and thread. You can teach me something else like basket weaving. I really would like to have it finished in my lifetime, and this woman is a fine quilter. I remember she finished a quilt for a friend of mine, and when I called her, she said she could start right away. That's why I want to get it off this morning." Faith was deliberately ambiguous as to name and place. Plus she never minded a few fibs in the cause of justice.

"I do understand, Faith, and it's such a lovely quilt, it deserves to be finished quickly. I wonder what color she'll choose for the backing. Did you tell her what color to pick?"

And they were off on a discussion of colors, patterns, and textures which took them through the checkout and into the street.

"Now for Part Two," Faith said under her breath as they strolled through the village with their packages.

Pix had something more on her mind. "You know,

you might enjoy basket weaving. It's fun and very relaxing. I could start you on a melon basket."

Faith knew where the thought was going. "Pix," she said gently but firmly, "I don't carry my melons in baskets. At least not in this country." Some ideas had to be ruthlessly nipped in the bud.

People with post office boxes generally came to get their mail in the late morning, and Sanpere Village bustled with their activity. Even if one's mail was delivered, there was always something to pick up. Something from Prescott's Hardware, the IGA, or The Blueberry Patch.

There were two other enterprises in the village, an art gallery started by an off-islander who now lived on Sanpere year round and an antique shop operated by one of the Sanfords, who purportedly got most of her stock from picking the dump. But these two shops were strictly for summer people and Faith and Pix walked by them quickly.

Jill stocked newspapers and magazines and had lately added a small section of paperback books. Faith stopped to buy a paper and managed to pass the news to the four or five people in the store, then conveyed it to three more in Prescott's while she picked up some batteries for one of the dozen or so flashlights that had come with the cottage, everything from penlight to searchlight. John Eggleston was busy buying nails, but paused to emit a bark of polite interest before turning back to the infinitely more fascinating display in front of him. Faith filed a thought to pull out later. It was unlikely that he had amassed much in the way of earthly goods as a minister, "poor as church mice" being the rule rather than the exception. Was he a successful enough sculptor to support himself? What did he live on?

By the time they walked up the worn wooden post office stairs, which had once been red like the rest of the building, it was almost pointless to keep talking. Most of the island, from the top of the old serpentine quarry at South Beach to the town wharf at Granville, already knew that Mrs. Fairchild was mailing that quilt of Matilda Prescott's up to Massachusetts to be finished.

There were only two people in the post office, but one of them was Sonny Prescott, and Faith and Pix went through the whole thing again for his benefit. The other was Eric, standing with studied care as far away as possible from Sonny as he could in the tiny room. It was to him that Faith addressed her remarks, with Pix providing backup.

Sonny left after a nod to the ladies. Possibly the conversation was not as riveting as they thought, but when the package, which had already made quite a journey, was finally sent on its way and they emerged into the sunlight, they were pleased to note Sonny earnestly talking into his CB in the cab of his pickup.

"Mission accomplished, *n'est-ce pas*?" Faith murmured to Pix.

"But *oui, mon capitaine*," she replied.

They both felt terribly smug.

Eric was following closely behind them, and they walked together toward Faith's car.

"I've decided to move into the Prescott house— my house, that is," he told them. "I think Roger would have wanted it."

"That's wonderful." Pix put her hand on his arm. "Of course Roger would have wanted it and we want it. You mustn't be driven away by all this."

"Jill is going to help me move later this afternoon. There isn't much. This morning I'm going to try to work again. I haven't been in the studio since all this happened, and I can't be a coward anymore."

"I don't think you're getting graded on this one," Faith commented. "Nothing on your permanent record."

Eric grinned. "Thanks, Faith. But it's now or never. Must be all those times my daddy made me get back up on the horse."

Faith remembered Pix had mentioned Eric was from Texas. Once more she blessed the fates for their wisdom in settling her near the bridle trails of Central Park, not the Panhandle.

He left them at the car and walked toward the causeway. The tide was out, and his house sat up on a knoll in fastidious contrast to the mud, rocks, and tangled seaweed below. Faith hoped he and Jill would get together soon. It seemed like a large and lonely place for just one person. Besides, there was safety in numbers.

She asked Pix if it was all right to take the long way home in order to replenish her liquor supply at Granville. Pix didn't mind, and soon they were on the shore road out of Sanpere Village.

The route provided an informal history of the island. The early settlers' few remaining clapboard houses were scattered among the large arks built by the rusticators at the turn of the century, more recent fishermen's cottages, trailers in varying degrees of repair, and finally sleek nouveau Robert A. M. Stern imitations built by the latest invaders. The gulls, pines, granite outcroppings, and wildflowers were the same in every yard.

On the way, Pix told Faith what Bill had told her when she drove him home earlier that morning. Faith had been right. Bird *had* returned to the cabin the night before to pack and also leave a note for

Andy. Bill and Bird were planning to get married as soon as they could get a license. It was going to be a simple ceremony in Bill's garden and he hoped they would both come.

"He's so happy, Faith. I don't have any sense of what she's like, but she'd better be good to him." Pix's voice brooked no opposition.

"I don't think you should worry. She's the embodiment of his imaginary princess and can do no wrong. I wonder what her life was like before she ended up here with Andy? It may be that the security Bill will provide is just what she needs—and wants."

"I hope so. It would be devastating for him if she got bored and took off with a younger man in a few years—or months."

"I'm sure that has occurred to Bill and he's willing to take the chance for the woman of his dreams."

As Faith said that, in her mind, she heard Eric's voice just the week before talking about the house of his dreams. So many dreams and a nightmare that touched them all. The sadness did not go away and she found herself murmuring "Poor Roger" as she parked in front of the old Opera House, which had once hosted traveling companies with such luminaries as Nellie Melba and now stood empty.

There were no other customers in the state liquor store. It was lunchtime. Native islanders were home and the summer people were picnicking or enjoying the chowder and pie at The School Street Rest. It was one of two places to eat in Granville, three if you counted the Italian sandwiches for sale at Baylor's Market. Bert Hamilton had painted an old bus blue and sold clam rolls and pizza in the parking lot next to the town wharf, but it didn't compare with The School Street. Pix had explained that

"Restaurant" hadn't fit on the original sign, and even when a new one was made, no one called it anything else.

Faith replaced what had been stolen from her tantalus. As they walked back to the car, she scrutinized the wrists of the teenagers sitting on the nearby wall. They were spread out silently in a row, unconsciously duplicating the immobile line of gulls perched on the roof behind them. The kids eyed Faith and Pix with expressions ranging from indifference to hostility. One of them had a face so devoid of affect that Faith suspected it was drug induced. He was definitely gone. She didn't see her bracelet. She didn't expect to.

They drove up the steep hill leading away from the harbor, passed School Street Restaurant, resisted the lure of fish chowder and black walnut pie, and hastened home.

Faith realized she was happy to get back. It had been an exhausting twenty-four hours, with the robbery and this morning's tour de force.

Samantha had fed Ben, and he was beginning to get drowsy. Faith could tell because he had an unusual amount of energy and was running around the kitchen trying to entice her into a game of tag. It was a final statement: "What, tired, me? Never!" She made herself a sandwich and a tall glass of iced tea, grabbed a banana for Ben, and led him outdoors. They sat in the grass, and soon Faith felt his body relax and lean into hers. She could hear the slight whistle of air as he breathed in and out. She could also, she suddenly realized, still hear the baby, Zoë, crying. Bird didn't seem like the kind of mother who suffered advice gladly, but perhaps the child was ill, and with no phone or car Bird couldn't get help. Of course, it wasn't far to Faith's, or Bird could even stand on the point and somehow attract Sonny Prescott's attention from the short distance across the water. And surely Bill was checking in. But his car was in the shop.

The crying continued. It was a high-pitched wail on one note that varied in volume. Faith sat and studied the calm horizon. She couldn't stand it anymore. Carefully she hoisted Benjamin into her arms and up the porch steps, depositing him in the portable crib that had been set up there for outdoor naps. Then she went into the house and called Pix.

"It does seem odd," Pix responded. "She seemed like such a placid little thing Tuesday in the cemetery. Why don't I come over?"

Pix arrived and listened. Samantha and Arlene were with her, waiting for a ride to the village. They agreed to sit on the porch steps in case Ben awoke while Faith and Pix went to offer maternal guidance to Bird.

"It could be indigestion. Bill said he was trying to vary their diet, and maybe Zoë was too used to brown rice," Pix suggested.

"Well, whatever it is, we'll find out. I just hope she doesn't take offense and think we're a couple of busybodies," Faith said as she turned up the narrow, rutted road that led to the shack, wondering at the same time when the word "busybody" had entered her vocabulary.

The shack appeared deserted. Some of the glass in the windows had been replaced with cardboard, and the siding looked like a good strong wind would send the whole thing tumbling down like a house of cards. A clothesline had been strung up between two pines, and a number of gaily colored articles swayed gently in the breeze. It was the only note of color in the scene.

Until Faith opened the door.

Blood was everywhere. The walls, the floor, and especially on Bird. Or what had been Bird. She was lying on her back on the floor, her long, silky hair spread out against the old piece of linoleum someone had put down in an attempt at housekeeping. Her head had dropped to one side. One hand rested on her cheek as if she had tried to ward off the blows. It had been futile. Her face was barely recognizable, a bloody pulp of something that had once been beautiful.

Faith slammed the door shut instantly, collapsed onto the granite step, and retched.

"Faith, Faith, what's the matter?" Pix grabbed her.

"Don't go in!" Faith screamed. "She's dead! Murdered! You've got to go get help!"

"What! It's not possible!" Pix started to open the door and Faith grabbed her arm.

"Believe me, Pix, don't go in! There's nothing we can do for her. Blood is everywhere and you don't want to see. I've got to get the baby, then I'll wait outside until you come back."

"Oh, dear God, think of Bill, Faith. This will destroy him!"

Pix sped off and Faith nerved herself to go back in. It was just as bad the second time. Zoë was in a basket cradle suspended from the rafters and was unharmed. Faith grabbed her and didn't linger to find fresh clothes. She stepped over the body and a chair that had been overturned. The shack was a mess, but not knowing how it had been before, Faith couldn't speculate on what was due to the struggle. Much of the blood was dry, as she had obscurely noted the first time.

Whoever had killed Bird was long gone.

Faith sat down wearily in the shade of a large mountain ash and held the baby close, rocking her. Soon Zoë stopped crying and began to suck her fist contentedly. Faith started to cry.

It wasn't that she knew Bird. She had never even held a conversation with her, but the horror of it all was overwhelming. First Roger, now Bird. Could it be a coincidence? All Faith's instincts said no, but what possible motive could tie them together? She gripped the baby tightly. Poor little thing. What was going to happen to her now?

Pix was back before the police arrived. She stumbled wild-eyed out of the car.

"Faith, this can't be happening! I called John and told him, so he could break the news to Bill. They have been close friends for years, and it would be terrible for Bill to find out from the police or someone in the village. It will be terrible enough. Oh dear, why did this have to happen and why now?"

"I know. It just doesn't make any sense. In either case."

"What do you mean 'either case'?"

"Bird and Roger. They both seemed like people with relatively uncomplicated lives who were just going their own distinctive ways not hurting anyone else. And unless Bird turns out to be some runaway heiress, neither had money a murderer would have wanted. And there aren't any jealous spouses around. All the traditional murder-mystery motives."

"Aren't you forgetting Andy? He's not a spouse, but pretty close."

Faith had forgotten Andy. Bird had been afraid of his temper, but would it drive him this far? Suddenly the unreality of sitting in the lovely landscape talking about whodunit while the very bloody corpse lay a few feet away struck Faith and she began to shiver.

"Faith, this is insane! You're still in shock. I've got to take you home."

"As soon as the police come. Remember, I've been through this before," she said grimly, "and they don't like you to leave the scene of the crime."

Fortunately they didn't have to wait long. Sgt. Dickinson screeched up, asked where the body was, and entered the house. He was out almost immediately and went into his car. They could hear him talking on the two-way radio, but not what he said. Finally he came over and sat down next to them. He looked pale.

"Gorry." He shook his head. "Somebody must have really hated that girl." Then he sat up straight, recollected his duty, and asked Faith to tell him what had happened. He pulled his notebook out and licked the tip of his pencil. She told him about hearing the baby crying all night and then coming over with Pix about twenty minutes ago to see if Bird needed some help. She *had* needed help. They were just too late.

"She was probably killed last night, if you heard the baby crying like that," Sgt. Dickinson reasoned. "You didn't hear any other sounds. Screams?" he asked hopefully.

Faith was forced to disappoint him and was tempted to add that although she was only a dumb summer person and a female at that, if she had heard screams she would have done something about it.

He asked if they knew anything about Bird. Where she was from?

"I've seen her only a few times," Pix replied.

"You probably know more than I do, since she's been living here all winter. Of course Bill Fox can tell you."

"Fox?" The sergeant seemed puzzled.

Before Pix could answer, Fox himself arrived, jumping out of John Eggleston's car before it stopped. He raced to the door of the cabin and almost had it open before Sgt. Dickinson reached him.

"You can't go in there, Mr. Fox. And I don't think you want to."

Pix and Faith, who was still carrying Zoë, hastened over. Pix put her arms around Bill, but he pushed her away roughly. He was angry.

"I have a right to see her! She was going to be my wife!" he shouted.

If the sergeant was surprised, he didn't show it, but he placed a hand on Bill's arm and led him away from the step.

"I know you want to do the right thing and that's to wait for the appropriate authorities to come with everything they need to track down who did this. We can't go in and mess things up."

Faith was impressed by his approach. It was common sense and, as it turned out, exactly the right thing to say to Bill.

"Well, I'm staying right here," he asserted.

"That's fine. I'm staying myself, and maybe you could tell me a little about your fiancée while we wait," Dickinson said in an even voice. He had appeared completely calm after that initial slip, and given the scene, Faith could hardly blame him. It was a scene she was trying desperately to obliterate from her mind with small success.

"I wonder if we could leave now, Sergeant? I can take the baby home. She must be starving and she needs changing," Faith said.

He nodded, and Bill Fox looked at Zoë. "The baby, I'd forgotten about the baby," he said dazedly.

"Come over here, Bill, and we can talk to the sergeant together." John had been standing off to one side. Now he was taking charge. Faith had trouble reading his expression. There was anger, but not sadness. Something else. Something like disgust.

She got into the car wearily and they left. The last thing they saw was Bill's face, immobile and uncomprehending.

The rest of the day was chaotic, but not immediately. Later the phone rang off the hook and they were besieged by reporters from TV and radio stations, *The Ellsworth American*, *The Boston Herald* and everything located in between.

But first it was just two women, two teenagers, and two babies to take care of. Samantha and Arlene immediately took charge of Zoë and fed, bathed, and dressed her in one of Ben's undershirts and an enormous toddler-sized Pampers. Faith fetched the auction cradle from the barn and put it by a sunny window in the living room. She placed some blankets inside and settled the exhausted child on top with a bottle, which she had discovered in the continuously amazing contents of the pantry off the kitchen.

The two girls immediately sat next to the cradle, Samantha rocking it gently while Arlene held Ben, who peered in delightedly. "Ben's baby?" he asked his mother in a beseeching tone of voice. The tone of voice he usually reserved for animal crackers.

"No, sweetheart. We're just taking care of her for a little while."

While the police scrape what's left of her poor mother off the floor of the shack and set all the wheels in motion that may or may not find her killer, but that will certainly find the baby a home, Faith thought as her insatiable curiosity took hold once again and she began to speculate. Bill had no legal claim, but he might try to get custody. And there must be relatives somewhere. Then there was Andy, but he didn't seem the paternal type.

Faith and Pix sat down next to each other on the sofa at the opposite end of the room. Faith looked at Pix and nodded at the scene around the cradle.

"Callous youth," murmured Pix. "They're happy to have a live doll to play with."

"They didn't know Bird, so it's understandable," Faith pointed out. "It's not like Roger." She realized that she felt sad, but the sadness was totally eclipsed by the horror she had witnessed, and it was hard to connect the blood-stained room and scarcely identifiable corpse with a real person.

"You have to call Tom, Faith," Pix admonished.

"I know. I've been avoiding it. But it will be worse if he reads about it in the papers or hears it on the news."

She glanced at the cheerful faces by the cradle and went into the kitchen to the phone. It was just after lunchtime and she might catch him. She did.

It was hard to know how to start. So she plunged in as soon as she heard his voice saying, "Faith, is that you?" He seemed to be chewing something.

"Yes, darling. Ben and I are fine, but I'm afraid I've found another body."

He choked. "What! Faith, you have got to get out of there immediately! I'll be there as soon as I can! What the hell is going on in Sanpere!"

"Really, Tom, it's not necessary for me to leave. I know it's hard to believe, but think of it as very bad

145

luck. Ben and I aren't in any danger. If I thought there was even the slightest hint of it, of course we would come."

"You haven't told me who was killed. The other potter?"

"No, not Eric. It was Bird—you know, the girl living in the shack on the next point. I only went over with Pix to see why the baby was crying." She hastily decided to omit a description of the body. "And there she was. It had nothing to do with me."

"Faith, please. You and Ben would have a nice time here."

"I'm sure we would, but it is lovely here. Perfect weather and there's really no reason to leave."

And every reason to stay, she thought.

"If I get nervous, I can always go to Pix's."

She could hear Tom sigh.

"But what about *my* being nervous?" he complained.

"I'll call. You'll call. And you'll be here soon."

They continued to talk, and Tom finally agreed—grudgingly. His misgivings took another five minutes and Faith hung up. The phone rang immediately and the chaos began.

The girls moved the cradle behind the sofa and Faith and Pix dealt with the onslaught on the porch. The press did not appear to know about the baby yet, and they were careful not to mention her. It was enough that Zoë had lost her mother in this particularly grisly manner without being spread all over the front pages herself.

Sgt. Dickinson stopped by during one of the rare hiatuses and told them the medical examiner and the state police had arrived. He seemed a bit left out, and Faith offered him some cold lemonade, which he gratefully accepted. While he drank, he told them that Bill Fox hadn't known much about Bird. She was from the midwest originally, but never mentioned her family or real name. The police hoped to find something in the shack. There was also an APB out for Andy. They did know his name, Andrew Collins, and he was from Rockland. Dickinson hinted that the police had been keeping an eye on Andy for some time.

"Drugs?" Faith asked.

"I wouldn't say no," he answered.

After he left, Pix went back to her house to get the quilt books and magazines. They had decided to fill the time trying to identify some more squares. Faith felt vaguely compelled to solve at least one puzzle.

While Pix was gone, she sat with Ben while he scribbled with crayons on the shelf paper she had taped to the top of the kitchen table. He was making car noises and covering the paper with lines that Faith assumed to be roads. She looked closely for signs of incipient artistic talent, didn't find any, and sank back into her thoughts.

Roger, then Bird.

She told herself that it was only logical to agree with the prevailing opinion that Roger's death was due to misadventure—that one of the Prescotts had meant to frighten but not kill him.

But there was no question about Bird. Whoever killed her meant it. Whoever?

Faith closed her eyes and felt sick. She opened them and was a little surprised to see the tranquil scene in front of her and not the mayhem in her mind.

The likeliest perpetrator was Andy. He was known to be violent. Pix had told her Bird had appeared with bruises and once a black eye in the previous months. He was also known to be jealous, and he might have gone berserk at the news of Bird's departure, especially if he had been on something.

And unlike the cases in fiction, Faith knew from Charley MacIsaac, the likeliest suspect is usually guilty—a husband, wife, someone who benefits financially or psychologically from the death.

But there had been two deaths on Sanpere, and much as she tried to reason with herself, Faith still couldn't squelch the notion that they were connected. After all, Roger and Bird were connected and had planned to be connected even more closely, it appeared. She tried to think how their deaths could have benefited anyone and came up with nothing. The Prescotts had no connection to Bird. Even if she and Roger had been secretly married, Bird would not have inherited Matilda Prescott's house, because of the way her will had been written. It went to Roger and/or Eric or issue. Faith wondered if Pix knew anything about Roger's will and resolved to ask her.

Ben was tired of drawing and went back to the cradle to gaze at the baby. The two girls—the "nannies," as Faith had begun to call them in her mind—were happy to have another child in their charge. Faith expected to see the two of them debating the merits of various soothing syrups as they rocked and knit serviceable garments.

Pix came back with lettuce, tomatoes, and some other vegetables from the garden. Faith put together a large salad for dinner, which they could eat with bread and the terrine of smoked mackerel she had made the day before. The nannies would probably want Bovril and toast.

They spread the photographs of the squares, which Faith had retrieved from their hiding place in the diaper bag, on the floor at the end of the living room and started to search for more names.

"Get out your list of the ones we know so far, and let's divide the photographs into two piles," proposed Pix, ever systematic. As she grew to know Pix better, Faith began to think all these lists and systems might be a hedge against basic absentmindedness, even out-and-out woolgathering. Nevertheless there they were.

"Fine. You read out the names and numbers, and I'll go through the photographs."

Pix had identified the tree square as Apple Tree and number nineteen, the chest, as Workbox. There were only five they didn't know.

"You know the island so well. Does any of this make sense, even without all the squares?" Faith asked.

Pix studied the list, glancing over at the photos as she did.

"We really need number four. Obviously she's telling us it's a puzzle since she starts out with Old Maid's Puzzle; then she goes to Harbor View, which must be where the hunt begins. But north on number three—the weather vane could be pointing almost anywhere on this side of the island—or even on the mainland."

"What about the next group? The Compass is pointing east, and it's the left road on Crossroads that's a different pattern. Does that help?"

"Yes," mused Pix, "and number six, Odd Fellows Chain, must refer to the Odd Fellows Hall. There's only one on the island. The problem is it's located almost equidistant between the two main crossroads. We still need number four to point us in the right direction. Matilda figured this pretty carefully."

"It looks like a bull's-eye. Does that suggest anything?" Faith asked hopefully.

"No, but it also looks like the spokes of a wheel, and that's easier. Let's look in the indexes for all the patterns with the word 'wheel' in the title."

Pix's strategy worked; fifteen minutes later Faith triumphantly cried out, "Here it is! Millwheel!"

"That's great! It definitely gives us our direction. There was an old mill across from Harborview, and what's left of the wheel is directly opposite the gazebo on the other side of the pond." She was getting excited. "So if we go north toward the wheel, then east, the Odd Fellows Hall is before the first of the crossroads."

"Then we turn left," continued Faith.

"And," finished Pix, "it's another square we don't know."

"Well, we have more than a week to figure it out before we go home."

The phone rang. Again.

"It could be Sam. He was in court when I called before, so we have to get it," Pix groaned. "Why don't you make us a drink while I find out who it is; then we can feed the kids?"

"Great idea," Faith replied, looked into the cradle, then moved toward the door.

Zoë was still sound asleep. She had roused briefly, drained a bottle, and immediately closed her eyes again. After a while even the nannies had become a bit bored with gazing at her cherubic, sleeping face and had taken Ben outside to play croquet. This was almost as hard as playing with flamingos and hedgehogs, since he chased all the balls and gleefully tossed them into the air. Between making sure he didn't concuss himself and trying to get their balls through the hoops, the girls were getting a fair amount of activity. They were happy to stop and eat. While they ate salad and what Faith had described as sandwich spread in order to make the terrine palatable, the two women sat on the porch.

"Why do we always sit on the steps?" Faith wondered.

"Because wicker is basically uncomfortable and the overhang cuts out the view."

It was after six o'clock, and everything was still. Hardly a leaf moved, and there was no activity on the water to ripple the surface. The sun hadn't set, but they could see the moon. The day's events seemed very far away.

But not too far.

"Pix, was that Sam who called? Did you get a chance to ask him about Roger's will?"

"Yes, I asked him the last time he called. Sorry, I forgot to tell you. Other things on my mind, I suppose. Anyway, it's public knowledge, all probated." She digressed, as was her habit, and Faith waited patiently for her to get back on the track. "You know it's hard being a lawyer's wife. Sam never tells me anything—and shouldn't—but there's so much I'd like to know. You probably have the same problem. Secrets of the confessional." She paused, then added hastily lest a whiff of incense escape into the Maine air, "Not that we have confession, of course.

"Anyway, it was as we thought. Everything goes to Eric. The only surprise would have been a small trust set up for Bird. But now we know how he felt about her. He also left a thousand dollars to his sister and two thousand to his mother."

"He made the will last spring, right?"

"Yes. He must have wanted to provide for Bird. He may not have thought she was going to leave Andy then, and that's why it's a trust and not money outright, which Andy could have taken over."

"Exactly what I was thinking," Faith agreed. "But what happens to it now? Does it go to Zoë or Eric or even the state of Maine?"

"I have no idea, but Sam will know. If Bird made a will, which I doubt, it would probably go to her beneficiary. But even without a will, I think it might still go to Zoë."

The day had seemed interminable, and Faith found it hard to believe that it was the same day she and Pix had taken the quilt to the post office. They went inside to eat. Sam called again, and then the phone was blissfully silent. The Fraziers had called earlier to tell them that Bill was at their house. They offered to take Zoë but quickly agreed that it would be better for her to stay where she was. Bill was in shock and refused to take the sedative Dr. Picot had prescribed. He had barely spoken since John had brought him to their house, except to refuse anything to eat or drink. "He seems very confused, almost as if he doesn't know where he is or who we are," Louise had added.

Pix was getting ready to drive Arlene home, although it hardly seemed worthwhile, since she and Samantha were virtually inseparable. Faith suspected Arlene's mother, who had uncharacteristically refused permission for Arlene to stay the night at the Millers', of wanting inside news of the murder.

The two girls went to take a last look at the sleeping baby. They had been disappointed that she hadn't awakened again while they were there.

"Can't we keep her, Mom?" Samantha pleaded. "She doesn't have any place to go, and you were just saying that the house will be so empty when we're all gone in a few years."

"Bird must have had a family, and they'll want her. Anyway, maybe I was looking forward to an empty house." Pix smiled. A fleeting image of time to herself with no car pools or soccer practices, and only Sam across a candlelit table, flickered across her mind.

"Mother!"

"Just kidding, dear. Now we have to get Arlene home."

"Ma would love to have her, Mrs. Miller. I can ask her tonight." Passion provoked Arlene to speak at length.

"I'm sure your mother has quite enough little Prescotts of her own underfoot—Arlene is the oldest of six," she explained to Faith. But Faith was focusing on the first part of her statement.

"Prescotts?" she asked.

"Yes, Arlene's last name is Prescott."

Faith looked at the pictures of the quilt and the books spread out on the floor where they had been working—right under Arlene's eager gaze.

"Why am I not surprised?" she said to Pix with a sinking feeling in the pit of her stomach. Pix clearly had no idea what Faith was talking about, until she followed her vigorous nod. She shook her head slightly and shepherded the girls out the door. Faith looked at them dismally as they climbed into the car.

Maybe the girl hadn't heard about the quilt or wouldn't connect the pictures to it. Maybe she wouldn't mention them to anybody.

Maybe there wouldn't be any tides tomorrow. Or maybe it would snow. Or maybe . . .

Seven

The children were crying. They had come across a baby robin, fallen from its nest, lying dead beneath a large oak.

Princess Ardea came up quietly behind them. They hadn't realized she was near until she spoke. "Come, we will bury it in the garden." She reached into the pocket of her gown, drew forth a blue silk handkerchief—the same blue as the color of the egg the bird had hatched from—and gently wrapped it around the still body.

They walked back toward the castle grounds, and Paul pointed to a bank of day lilies in bloom. "This might be a good spot." The princess nodded, and he dug a small hole with a stick.

"The bird never had a chance to live. It didn't even know it would have been able to fly someday," Julie said.

"It isn't fair." Her brother scowled. "Why do things have to die?"

"To make room for other things," Prince Herodias answered as he approached from the river, where he had been watching the herons.

"And must everything die?" asked Julie.

"Yes, that is the way," he replied.

"Even you?" she persisted.

"Even us."

"But not for a long, long time?"

"No, not for a very long time. Time passes very slowly here."

Then he took her hand, and they went to stand by the others to lay the bird to rest.

Nightfall in Selega, WILLIAM H. H. FOX

Zoë slept through the night, which Faith had not expected. She had not expected that she would either, but aside from a brief time of semiconsciousness listening for the baby when she first got into bed, Faith slept too.

Now it was after breakfast and she was sitting on the lawn watching the two children communicate contentedly in a language all their own. She had spread a blanket and put an assortment of Ben's toys on top, but Ben seemed to think Zoë was the best toy of all. He had taken to crawling to keep her company after trying valiantly to pull her to a standing position before toppling over in a heap. Zoë was wearing another of Ben's shirts, which reached her ankles, and one of his hats. Although it was slightly overcast, Faith didn't want her to get too much sun. Ben was brown as a berry, and next to him Zoë reminded Faith of one of those Poor Pitiful Pearl Dolls before the transformation.

Was it just yesterday morning she had heard Zoë crying? Less than a day since finding the body? She suddenly felt exhausted and shivered as she contemplated the violence that must have preceded Bird's death. Who could have hated her that much? Faith had been turning this question over and over again in her mind. There was no question of burglary. Poor Bird had had nothing worth stealing. It was hate. Or insanity. Or both.

There had been three phone calls before Faith took the children outside. First, of course, was Pix. The "nannies" wanted to know if they could come over, and Faith was happy to agree. She asked Pix to stop and get some smaller diapers and another bottle, preferably postwar, to supplement the one from the pantry.

Sgt. Dickinson had called shortly after and asked Faith if she could keep the baby a little longer. They had not found much in the cabin, but the police down the coast had picked up Andy, and they hoped he might be able to tell them who Bird was. Dickinson had spoken rapidly, and Faith had had the impression that he was short of time—or someone who matched a face on the post office wall had just passed by his window.

Finally, Louise Frazier had called. Bill had not slept and was still sitting silently. John Eggleston had come by the night before and tried to talk with him, but Bill had waved him away. John was coming back today. Not whom she would have chosen as a comforter, Faith reflected; rather like having Captain Ahab offer solace, but they had known each other for a long time. Bill had roused himself only once, to ask about Zoë, and had appeared to be satisfied with the arrangements.

Faith looked at the horizon with what she thought was an increasingly nautical eye. They hadn't had any rain in a long time, and it appeared there might finally be a storm.

By the time the Millers and Arlene arrived, the rain was pelting down and Faith and the children had hastily moved into the living room.

"We certainly need this," Pix said as she removed

her dripping-wet foul-weather gear. "But I hope we don't lose our power. I left the pump on."

"What do you mean?" Faith wanted to know.

"When the power comes back on after being off, it surges and can destroy the pump."

"Just another one of the perils of living in the country."

"Have you ever tasted better water?"

Faith had to admit that if the Millers ever got around to bottling their spring, fifty million Frenchmen would toss their Perrier and Evian bottles out the *fenêtre*.

But Pix had more on her mind than water.

"Faith, how about a cup of coffee?" she asked, and seemed barely able to contain herself before they got into the kitchen. She closed the door quickly.

"I didn't want to gossip in front of the girls, but when I stopped to get some of Mrs. Kenney's doughnuts this morning, she told me there was a big drug bust last night! She heard it all on her CB. The Coast Guard seized a boat out beyond Osprey Island, and the hull was loaded with bales of marijuana.

"Mrs. Kenney said they were probably going to land it on Osprey, which is uninhabited, divide it into smaller amounts, and then bring it into Camden and Bucksport on several other boats."

"So that's why Sgt. Dickinson was in such a rush this morning. He barely said two sentences. But he did tell me they had located Andy. Maybe he was on the boat!"

Pix slumped into a chair. "What an amazing summer! Believe me, Faith, in all the years I've known this island, there hasn't ever been this kind of trouble."

"I certainly hope not," Faith said, as she filled the

pot with water and set it on the stove. "But I'm beginning to think there was probably a lot going on you didn't know about. And what about the old days—during Prohibition? Things must have been pretty lively then."

She sat down next to Pix to wait for the pot to boil and studiously avoided watching it. Her mind was racing. If Andy had been on that boat, where had he boarded it and did his presence mean that he was not a suspect in Bird's murder? And if he wasn't a suspect, who on earth was? Itinerant tramps suddenly gone amok were always possibilities in books, but unheard of on the island. Everybody knew everybody else, and if there had been a stranger around the last few days, they, or rather Pix, would have heard about it by now.

And there was something else. Bird had been attacked face on. The murderer had not crept up behind her. This suggested that they had been talking. It also suggested it was someone she knew.

The whistle blew shrilly, and Faith ground some beans for the Melitta. Nothing was getting any clearer. Except for one thing.

She and Pix had better hurry up and figure out Matilda's clues before word spread too rapidly that she had kept the quilt photos. She doubted that Arlene's branch of the Prescott family had had anything to do with the break-in, or with Roger's death for that matter; but she wasn't going to count on word not leaking out. Anything to do with Matilda's quilt, which might just happen to be a treasure map, was bound to reach the wrong ears at some point. The drug raid might squeeze it off the grapevine today and give them time to name the rest of the squares and find whatever they were seeking. She said as much to Pix, and they spread their things out on the kitchen table.

"Only four more." Faith put the photos in a row. "What do they look like to you? Number eight could be a spider's web, or a ripple in a pool with concentric circles."

"And number twelve looks like mountain peaks. Let's try those themes."

It worked for number twelve. Pix located it in one of the quilt books soon after.

"Hill and Valley. That should be easy—North Star is just before and it's not marked in any way, so presumably it means go north, and Apple Tree is before that, so we look for a tree or orchard."

"Pix, I think we should go out for a drive when the rain lets up and see what we can figure out with what we have. The children will be fine here, and we could spend weeks at this. We don't even know that they are all in these books." Faith was also starting to get a little bored with the current approach.

"True. I agree. We can follow the clues to square eight and then see what choice we have. The Schoolhouse square should give us a clue, but again there were quite a few of them when the island population was greater. At the turn of the century there were fifteen hundred residents in Granville alone."

"Let's give the kids an early lunch, then take off. I want to do some cooking this afternoon. I feel like eating something good tonight, and it also calms the spirit."

"I know," Pix responded. "Comfort foods—like shepherd's pie and macaroni and cheese."

"No, like seafood mousse or maybe lobster en gelée."

"Whatever."

It was shortly after noon when Faith turned the Woody around in the driveway at Harborview and said, "Go," to Pix who sat next to her with the list and the photos discreetly out of sight in her lap.

"Drive back through the village and turn right up the hill. At the top, you're as close to the mill wheel as you can get on the road."

They drove on, turning east when the road divided, and paused at the Odd Fellows Hall.

"That casserole supper seems like a long time ago," Pix remarked. "Although it's been less than two weeks."

"I was just thinking the same thing."

And thinking of the way Roger and Bill had looked at Bird when she had come in with Andy.

Faith tried to remember more about what Andy looked like, but she had been so distracted by his outfit that she didn't really remember much about his face, although she had had a general impression that he regarded the world at large in a smug, lordly way. Almost as if he knew what the other men yearned for and only he had. Now no one had her.

"What's next?"

"Go straight and turn left at the crossroads."

They encountered few other cars. Most people were eating lunch. Traffic on Sanpere was never very heavy, except on the Fourth of July when everyone left the parade at the same time for the chicken barbecue. And then they had two auxiliary policemen, each authorized to wear a special armband and carry a piece.

A blue Ford pickup roared past them going the other way, and the driver raised a few fingers from the wheel in the traditional island wave. Faith was flattered. She might almost live here. But what was she thinking of? Tom, that's whom she was thinking of. He had noticed the wave the first day and thereafter raised his fingers, getting a response each time. He liked to be at home wherever he was. She took a deep breath. Labor Day was still a long way off.

"Come on, Pix, right or left?"

The road forked, and each branch beckoned with a claim of its own.

"I can't tell you. It's number eight. The square we don't know."

"All right, we'll wing it and go down each. Maybe something will suggest itself." She turned left, and they drove past a series of wood lots, a few trailers, and one or two farmhouses before the road again split.

"I think we should try the right-hand one first. Remember, Winding Ways with the upper right section indicated comes next, followed by Apple Tree. If we see any sign of apples, we'll know we're on the right track."

They weren't, and Faith suggested they go back to the original fork and try that one. Pix agreed. "And I thought I was figuring it out so cleverly."

"You are. Keep it up."

The right turn dipped down toward the shore. The rain had not completely stopped, and as Faith looked at it breaking the surface of the water, she was sure this was the correct choice.

"Look at the water. The waves look just like the square. I'm sure of it—look at the way the wind ripples the surface of the waves." She put her foot down on the pedal, and they shot forward. The road twisted and turned.

"Winding Ways," Pix muttered.

"Ayup." They came to a fork that showed the remnants of logging tracks, and they stayed on the road, turning right. When they saw the old apple orchard, Pix grabbed Faith's arm. "It really is like a map!"

"Of course it is, and what's more I'm sure the gold, or what's left of it, is at the end. She must have put it there before she became bedridden, intending to tell someone, but then decided this would be more fun."

"Or maybe the gold has been there since her father's time." Faith stopped the car again to have another look at the photos.

"Maybe we should get rid of the ones we've identified and just keep a list of the names."

"I think we should hold on to them. There's always the possibility we've identified something incorrectly, or by one of its other names."

They sat in silence for a moment, which Pix broke somewhat hesitantly. "It's been a bit like a game up to now. If, a very big if, we do find something valuable, what are you going to do with it?"

Faith realized she had been thinking primarily of the journey and not the arrival. Although from the moment she had seen the spidery handwritten "Seek and Ye Shall Find" at the Fraziers', she'd been convinced it was some sort of treasure.

"*Us*, not me. Let's get that understood. I never could have identified all these squares without you or known where they led. But I'm sure it's the gold, Pix, and I know you don't just mean we'd never have to worry about our children's college tuitions or wardrobes again. You must have had as much Sunday School as I did." Faith pictured the pin with all the bars for perfect attendance, which grew steadily longer on the lapel of her navy-blue coat from B. Altman's as the hem of said garment kept pace. She was sure there was a similar bijou in Pix's past. Along with all those "Do what you think is best, dear" remarks from parents who would have been astonished if you had. It was a burden that Faith had been endeavoring to unload for some time. Now might be as good a time as any, but she still said to Pix, "You mean what is the *right* thing to do."

"I suppose I do. Of course, we may never find it."

Neither of them believed that for a moment any longer, and the look they exchanged said as much.

Faith continued wrestling. "Probably the morally correct thing to do would be to split it with the Prescotts. Take a finder's fee. Or give the whole thing to some worthwhile cause."

"Legally, of course, I think it would be ours. Abandoned property or something like that."

They laughed. "I wonder what our husbands would advise," Faith mused. "Representing God and Mammon."

"I wouldn't say that exactly." Pix was a little peeved. "Sam does plenty of pro bono work."

"You know what I mean. I only thought it would be funny if Tom said finders keepers and Sam said give it away."

"This is all castles in the air until we locate what is in that last square."

"Very nice castles, but you're right. Let's get going."

She pulled out onto the road, and they followed it for almost a mile before another choice presented itself. The next square was North Star and Pix told her which way was north. Faith said a silent prayer of thanks to the Girl Scouts or whomever for the thorough training Pix had had in her youth. The road suddenly plummeted, and they careened up and down two hills. The burned-rubber tire tracks in evidence indicated it was a favorite spot for those island youth possessing cars, and Faith could see why. She looked forward to driving it again herself, slightly faster this time. "Hill and Valley it is," she noted jubilantly.

When the road took them past an old schoolhouse that a summer person had painstakingly restored, they felt the treasure was almost in their grasp. But not quite.

Faith stopped the car again.

"Let me see the next square. Jacob's Ladder? How does that fit in? Are any of the rungs a different pattern? Or does it seem to be pointing a certain way?"

"No, it's all the same. Very regular and there are three possible roads here and all these woods."

"Fern Berry doesn't give us much help either," Faith observed dismally as she looked at the lush ferns, bright red bunchberries, and other bracken that grew along each roadside.

"And we don't know the one after, and the one after that is Shady Pine."

They looked up glumly at the awning of evergreens surrounding them.

Pix sneezed.

"It looks like it's back to the books and back to the antihistamines for me." She was allergic to ragweed, and this was the worst time of year for her.

"I thought the rain was supposed to drive the pollen out of the air," Faith commiserated.

"So did I." Pix sneezed three times in rapid succession.

Faith started the engine. "There are only two more squares to identify now. Even if we didn't name that spiderwebby one, I'm sure it had to do with that ocean view. And if worse comes to worst, we'll go down each of these and look for noticeably shady pines or ferny berries."

Pix laughed and sneezed at the same time.

"We're in the right spot, though. No question."

"What makes you so positive?"

"This spit of land is called Prescott Point, that's why."

Faith was impressed.

As they passed the turnoff for Prescott's lobster pound, Faith said, "Do you mind if I stop to pick up some fish?"

"Not at all. I'll see if Sonny has any scallops today. Scallop stew is Samantha's favorite."

Faith parked the car next to the bait shack and tried to keep upwind of the smell. Sonny was at the end of the dock where two boats were unloading their catch. Faith regarded the still-quivering, glistening bodies in the hold with anticipation. The only way she'd ever get fresher fish would be to catch it herself—an unlikely prospect. She selected what she wanted and followed Sonny into the office, where he weighed it out. He was a small man, but trim and muscular. His blond hair was crew cut, since he had never bothered to change his hairstyle after his military service. Faith had heard he was the star pitcher and coach for the Fish Hawks. She wondered if he'd given the team its name. As he wrapped the fish, she noticed his nails were bitten to the quick and his hands were red and chafed from his work. He handed her the bag.

"It will be delicious," she commented.

"Waal, can't say I ever cared much for the creatures. I like a good steak myself," he said.

"That's got to be a bit harder to find than fish on this island." She smiled.

"Ayup, but we always want what we can't get, Mrs. Fairchild." The intensity of his glance full in her face seemed to pin her against the wall next to some coiled rope, netting, and a long fly trap black with prey.

"I suppose so," she said without looking away. She paid and joined Pix on the dock, wondering as she did whether what had just occurred was an oblique reference to Matilda's house, the quilt, or a come-on. Maybe all three. She'd never heard him say "Ayup" before either. A reminder of turf?

He stood in the doorway and watched them go to the car.

"I'm sorry he didn't have any scallops. Maybe Monday," Pix said.

"What do you know about him? He seemed almost sinister today. The last time I was here, he was full of jokes and talked my ear off. Do you think he's heard about the quilt?"

"No, or he would have said something. Sonny and Margery Prescott are as honest as they come. We've known them for years. He's probably worried about the catch today, or maybe he's not feeling well. You know there *can* be logical explanations for things, Faith. You're beginning to imagine bandits behind every bush."

"I suppose you're right. I do feel surrounded by a kind of cocoon of suspicions. I keep looking at people and wondering where they were when Bird was killed, or the house broken into, or even if they have the kind of drill that made the holes in Roger's boat.

"Well, Sonny certainly has a drill like that, I'm sure. And I'm equally sure he didn't do it." Pix's mouth was set in a firm straight line. It reminded Faith of the lines they used to have to draw under the predicate with their rulers when she was in grade school. The line suddenly curved toward the rest of the sentence.

"I thought this was going to be the perfect vacation for you and you'd fall in love with the island. How wrong could a person be?"

"Not very wrong at all! I do love the island, and while it certainly hasn't been the perfect vacation, it hasn't been dull. And anyway, nothing more is going to happen, except when we find the treasure." Faith was surprised to hear her declaration of allegiance to Sanpere and even more surprised to realize it was true.

Both children had gone down for naps when they returned. Pix decided to go home, take an allergy pill, and lie down too. The "nannies" reluctantly relinquished their role and went with her. Pix had promised to take them to the dance at the Legion Hall that night, and they had to decide what to wear. This could take all afternoon.

As Pix was leaving, Faith said, "If you don't feel up to it, I can take the girls to the dance for a while and you can lie down here."

"Oh, I'm sure I'll be all right. These pills are magic, though I do hate taking them. They make me so dopey."

Pix was loath to take even an aspirin and was driven to any form of medication only if in dire pain. Faith had found this to be characteristic of New Englanders. They seemed to revel in the antique remedies enjoyed by their foremothers and -fathers, righteously avoiding the relief provided by modern medicine. "Let Nature take its course," one parishioner was fond of saying whenever she heard of an illness in the congregation. Faith reflected if we had let Nature take its course unhindered all these years, most of us would be dead.

"Call me if you need me," she shouted after Pix. "Otherwise, I'll talk to you tomorrow."

After they left, she felt a certain relief. The children were asleep and it was nice to be alone. It would have been nicer if Tom was there—he had called early in the morning to make sure she was still alive and kicking, or so she had accused him. She was extremely happy to hear his voice, though, and they agreed he would call at the same time for the next few days.

Now, after the intensity of the last twenty-four hours, she was content to go into the kitchen and poach some fish for the mousse. She decided to bake some bread too. The real comfort food. The real comfort smell.

She couldn't keep her thoughts away from the scene in Bird and Andy's shack. She plunged her hands into the dough, trying to knead away the memory of all that redness, all that blood. As she built up the rhythm and felt the dough smooth into an elastic texture under her hands, she wondered how Bill Fox was. The Fraziers hadn't called. His silent grief had a self-destructive quality, or perhaps it was self-preservation—if he gave way to what he was feeling, it would be impossible to be whole again. Either way it was terrible. She tried to think about Bird. Who was she? Was it simply her startling beauty that had enthralled Bill and Roger, or had it been more than that? Faith had categorized her immediately as the flower child of parents poised in the sixties forever, picturing Bird's mother in black tights, ballerina flats, sack dress, and Student Peace Union button, teaching little Bird to weave, silk screen, or whatever. Or maybe Bird was as romantic in her way as Bill, yearning for what she imagined the sixties to have been like and re-creating them in her person. Whatever she had been, she had a kind of consistency Faith admired—from afar. Bird had decided to live a certain way and had not merely adopted a few surface trappings—the beads, the hair, and inevitable water-buffalo sandals.

Faith put the bread to rise again and went upstairs. Zoë was lying in the cradle awake and talking softly to herself. Faith leaned down to pick her up and thought how much simpler it would be to adopt Zoë than go through the whole tedious business of pregnancy again. Maybe it wasn't such a crazy idea. It could be that Bird didn't have any family, or perhaps if she did, they wouldn't want the child or be able to take her. And Andy had told the police he wanted nothing to do with Zoë, that she was all Bird's idea.

Ben was up too, and they all went outside again. He taught Zoë by example how to roll down the little hill behind the cottage and soon they were shrieking with delight.

It was late in the afternoon and Faith was gathering her small charges for mousse when the phone rang. She grabbed them to hurry inside before it stopped—something that happened with irritating frequency.

It was Pix, or some approximation of Pix. Her nose was so stuffed up, she sounded like a caricature of herself.

"Faith, cud you ruddy tage de gurls to de danse?"

Faith hastened to interrupt her. It was a horrible sound.

"Don't say another word. Please. Of course I can take them. Why don't you plan to spend the night here, both of you? Then you can get settled in bed when the kids go to sleep. You know there's plenty of room."

In between major trumpeting into possibly an entire box of tissues, they established that Pix would come over after dinner and spend the night. Samantha was going home with Arlene, and Faith could drop them there no later than eleven o'clock, which Pix and Arlene's mother had established as a reasonable curfew.

Faith hung up the phone and turned her thoughts to what to wear. It wasn't going to be Capote's Black and White Ball, but she didn't think she should turn up in jeans. Pix had told her that there would probably be a few square dances sandwiched between the band's renditions of Pink Floyd and Lawrence Welk favorites. The Saturday-night dances attracted a wide age range. Faith lacked the requisite circle skirt and petticoats for do-si-do-ing, but she thought she would dress for the spirit of that part of the soiree and decided on a pale-blue Eileen West sundress with a wide skirt. At the last moment she tied a black ribbon around her neck and promptly took it off in the car. It had been a close call.

The girls sat together in the backseat, which made her feel only slightly ancient, and they spent the whole trip talking about what they should have worn and each reassuring the other that what she had on was perfect. Faith wondered how many permutations a wardrobe that seemed to consist chiefly of oversized khaki pants, form-fitting Guess? jeans, and extra-large T-shirts could allow, but evidently enough to cause concern. Arlene had a black barrette with rhinestones in the shape of a star on it that was destined to appear and disappear from her hair all night as clouds of doubt rolled by.

Faith pulled into the parking lot in front of the Legion Hall, a large, barnlike structure that had been used for everything from dances and band concerts to basketball games and graduations in various incarnations. She parked next to a Corvair. You could spot cars of virtually every era on the island, and although pickups were the vehicle of preference, she had seen everything from a Model T to a Mercedes traveling along Route 17.

They walked in, bought their tickets, and were enjoined to guard their stubs for the raffle. Arlene and Samantha were trying to enter as nonchalantly as possible, walking behind Faith and using the abundant fabric of her skirt as a shield.

"There's Becky!" Arlene cried, and they scurried over to a group of girls who were leaning against the wall, pretending to look bored.

Faith looked after them. She wouldn't return to adolescence for a second. Well, maybe a second out of curiosity, no longer. It wasn't as if your own trials and tribulations were enough; everybody else was your age and having them too. And the boys' palms were always sweaty. She sighed. Even a boy with sweaty palms might have been welcome. What was she going to do for three and a half hours?

She sat down on one of the folding chairs set against the wall and spread her skirt out in an attractive manner. She loved to dance, and she hoped someone would have the courage to ask her. She smiled encouragingly, then decided she looked like a lunatic sitting there grinning and fell to studying her surroundings instead.

It was not dark inside, but it was quite dim. In the center of the room a huge ball covered with tiny mirrors slowly turned and sprinkled the dancers with irregular patches of light. Up on the stage the band had blue spots trained unsteadily on them, and the air was thick with cigarette smoke. It didn't look much like the island. More like *The Blue Angel*. Marlene Dietrich's role had been usurped here by a young woman, with short platinum-blond hair, dressed in leather. She was wailing some lyrics into the microphone, but there was too much noise for Faith to decipher them. The band had energy and was good and loud. She squinted through the smoke and saw from the name on the drum that they were The Melodic Mariners. Two of them looked to be in their forties, the rest somewhere between fourteen and twenty-one. They were all having a hell of a time, to judge from their expressions.

The music stopped, and with barely time for "A one and a two and a three" they launched into the slow cadences of "The Blue Danube." Nobody seemed to find the change disconcerting. A few stood up to dance, a few left the floor, but mostly they stayed, stopped boogying, and waltzed.

Faith turned her attention to the crowd to see if she recognized anyone. Pix had been right. It was all ages. Small children were dancing on their fathers' and grandfathers' shoes. Middleaged women were dancing sedately together in perfect step. The teenagers were using the music as an excuse to make out on the dance floor, rocking slowly from side to side when they remembered they were supposed to be dancing.

Faith spotted Sonny and Margery Prescott on the floor. They weren't Ginger and Fred, but they weren't half bad. They danced in that practiced, semiprofessional way people who like to dance and have been married for a long time do. She also saw Nan and Freeman Hamilton sitting next to an enormous fat woman dressed in trousers with a skinny man perched comfortably on her knee. She'd *have* to ask Pix who that was. Paul Edson and his wife, Edith, were on the other side of the Hamiltons. They were staring at the crowd. Paul probably liked to keep close tabs on everyone's physical and financial well-being. He seemed to be studying one couple in particular. Looking to see if she was still wearing all her jewelry or if hard times were setting in? Maybe they'd like to get rid of their small camp down by the shore that they never used? Faith imagined this was what was going through his mind and wondered why Nan and Freeman hadn't moved away from them. Then she remembered Edith had been a Hamilton and on the island, kinship mattered more than real estate transfers. Nan and Freeman didn't seem to be paying them much mind, though. Paul was the only man Faith had seen wearing a suit. There were a few ties of various natures, some dress pants, even a few neatly pressed jeans, but no suits. He must know the mores. Maybe he liked to set himself apart, in which case Faith thought he could have picked something more distinguished than the navy polyester model he was sporting. Edith was wearing a lilac pants suit, no doubt of similar venue, and they looked like bookends.

There seemed to be a lot of activity around the rear door to the outside. Faith noticed the people leaving for a breath of fresh air were returning with very rosy cheeks. The dances were dry, not even BYOB, so those desirous of refreshment drank it out in the parking lot or made do with the punch ladled out of a large pot sitting on the pass-through into a small kitchen. She hoped Arlene and Samantha didn't disappear out the back door. She was there to chaperone, but it was not a role she relished. They were still glued to the wall with a steadily increasing group of girls. An equal and opposite number of boys was gathered by the entrance.

The time passed more quickly as she became engrossed in people watching. Those returning from the outside began to be a bit unsteady. The room got warm, and people who had arrived in freshly pressed shirts and dresses began to sweat and wilt. The smoke grew even denser, and the Mariners announced they would be taking a break. The floor cleared, but many of the dancers stayed and arranged themselves in two long lines facing each other.

Freeman mounted the stage and took the mike in his hand.

"Get ready for 'The Lady of the Lake,'" he called out. "And if you don't know it, don't worry. The person next to you does."

Faith joined the ladies' line and saw Arlene and Samantha follow suit. Two boys quickly placed themselves opposite them. Faith looked across. She was opposite Joe Prescott. The one who had tried to attack Eric and Roger at the auction. He smiled encouragingly at her. Well, she reflected, if she thought someone was trying to get away with what she believed to be hers, she might try to throw a punch too. Besides, bygones were bygones. In some cases anyway.

The music started. It would have been impossible to sit still, and she was glad she had decided to dance. An old man with a string tie was playing the fiddle. Another man was plucking a flat-backed mandolin, and a woman named Dorothy was on guitar. Faith knew her name because every once in a while someone would shout, "Hit it, Dorothy." She was obviously a local favorite. Freeman was a good caller, and Faith had no trouble following. Over the years the dance must have been performed countless times under this roof. Skirts swirled, feet stamped, and hands clapped. Two more dances followed, then they played "Soldier's Joy" for Nan Hamilton and "Red Wing" for Freeman, who demanded equal time. The Mariners returned and Faith collapsed breathlessly on the nearest chair. Sonny and Margery were next to her. Sonny grinned at her. "Don't get much of this up to Boston, do you?"

"No. In fact, I've never been to a dance like this before."

"A few years back they wanted to cut out the old dances. Said the kids didn't want to do them and would stop coming, so we tried for a while. They were the first ones to complain," Margery said.

"I think it's important," Faith told her. "Otherwise they would never know how to do them and a whole part of the island's history would be lost. I hope there will be some more, and the musicians were wonderful."

Sonny looked at her appreciatively. "They just do it for fun. We have an awful lot of good times in the winter. Those three will come by and we'll have a musical evening. There was an English lady here last summer, and she heard them play down to the inn. She said a lot of the songs were old English and Scottish ones. And here we thought we'd invented them on the island. Anyway they've been here a long time."

Sonny was being his friendly and loquacious self, and Faith didn't think it all could be chalked up to the nips he was having out by his Chevy. By dancing she had taken a step away from being an off-island onlooker to becoming at least an appreciative outsider. She thought of the quilt. Little did they know how much and how well she was getting to know the island.

Sonny and Margery excused themselves to dance, and Faith was lost in thought when she heard a familiar voice.

"You were stepping pretty lively from what I could see, Mrs. Fairchild, and I hope you'll give a poor old man a dance." It was Freeman.

"Show me the poor old man first," answered Faith.

"Now that's what I call kind." He pulled her to her feet and energetically steered her onto the dance floor. It was "The Beer Barrel Polka" and fortunately it was half over. After they had spun around for a while, there was another of those abrupt changes of direction and the Mariners segued into "The Tennessee Waltz."

"My favorite," said Freeman. "Are you game for another?"

"Absolutely."

The waltz afforded more opportunity for conversation, and after they had maneuvered over to wave at Nan, Faith commented that the Edsons didn't seem to be dancers.

"I guess that's true," observed Freeman. "Come to think of it, I never have seen Paul dance. Edith used to be pretty spry when we were younger."

"Maybe he likes to sit and take the lay of the land."

Freeman slowed down a bit and appeared to be thinking of something. When he responded, his voice had lost some of its teasing quality.

"You seem to have gotten pretty interested in this island in the short time you've been here. I don't deny that a lot has happened to you that sort of dragged you in. But sometimes it isn't always good to know too much about a place too fast."

Faith was startled. Was this some kind of warning? Did Freeman know about the clues in the quilt? Or was it the normal reaction of someone who liked her to the fact that she had come upon two corpses and had her house broken into in less than a week?

She spoke slowly. "I'm not sure I understand what you mean, but I certainly don't mean to push myself in where I'm not wanted."

"Now, now it's not that. Not that at all. Just take it slow, Faith." He smiled broadly at her. "Since you're so interested in things, I'll tell you what we say about Paul Edson around here. He's what we call a 'self-made man,' and that lets the Almighty off the hook. Now I'd better dance with my wife or the whole island will have me in divorce court on Monday." He gave her hand a squeeze as they walked over to Nan. Faith felt as if she had been stood in the corner and given a star all at the same time. She greeted Nan. "Thanks for the loan of your husband. He's a treat to dance with."

"He's a treat, all right," Nan said as she glanced lovingly at Freeman. "You can borrow him anytime. He's awful good at weeding the garden and chopping wood too."

"Now Nan," protested Freeman. "One female slave driver is enough!"

The three of them laughed and Faith went back to her chair. She had told the girls that was where she would be if they needed her for anything, and she didn't want to desert her post for too long.

Nobody asked her to dance, and the next half hour dragged a little despite the excitement of the raffle drawing. Seven-year-old Missy Sanford drew her own grandmother's name and everybody cheered as Missy solemnly presented her with a large canned ham and got a big kiss in return.

Faith's chair was near the door, so she saw Eric before he spotted her. He was wearing spotless white Levi's and a navy polo shirt open at the throat. He looked cool, crisp, and very handsome. She automatically looked for Jill, but he appeared to be alone. Maybe he was meeting her at the dance. He certainly seemed to be looking for someone, standing in the door and letting his eyes travel across the crowd. At last they landed on her, and he smiled and made his way over.

"Faith! What on earth are you doing here all by your lonesome?"

"Gooseberrying. You know, the honorable role of 'chaperone.' Pix is having one of her allergy attacks, so I'm here to keep Samantha and Arlene on the straight and narrow. A pretty easy job."

"Poor Pix. This smoke would have been murder for her. I always stink after one of these things."

He was speaking clearly, but Faith had the definite impression Eric had been drinking. It was the way he shaped his words—precisely and with extra care. He asked her to dance and stumbled slightly as he gallantly reached for her hand to pull her to her feet.

"Love the band, don't you? Good beat and easy to dance to. I give it a seven and a half." He laughed.

Maybe Jill didn't like to dance, Faith thought. Or maybe Eric liked to have a few beers and go solo. As was often the case with Faith, to speculate was to query.

"Where's Jill tonight?"

"We're not married, you know," Eric answered peevishly, then modified his tone. "Not yet, anyway, but I hope it will be soon. This is strictly *entre nous*, Faith, not even Pix. She'd be arranging showers and trousseaux or what have you if she knew."

"I'm so pleased, Eric. For both of you. It's been

such a difficult time for you, and you deserve some happiness."

He pulled her closer and said, "Thank you, Faith. Thank you for understanding."

The band was playing and Eric hummed along. He pulled Faith a bit nearer, and while one part of her was definitely enjoying the feel of his lean, muscular body, another was slightly uncomfortable at the increasing proximity and the fact that he was slowing down to a standstill. She could count on the band, though, and as they zoomed into "Twist and Shout," Eric broke away abruptly and began an extremely athletic version of the old classic. After a few minutes Faith said, "I've got to sit down, Eric, and it's getting close to eleven. The girls will be looking for me. That is, they'd better be looking for me."

"Go do your duty, my beautiful duenna," he replied, and walked over to the wall and grabbed the first woman he saw. She looked pleased and began to match him step for step.

Definitely feeling no pain, Faith reflected in amusement. It was good to see him letting loose and having some fun.

Samantha and Arlene were dancing at last. With the two boys from the "Lady of the Lake" square dance. Ten more minutes. Faith was sure they would be good about going, and she was ready to leave herself. The band decided to continue the frenzied momentum they had created and started in on "Louie Louie." Eric was still dancing with the same partner. Sonny and Margery gyrated alongside. Both couples were not far from where Faith was sitting.

Suddenly Eric seemed to register the fact that

Sonny was there. He turned and said something to him that Faith couldn't hear. Sonny said something back, and the two women seemed to be trying to keep the men dancing. Margery put her hand on Sonny's arm, and he angrily shook it away. The couples around them gave them a wide berth.

Sonny was shouting at Eric now, and Faith could hear Eric calling him a "son of a bitch." "Motherfucker" was next, and Sonny tried to land a punch, but a number of men had closed in and were swiftly escorting them into the parking lot.

Samantha and Arlene came running over to Faith. "Do you think Eric's all right?" Samantha asked.

"I think the men who took them out will take care of things, but maybe we should go and see if he needs a ride home"—and see what's happening, Faith said to herself, although the part about the ride was true. Eric should definitely not be driving in his condition.

The philosophy on the island seemed to be to let the men fight it out, just get them away from the women and children, and to a place where they couldn't do damage. When Faith and the girls walked into the parking lot, Sonny and Eric were rolling on the ground. Margery was standing to one side. Faith went up to her.

"This is ridiculous. They could seriously hurt each other. Can't we do something about it?"

"I think 'hurt each other' is what they have in mind, Mrs. Fairchild, and if I could stop Sonny, I would. Besides, if they didn't do it here, they'd do it somewhere else."

But some of the men seemed to think enough was enough. Freeman was among them.

"That's it," Faith heard him say, and he waded in between them. They were still screaming at each other. Eric's white pants were covered with dirt and streaked with blood from a cut on his cheek. Sonny's nose was bleeding and looked a little crooked. "Fuckin' faggot!" he yelled as he tried to get away from the two men who held him. Margery walked over and stood slightly behind him.

Faith didn't know what to do. Eric was in no condition to drive, but she was unsure how to approach the situation. Freeman must have had the same thought and was offering Eric a lift. "I can drive myself, thank you," he replied with exaggerated politeness and crawled into the front seat of his car. Freeman pushed him to the passenger side and they took off. Nan climbed into their car and followed.

Faith took a deep breath. "I'm sorry you girls had to see this."

"Don't worry, Mrs. Fairchild," Arlene assured her. "We have fights like this at every dance. They drink too much, then they get rowdy."

Eric wasn't going to feel very rowdy in the morning, although he probably would feel a lot of other things, Faith thought. They walked toward the Woody, passing Sonny and Margery with a cluster of friends and relatives around them. Sonny was slumped against the side of his car, but he didn't seem to be injured. Margery had pushed up the sleeves of her shirt and was busy holding a handkerchief to his nose. As they passed, Faith paused to say something, couldn't think of an appropriate remark, and kept going with a brief nod and slight smile to Margery that vanished immediately when she got a closer look at Margery's left wrist.

She was wearing Faith's bracelet.

The silver cuff bracelet Tom had given her.

The one missing after the break-in.

Faith gasped and increased her speed, almost

pushing the girls into the car. Although it was possible that Margery had bought one like it from the same silversmith on the island, it was not possible that she had deliberately made a scratch on it. No, Ben had done that with a fork when Faith had left the bracelet on the kitchen table one day.

Faith's mind was in a whirl. Margery and Sonny the burglars? It seemed reasonable if they had known about the quilt, but how did they know about the quilt? The image of Margery standing in the Fraziers' doorway flashed into Faith's mind. Of course, she had overheard them discussing "Seek and Ye Shall Find." But to wear the bracelet to the dance, what gall! Of course she would not have expected to see Faith there. And she had been wearing long sleeves. Faith tried to remember. Was it overactive hindsight, or had Margery tugged on her left sleeve when Faith had sat next to them?

She was driving fast, but Arlene and Samantha, already beginning the dissection of the evening that would be the main topic of conversation for the next few days, didn't notice. She had to finish identifying the quilt squares. The Prescotts might not know she had made photographs, but Arlene could let something slip, and it was only a matter of time before they would. Then there would be another break-in—or worse.

Driving back along the causeway after dropping the girls at Arlene's, Faith didn't see a single light. There were only two streetlights in the village, and then you were plunged into darkness. She slowed down. There were no other cars on the road and she didn't know whether to feel relieved or anxious. The last thing she wanted now was a pair of headlights following her down the long dirt road that led to the isolated cottage. But Pix would be there waiting, and she relaxed when she remembered.

Pix and the dogs.

Faith let herself in quietly. The dogs barked dutifully and briefly once they recognized her. Only the porch and kitchen lights were on, which meant Pix must have gone to sleep. She debated waking her, but decided to wait until the morning. She wanted some time to think what it all meant. Eric's behavior at the dance, then the fight, and the bracelet. She looked in on the two children soundly asleep in Ben's room and took a peek at Pix, who was also soundly, but more noisily, asleep.

She got into bed and revolved the various scenes of the evening around her brain. In less time than it takes to go Loupty Lou, she was asleep too.

Asleep, that is, until she heard the dogs begin to bark.

Eight

Dusty had been joined by Henry and Arthur. Pix never liked to leave the dogs home alone. Surely she must be awake with all the barking! Faith quietly crept out of bed and moved quickly to the door, pausing to pick up the brick doorstop that had been disguised with needlepoint. Then she ran down the hall into Ben's room. She had no time to waste.

The children were sleeping peacefully. She closed the door and positioned herself behind it with the brick raised in her hand. She'd have the element of surprise on her side. Whoever it was downstairs would have everything else. She couldn't hear any footsteps, and the dogs had calmed to occasional whimpers of delight, as Pix had predicted. Maybe the intruder had brought snacks.

The house was quiet again and she waited. She had time to be afraid now, and she was terrified. Finally the boards on the stairs creaked. The intruder was coming up.

She heard the hinges groan as the door to her room was pushed slowly open. Then nothing.

The steps began again and moved down the hall past the room Pix was in. They were making straight for the nursery.

The doorknob turned slowly. She watched it,

hypnotized with fear. The door began to move. Faith got ready.

"Faith," came a soft voice, "Faith, are you in here?"

She yanked the door open. It was Tom.

"What the hell do you mean giving me a scare like that!" she whispered angrily at him, then threw herself into his arms.

"I tried calling, but there was no answer. I'm sorry, honey, but I was getting too edgy down there. They didn't need me tonight or tomorrow, and I wanted to see my family. Intact, as it were."

"You were the one destined for injury," Faith said as she dropped the brick that had become cemented into her palm.

"Why don't we go to bed and you can tell me everything in the morning?" Tom suggested as he lifted Faith up in his arms and walked toward their bedroom. "Just one question. What are all those dogs doing here?"

"I'm beginning to realize there are few easy explanations on this island, but this one is fairly straightforward. Pix had one of her allergy attacks, so she stayed here and I took Samantha and Arlene to the dance tonight. Of course, the dogs couldn't stay all by themselves at the cottage."

Tom lowered Faith onto the bed and started peeling off his clothes preparatory to following her. He started to climb in and stopped. "I didn't even look at Ben. Just a minute, darling, I'll be right back."

And he was. In seconds.

"Faith Sibley Fairchild. There are two children in Ben's room! Would you mind telling me where you got that other baby?"

Faith gasped. Surely she had mentioned to Tom that she was taking care of Zoë, hadn't she?

185

"Oh Tom, I'm sure I must have told you I was taking care of Zoë until the police can find out who Bird was and if she has any family."

"No, you omitted to mention that fact." Tom started to laugh. "Of course it's fine to take care of her, but you have to imagine what it is like to bend over Ben's crib and realize there is a fairly new baby in a cradle by the side. Nice cradle, too."

"I'm glad you like it. It's ours. I got it at the auction."

Tom beamed. He wanted a big family. "That's great, sweetheart. Now, why don't we do something about filling it? Presuming, of course, that Zoë is not a permanent resident."

"Well, it would make life simple, and what if they can't find any relatives? I do feel responsible."

"Because you had the misfortune to find the body? Why don't we wait and see what happens." Tom reached over and turned out the light. "We've had enough surprises for one night."

"Don't be so sure," Faith said as she began to kiss his ear. She was very fond of his lobes.

Sunday morning dawned fair and fine. Pix left after consuming a stack of blueberry pancakes. She hadn't heard a thing the night before and vowed never to take an antihistamine again, no matter how miserable.

"What if it hadn't been Tom? I would have been useless!" she wailed.

"I don't think this particular situation will arise in the near future, and I'm sure you can sleep safely with or without your hay-fever medicine," Tom said.

"No, if I can't even hear the dogs or the phone, it's too strong. I'll have to get something else from Dr.

Kane when I get home." Pix was adamant. "I have to get Samantha now. See you in church."

They waved good-bye from the porch and settled down on the lawn with more coffee and the two children.

"Okay, Faith, tell all. I want to hear everything you've been sticking that pretty little nose of yours into." Tom sounded firm.

Faith felt it was a bit unfair to accuse her of idle curiosity when both bodies had virtually found her. But she started from the beginning and told him everything. Or almost everything. She glossed over the quilt, sticking it in the midst of Bird's murder and making only a vague allusion to the map and treasure. It was, after all, supposition. To assuage her guilt, she mentioned the break-in. Tom got up and paced around the yard.

"I really wish you and Ben—and Zoë if you feel you must—would come back with me. It's only a few days, and I'd feel much better knowing you were safe. We can still be here for Labor Day."

"I am safe, Tom. Sgt. Dickinson was sure it was kids looking for liquor and it's not likely to be repeated. Remember, they picked a time when I wasn't here. And what would I do down there? You'll be busy and I'd rather not attend the workshops."

"There's a beautiful lake and you could sit on the beach with the kids," Tom pointed out.

"All day? No thank you. And what about the food? You said yourself it was abysmal," Faith protested.

"Food isn't everything, Faith."

"Bite your tongue!"

They glared at each other a moment; then Faith took Tom's hand and stroked the back of it gently.

She loved the fine reddish hairs that grew there. "I know you're worried and I love you for it, but I'm a grown-up too. If I thought it was dangerous, I'd leave."

"Promise?"

"Promise."

They went inside, got ready for church, and were in good time for the service. The bell, hung high in the pointed steeple of the small white clapboard church facing the harbor, was just starting to peal as they drove over the hill into Sanpere Village. Ben and Zoë were deposited in the child care overseen by volunteers, among them Samantha and Arlene, who reached for the children delightedly. Faith raised an eyebrow at Tom. "And what about babysitters in New Hampshire?"

"All right, all right, I've already given in. Put your life in danger just so you don't have to search for a baby-sitter."

"Women do it all the time, Tom."

Faith sat contentedly in a pew. The sun streamed in the long, plain-glass windows. The only ornament was a large bouquet of flowers on the simple altar in front of the cross. Prize gladiolas from someone's garden were mixed with ferns from the woods, Queen Anne's lace, and other wildflowers. The glads, never Faith's favorite, looked definitely out-classed.

The sermon was as unadorned as the church, and Faith enjoyed the service. A few well-chosen words, a rousing hymn or two, a quiet moment for prayer, then they were out in the bright sunshine greeting friends and neighbors. In Faith and Tom's case, this meant saying hello to Pix again and nodding to Nan Hamilton. She came over and Faith introduced Tom.

"I'm afraid my husband is not a great one for church, Reverend Fairchild."

"There are many ways to worship," Tom said.

"Now, that's just what Freeman always says. You two ought to get together sometime."

"I'd enjoy that."

They collected Ben and Zoë and drove back through the village and turned at the Fraziers' house to get onto Route 17. The cars in front of them appeared to be slowing down, and Faith rolled down her window and leaned out to see what was happening.

"Pull over, Tom! There's a police car in the Fraziers' driveway and some cop is putting Bill Fox in the backseat! I've got to find out what's going on."

"They may only be bringing him in for questioning. He was going to marry the girl and presumably he knew her very well."

"But they could do that here. Why take him some other place?" Faith sprinted along the road and was in time to see the police car pull out and turn left, the way off the island. The Fraziers were standing on their porch. Louise was crying.

Faith walked slowly up to them, unsure now whether she was intruding, but Elliot called out, "Oh Faith, this is terrible. I'm glad you're here. We can't believe it." She climbed the stairs.

"They've taken Bill to Ellsworth. They think *he* killed Bird!"

"That's incredible. What possible reason could they have for accusing him?"

Louise spoke, her normally soft voice a whisper. "They found the weapon in his tool shed. They also found a drill and some corks."

"You mean they think he killed Roger too?"

She nodded.

Faith thought rapidly. "Let me tell my husband what's happened. He can leave the children at the Millers' and come back with Pix. Sam is Bill's lawyer, isn't he? I think Pix should get in touch with him right away."

The Fraziers seemed grateful for her help, and when she came back from telling Tom, they moved inside and sat in the kitchen.

"What did Bill say about the evidence?" Faith asked.

Louise paused to pour some tea, and having a mug to hold on to seemed to allow her to strengthen her voice.

"Nothing, absolutely nothing at first. He just stared at them as if they were crazy, which of course they are," she answered. "Then he stood up and said, 'I guess you want me to go with you,' got his jacket, and went. We told him we'd follow and he said not to bother, but as soon as we've talked to Pix, we'll go up there."

The two of them looked terribly frail and all of their years. Faith knew that Tom would go with them. He could leave for New Hampshire from Ellsworth. After the events in Aleford when Faith had discovered Cindy Shepherd's corpse, Tom had become an old hand at police procedures and comforting the incarcerated and their friends and families.

"Did the police say what the weapon was?"

"They had it with them, all wrapped up in a plastic bag. It was a small hatchet and there was no doubt it was Bill's. Had his initials on a little brass plate. His mother and brother had given him a fancy set of garden tools last Christmas. He thought it was sweet of them, but he liked his old ones best and I doubt he ever used these."

Faith flashed back to the bloodstained shack. Hearing about the weapon added the final touch of horror to the scene. It had not been an easy death.

Pix rushed in the back door, followed by Tom. She put her arms around Louise. "How could they possibly think Bill had anything to do with this? He *adored* her."

Elliot spoke. "I'm afraid that's what they think the motive is. They confronted him with the drill and the corks, and I think they're going to charge him with Roger's death. I imagine they think he killed Roger so he could have Bird."

"Even admitting that, which I don't," Pix said, "we still come back to Bird. Why destroy the one thing you love?"

You might have to, thought Faith, if she had somehow discovered the earlier deed. Or she might have decided to go back to Andy and wasn't in the cabin packing, but there to stay. She decided it was neither the time nor the place to air these opinions. And it was Bill Fox they were talking about. The man who had created the gentle world of Selega couldn't have done either of these murders. It just didn't feel right, and Faith was a great believer in hunches.

"I called Sam and he's going to try to find out what's going on in Ellsworth. He has a lawyer friend who summers in Blue Hill, and he's going to ask him to go straight over. Sam won't be able to get away himself until later in the week, unfortunately, but we're to call if we need him and he'll drop everything. He's fairly certain they won't charge

Bill now. It's all pretty circumstantial." Pix was starting to run on and on. Tom interrupted.

"I don't know Bill Fox, but if you'd like me to come to the jail with you, I'd be happy to be of help," he told the Fraziers.

"That would be wonderful. We really would like someone to come along with us, and I have the feeling you are the perfect choice," Elliot said.

Faith thought so too. Calm, unobtrusive, firm. That was her Tom.

"Oh, dear, we should tell John. He'll probably want to come too," Louise remembered.

"Would you like me to tell him on my way back?" Faith offered.

"That would be a big help, because we should be leaving, and in any case, I hate to break news like this over the phone—not to mention our party line. It will be all over the island soon enough. Poor Bill. He came here for privacy, and now it looks like that will be at an end for some time."

Pix followed the Fraziers out the front door. She was going along too. Tom and Faith lingered on the porch a moment.

"I know," said Faith. "It's always something."

Tom held her close. "Be careful, darling. I'll be back before you know it, and then we really will have a vacation."

"Pix should drive with you so you won't get lost."

"That's a good idea, and she can tell me all the things you didn't on the way." Tom shook his head. "I never met Fox, but I read all his books when I was a kid, and I feel like I know him. What do you think. Could he possibly have done this?"

"I think he was obsessed by her and he might have been driven to some kind of passionate act, but

I don't see him plotting to do away with Roger. Or killing her so brutally. He'd have been more likely to give her a poisoned apple and watch her slip into a sleeplike death."

"I'd better get going. I'll call you from New Hampshire tonight. Try to take it easy today. Play with the kids. Cook."

Faith kissed him. "Drive carefully. I love you."

She watched as the tiny caravan took off, then got into Pix's car. For a moment she was daunted by the number of things confronting her on the Range Rover's dashboard—there was even a compass. Then she set off for John Eggleston's house in Little Harbor, curious to see how the former clergyman lived.

She pulled into his road and swerved immediately over to the side to avoid the large Lincoln Town Car speeding in her direction. As it careened past, she saw Paul Edson at the wheel with Edith sitting stiffly beside him. They were not smiling.

Now what could they want with John Eggleston? Faith wondered. A spiritual crisis?

He was standing in front of his house. His face was more ruddy than usual and his angry expression softened only slightly when he realized it was Faith.

It was a small white farmhouse in perfect repair. Peony bushes lined up like choirboys across the front, and a purple martin multiple-dwelling birdhouse adorned a huge pine that stood to one side. There were no other flowers. No lawn decorations—no whirligigs, clam-basket planters, old tires filled with marigolds, or the ubiquitous posterior of a fat lady bending over that had sprouted on many local lawns this summer, the only variation being in the color and pattern of her bloomers.

It was all pretty stark, until you looked past the house to the view.

John Eggleston had one of the choicest pieces of waterfront on the island. The backyard stretched out to a salt marsh, and beyond that was a wide, crescent-shaped beach. And beyond that was the sea, a westward view of the islands. They looked like plump green pincushions today beneath a cloudless blue sky. Faith knew why the Edsons had been there and why John was not in the mood to love his neighbor. They'd been trying to get him to sell, and they must have had a reason to think he would.

She re-collected herself and the job at hand.

"Is there somewhere we can talk? I'm afraid I have some bad news. They've arrested Bill."

"I'm not surprised," he said, and started walking toward the small gray-cedar-shingled barn at the rear of the house. Faith trotted along behind him.

She waited for amplification, realized it would not be forthcoming, and asked, "Why do you say you're not surprised?"

"Because they're all a bunch of fools. Bill included."

He opened the door, and they stepped into what was obviously his workshop.

"They're a bunch of fools to think that Bill could do it, but they haven't the brains to figure out who did. And Bill's a fool for getting involved with the girl in the first place."

He picked up a chisel and a mallet and started to hack away at an enormous piece of wood on his workbench. Faith perched on a stool and looked around. There were a number of pieces in various degrees of completion. She needn't wonder about how he supported himself anymore. He was obviously very competent at his craft. She noted the irony that many of the pieces seemed related to religion. There was a beautiful menorah, and an altarpiece with a crucifix surrounded by flamelike spirals. He followed her glance.

"Most of my commissions come from churches and synagogues. I had started doing this when I was a priest, and just because I am no longer active in the church doesn't mean I should stop doing what I know best—or stop believing either."

He was chipping away for dear life, and Faith noticed how sharp he kept his tools. The metal edges gleamed on the bench, mixing with the shavings that were flying all over the barn. He was certainly a muscular Christian.

He didn't seem inclined to talk about Bill, and she didn't feel like leaving. If she was ever going to find out anything about this man, she'd have to ask. He wasn't going to give anything away.

She plunged in. "Why did you leave the church?"

He glared at her, then turned back to his work. "I should say it's none of your business and it's not, but I'll tell you and you'll see why I think Bill has been such a fool. That girl would have brought him nothing but unhappiness. Has, in fact."

Faith waited patiently.

"My grandfather had been an Episcopal priest, and I loved and respected him more than anyone in the world. I never had any doubt that that was what I wanted to be. He was at peace with himself and the world. And he gave that peace to others. But I lost it. And it was all because of a woman." He gave the wood a particularly violent, vicious blow, and Faith drew slightly away.

"I'm not saying it wasn't my fault too, but let's just say I had a Bird. She was in my congregation and I was drunk with love of her. We were going to get married when she announced she was pregnant and we'd have to move the date up. Now I knew for a fact that baby wasn't mine, but it wasn't long before the parish got wind of it and began to agitate for my removal. Like a fool I still wanted to marry her, and we decided to go to the next parish, where a friend of mine would perform the ceremony. Well, she never showed up. I heard later she'd gone to Atlanta with some man. By then I'd come to my senses, but I had to leave my church. The church I had led for ten years. I wasn't at peace anymore. Not with myself, my congregation, or my heavenly Father. I've been searching for it ever since. Thought I might find it here. But it remains out of my grasp."

He was grasping the chisel so hard, his knuckles were white. "And now Edson is breathing down my neck. How he found out I'll never know. Must steam open the mail somehow—you see, that woman is filing a paternity suit. The baby is nine years old and the mother wants all the back child support. Of course she won't win, but it's going to cost me a lot in lawyers' fees."

"Maybe Sam can give you some advice," Faith suggested.

Eggleston jerked his head up. He appeared to have forgotten she was there.

"Maybe. Anyway, I'll be damned if I'll sell even an inch of this land."

There was a large window in one end of the barn.

"I don't blame you," Faith said. "It's some of the loveliest land I've seen on the island."

He carved in silence for a few moments, then set down his tools and ran a hand through his hair, leaving wood shavings mixed in with his own curls.

"I guess I better get up to Ellsworth. Bill's never

going to be the same again. Damn that girl!" He blurted out the words vehemently.

Faith got down from the stool and followed him across the lawn. He whirled around and faced her. "Did you read his books?"

"Yes, many times."

"So you know what it means, Selega and all that."

"It's just a made-up word, isn't it?"

"Spell it backward," he said grimly, and without saying good-bye strode into his house and closed the door.

Faith stood and looked at the shore. She could hear the gulls screech as they dropped mussels and sea urchins onto the rocks to crack them open.

Selega.

Ageles.

Ageless.

She sighed, got into the car, and drove to the Millers'.

Efficient as always, Samantha and Arlene had fed the children and put them down for naps. Faith was beginning to think the two of them might do a far better job at parenting than Tom and she ever would. It might be wise simply to turn Ben over immediately. She sent them off for a bike ride and told them she would take care of things. They seemed a bit dubious, and she half expected them to leave a list of emergency numbers, but they took off and she was pleasantly reassured to hear some adolescent giggles and horseplay as they left the drive.

She made herself a sandwich. Pix seemed to go in heavily for tuna fish, so tuna it was. Hunger will do that. Then she wandered about at loose ends. She didn't want to be out of earshot and she didn't feel like reading. The morning's events had made her edgy. She wondered what was going on up in

Ellsworth. And John Eggleston's revelations had been pretty startling. A genuine misogynist. She felt somewhat uneasy as she thought about the way he was cleaving the wood sculpture.

Pix had taken the quilt books and magazines back to her house along with the photos to work on some more. Faith didn't know where Pix had hidden the pictures. Probably in her freezer, marked "mystery," but the rest of the stuff was in a pile by one of the large easy chairs set in front of the fireplace.

Faith didn't need the photos anymore. The three squares they had not yet identified were permanently etched in her memory. She was sure number eight had something to do with ripples and turned to the index to look up any references to sea, ocean, pools, anything with water. After searching through several books, she found Wild Waves, only to be disappointed. It didn't look anything like Matilda's square. Ten minutes later she had it: Ocean Wave. They *had* been on the right track. She found a piece of paper and sketched the other two. Maybe if she stared at them long enough, inspiration would strike. Number fifteen looked like someone had placed four squares of diminishing sizes on top of each other. It didn't look like anything. Neither did number seventeen—two large diamonds surrounding two smaller ones. She decided to try Pix's method. Seventeen was a four-patch divided in half. She started to go through the books looking under four-patch designs and was making some progress—that is, she had eliminated a whole lot of squares—when she heard Ben's familiar "Mommee! Up!" Zoë was not far behind, and it sounded like an "I'm wet and hungry" cry.

Maybe one child was enough.

She changed the baby and decided to go back to

her own cottage for the rest of the afternoon and left a note for Pix telling her to call and relating Faith's success with the square.

Walking back through the woods weighed down with Zoë on her hip, the tedious job of trying to keep Ben from straying too far afield, and the cares that refused to go to the back of her mind, Faith decided to take Tom's advice and spend the afternoon playing with the children outdoors. She knew if she got into the hammock, she'd be asleep in no time, so she spread a blanket on the grass and dumped blocks, cars, whatever she could find in the middle. Maybe later, when she had regained some energy and *joie de vivre*, she'd bake some cookies. Ben and Zoë could bang on the pots and lick spoons. But all she wanted to do now was collapse.

Pix arrived about four.

"I'm exhausted, and I didn't stop to eat anything, but I know I've come to the right place. Please feed me."

"My pleasure. We just finished making these oatmeal cookies, but I have the feeling you need something heartier."

Pix picked up one of the crisp, lacy cookies and took a bite. "Ummm, delicious. I'd probably finish the plate."

Faith was busy taking things out of the fridge and putting them in front of Pix: a salad of the tiny lentils from LePuy in vinaigrette, some tapenade, tomato slices, and hard-boiled eggs. She grabbed a loaf of bread, cut a few slices, poured two glasses of an '82 Minervois, deposited the children by the large clothes basket of toys she kept in the kitchen, and sat down to listen.

"Tom left after an hour or so," Pix said after a large mouthful of the salad and a gulp of wine. "Nobody could see Bill, but Sam had gotten hold of the lawyer from Blue Hill, and he arrived before we did and stayed with Bill the whole time. I'm glad Tom was there. The Fraziers are terribly shaken, and he was able to comfort them. They came home the same time I did. We left messages for Bill, but there was nothing we could do. Oh, John appeared just about when Tom was leaving. He looked wild. His hair was even more on end than usual."

"I think he is an extremely angry man, certainly bitter. I had a very interesting conversation with him when I went to tell him about Bill. It turns out that the reason Eggleston left the ministry was a woman. And a parishioner at that. She got pregnant while they were seeing each other—not by him, he claims—and the congregation found it difficult to condone. He still wanted to marry her—why I can't imagine, since she was evidently traveling many garden paths at the same time—but he did; then she left him standing at the altar—not his own. He had to leave his church and now she's slapped a paternity suit on him."

"But there must be some sort of statute of limitations on these things! Did you believe him when he said he wasn't the father?"

"Yes. He seems so ruthlessly honest. Besides, he's quite confident he'll win the case, but he is worried about the costs. And the plot thickens. I saw the Edsons emerging from his drive. It's uncanny the way those two can nose out financial hardship. They were after his waterfront."

"I can imagine what he said, or even did."

"They didn't look pleased, but they did seem to be in one piece."

Pix laughed. "They do look like one piece, joined at the seams."

Faith had finished her wine. She took Zoë on her lap and Ben ran over to wiggle the baby's toes. "One piggy, two piggy, market."

"That boy is a genius," Pix commented.

Faith smiled. There were these moments.

"Eric left a note at the house inviting us for drinks in the gazebo. He's all moved in," Pix said, "but I'm too tired to go."

Faith was tired too, but she wanted to see Eric after last night's contretemps at the dance. She'd told Pix about the fight, and she'd been inclined to dismiss it as too much Coors too fast. Faith hadn't told Pix about the bracelet. She wasn't altogether sure her friend Mrs. Miller could keep her mouth shut with Tom around, and she knew they would both worry.

"Come on, Pix, we'll just stay a little while, and it will be a good distraction. Heaven knows we need it."

"You don't usually say things like 'heaven knows,' so you must have a reason for wanting me to come. But I want to be in my bed and asleep by eight."

Faith wasn't sure she had heard correctly.

"Eight o'clock? That sounds obscene. I'm sure all that sleep can't be good for you."

"It is tonight," Pix answered.

"All right, I promise. Do you want to pick me up? And I almost forgot, can Samantha baby-sit?"

"Yes and yes."

Faith had a momentary pang, followed swiftly by an unwelcome realization that that utterance might lend validity to it. She bravely voiced it anyway.

"You don't think I'm asking Samantha and Arlene to watch the children too much, do you?"

"No, my dear, and you don't either. It is your vacation, though I must say it hasn't seemed like one. Besides, you're paying them very well for their labors, and I happen to know Arlene has opened an account at Bar Harbor Trust and all this is going toward college, so she's very pleased."

"College?"

"Yes, Arlene wants to be a biochemist."

"Still waters run deep. I'll see you later. I suppose we should wear our sprigged-lawn afternoon dresses or white muslins with the trim we tatted last winter?"

"Mine need airing, so I'm going for a denim skirt and that striped blouse you made me get. See you soon."

The fog had started to roll in late in the day, and by the time they got to Eric's, it had stopped coming in wisps across the horizon and settled in a thick blanket that effectively obscured any dramatic sunset they might have glimpsed from the gazebo. Yet there was a cozy, mysterious quality to it. They followed the red sun faintly piercing the fog as it slipped into the sea while they sipped some wine and nibbled the cheese straws Jill had made. She seemed very much the mistress of the house, and Faith, remembering Eric's words the night before, hoped she would be in name as well as deed soon. Eric appeared none the worse for wear, except for a large bruise on his left cheekbone. Neither Pix nor Faith said anything about it and studiously addressed their remarks to his good side.

"You two are so discreet," he said, laughing. "I really made an ass of myself last night. Faith can bear witness." He grabbed Jill around the waist. "That's what happens when I go anywhere alone."

Seizing the opening, Faith hastened to ask, "What were you fighting about?"

"You name it. The house, the weather, politics, religion," he replied vaguely, and she had to be satisfied with the response, especially as Jill firmly proceeded to close the subject.

"I don't want to hear any more about it," she said. "Two grown men acting like children." She was angry herself. Bright-red spots rose on her cheeks. Faith was surprised at her intensity, then recalled that Jill, unlike the rest of them, was a true islander, and it must be embarrassing or worse to have the man she was in love with at odds with the Prescotts, a significant percentage of Sanpere's population.

Eric looked sheepish. "Tell us more about what's happening with Bill, Pix. Did you get to see him?"

"No, but he has a lawyer, James Lyman—a friend of Sam's from Blue Hill—who's been with him. When Jim leaves, he'll call Sam and we'll know more—whether Bill will be formally charged or not."

"What the hell are they doing wasting their time on Bill instead of finding out who really did this? It's typical of the way things run around here!" Eric exploded. "He's from away, so he's suspect!"

And they *did* find the murder weapon in his shed, Faith added mentally. It seemed Eric and Jill hadn't heard that the police had also found a drill and corks in Bill's shed, and she decided not to mention it if Pix didn't.

Pix didn't.

"I've known Bill since he came to the island," Jill said quietly. "It must have been twelve years ago. He was always a bit moody. There would be times when we wouldn't see him for a while. Usually it was when he was between books. When he was writing, he was engrossed but happy. I can't imagine that he would do something like this."

But somebody had, and it was clear from the expression on each of their faces that that was what they were thinking. Pix stood up.

"This has been lovely, but I really have to go. I hope you'll excuse me, but I am so-o-o tired."

Eric put his arm around her. "Of course you are, after the day you've had. But at least stay and have a bowl of chowder. You have to eat."

"Thank you, but I've been eating so many of these cheese tidbits, all I want is a cup of Sleepy Time tea and bed."

Faith was a little worried. The words "unflagging," "indefatigable," "robust," had all been coined for Pix. "Tired" was something that happened to other people.

"I know what you mean," Jill said. "I'm tired too. Not my body. That can keep going on automatic pilot, but I find myself wanting to sleep so I don't have to think."

Faith was relieved. Of course that was it. The engine was fine; it had just been flooded.

"We'll have a grand dinner party Labor Day weekend, an end-of-summer party," Eric offered. "Cocktails out here, then we'll retire to the dining room, which should be finished by then."

"Eric is stenciling a frieze around the walls," Jill explained. "Kind of a cross between William Morris and Peter Max."

"Sounds interesting," Faith said.

"Take a peek before you go," Eric urged.

Faith looked at Pix.

"One peek," Pix said, and they started to walk toward the house.

"Did you grow up in an old house?" Faith asked Eric.

"Anything but. It was a trailer that my father set on concrete blocks and later enclosed in siding. Then when my parents split up, I lived with my mother in an apartment in Houston. But by then I was a teenager and on my way out."

And up, Faith thought. No wonder he loved the Prescott house so much. It was still the Prescott place, and even when Eric was ninety, it would be known as such. She wondered what he thought of that.

"And where did you live?" Faith turned to Jill. "I know you grew up here, but which part of the island?"

"I'll show you sometime. A relative of mine still lives there. It's a tiny old farmhouse on the shore near the causeway. It faces the reach. I'll always miss living there. It seemed perfect when I was growing up. This house"—she gestured toward Harbor View, draped in fog and looming larger than life with nothing visible nearby for comparison—"this was like a mansion to us, although the Prescotts weren't snobbish. We just never had much occasion to come here."

Not exactly on the trick-or-treat circuit. Somehow Faith couldn't see the Matilda she'd heard about dropping Hershey bars into small outstretched hands.

They walked into the dining room and Eric switched on the lights. He had done a great deal in a short time. The walls were painted a warm coral, and across the top stylized Morris leaves and berries in gold joined turquoise geometrics. Words in deep green, some in gothic script, some in block letters, ran across the bottom.

"What does it say?" Faith asked. She stood and looked up at the wall and read aloud. " 'Here too in Maine things bend to the wind forever.' That's very beautiful."

"It's Robert Lowell's 'Soft Wood,' a favorite of Roger's and mine. It seemed to suit the house and Matilda too. It was written for Harriet Winslow, Lowell's older cousin who lived in Castine, not too far from here."

Faith was deciphering other lines. She liked the sound of "illimitable salt" and decided to look for the poem in the little Sanpere library.

Eric had purchased an Eastlake dining-room set from a dealer in Northeast Harbor, and it looked perfect against the color of the walls. She walked slowly around the room, reading the poem, then stopped abruptly. Over the lintel, by accident or design, two lines stood alone: "This is the season/when our friends may and will die daily."

The phone rang. Eric excused himself. He was back quickly, ashen faced and the words spilled out. "That was Louise. Bill Fox has killed himself."

For the first time in her life, Faith passed out.

Nine

Whenever Faith recalled that juxtaposition of reading Lowell's lines and Bill Fox's death, she thought she understood what the phrase "a clashing of the spheres" meant. It was as if two universes had collided, the written and the real—with Faith caught in the middle, one foot resting unsteadily in each.

She didn't believe in portents, but for an instant it seemed the words had killed him, stabbing him with the sharp strokes of painted prophecy.

But he hadn't used a knife. He would not have been allowed that. What he had been permitted was paper, a pencil, and a lamp. Young Officer Gibson, who was on duty, saw no reason to deny his request. Gibson had heard the guy wrote books and figured he probably wanted to work or write to somebody.

Bill did write—a long, incoherent letter addressed to the Fraziers in which he confessed to the crime: "My princess is dead and the guilt is mine." Then he stripped off the end of the lamp cord, wrapped one wire around each leg, plugged the other end into the wall outlet, and electrocuted himself. It was a swift death. They found him, lifeless on the floor, when they came to bring his dinner.

If it had not been that way, it would have been another.

The fog was even thicker on Monday morning than it had been the night before. Faith looked out the window, and only the fact that she had two importunate children to care for kept her from crawling back into bed and pulling the covers over her head for a long, long time. She felt numb as she dressed, fed, and even smiled at Zoë and Ben. It was an out-of-body experience.

Pix had called. She was on her way to the Fraziers' and Samantha was in her room. Bill had been her idol. She had a complete set of his books, all personally inscribed. She had told her mother there was no way she would ever believe he was a murderer.

Faith was inclined to agree. An ambiguous suicide note written in the throes of intense grief did not exactly amount to an ironclad confession. But if not Bill, who? Andy, her favorite choice for a suspect, was apparently being ruled out. He had been on the boat raided by the antismuggling task force. But the boat was wandering around the islands close to Sanpere. How hard would it have been for him to put ashore? Andy had stated to the police that Bird never intended to marry Bill, that she was in fact at their cabin because she was coming back to Andy—had never really left. He reportedly regarded Bill as a demented old man. But it was his word against Bill's, and now Bill wasn't around to speak for himself. Nor was Bird. Or Roger. Faith felt an instant of panic. Death shrouded the community like the fog lying thickly in the cove.

Bill's mother and brother were flying to the island to take Bill home. He would be buried next to his father in the family plot in a small cemetery near their North Carolina farm. He'd been from away. Like Bird and like Roger. Could there be a connection there?

Faith slogged through the morning and planned on a nap when the children took theirs. She had tucked them in—marveling at the quirkiness of fate that for once had smiled, sending Zoë and Ben to sleep at almost precisely the same moment—and stretched out on her own bed. She was drifting off to sleep when she heard a car drive up.

She ran to the front hall window and looked out. It was too foggy to see the plates, but she could see the driver as he approached the house—a large man about sixty with thick white hair. He was alone. He stood on the porch uncertainly, then knocked and called out, "Is anybody home?"

Faith went downstairs and opened the door. As soon as she saw his face, any fears she had quickly vanished. It was a kind face and a tired-looking one. It was also slightly familiar. She knew immediately who he was, and a wave of contradictory emotions swept over her.

"Mrs. Fairchild? I am George Warner, Bird's father. I've come for my granddaughter."

So, Faith realized, Andy *had* known Bird's real name and where she came from. "Please come in and sit down. Zoë is taking a nap. We can wake her, but perhaps you'd like to have a cup of coffee and wait. She won't sleep much longer."

"Oh, I don't want to wake her, and a cup of coffee would be wonderful. I drove straight from the airport to the police and then couldn't wait to see her."

"That you can do right away. She won't wake up, and neither will Ben—that's my little boy. They're in his room."

She led him up the stairs and stood to one side as he looked down at the tiny child asleep in the cradle. He turned to leave and there were tears streaming down his face. In the hallway he said to her, choking on the words, "She looks just like her mother."

"Please, come down and sit in the kitchen while I make some coffee. And I'm sure you must be hungry too." Faith always assumed people were hungry. Especially in times of crisis.

"That would be very kind."

He sat at the kitchen table in silence and watched Faith as she heated up some scallop bisque. She set a steaming bowl in front of him and quickly spread some thick slices of bread with cheese to run under the broiler. He ate swiftly, and it was not until she had placed a cup of coffee in front of him and sat down herself that he began to talk.

"Her real name was Laura Sue. She never liked it. We took both grandmothers' names." He paused. "Did you know Bird well?"

"No, I'm sorry, I didn't. We have been staying here only since the beginning of the month. I've seen her. She used to gather seaweed on the beach in front of the cottage, but we never actually spoke." Faith did not feel it was necessary to describe the scene in the cemetery or remind Mr. Warner that she had found the body. Perhaps he didn't know.

"We lost her mother when Bird was twelve. Cancer. It was pretty rough on Bird. They had been so close. Rough on me too, but I was more used to death. My parents, a brother. For Bird it was like the world had come to an end. She had always been a little different from the other kids. Always reading books."

Probably Bill's, Faith thought. This view of Bird's

childhood was different from what she had imagined. Lonely. Somehow the self-assurance her beauty had projected had never suggested that.

"She used to hang around with the older kids at school. That's how she knew Roger."

"Knew Roger? You mean Roger Barnett?" Faith was astonished.

Bird's father nodded. "Oh yes, he's from Blakesburg too. Iowa born and bred. Known his family all my life."

"But Roger would have been quite a bit older than Bird," Faith said.

"Only five years. She and Roger were always close. I'd say like brother and sister, and maybe it was for Roger, but not for my daughter. She never looked at any of the boys in her class. If she went to a dance, it was with Roger or not at all. When he went away to college, she was very unhappy. He'd come home from time to time, but it wasn't the same. Then there was a while when his mother didn't know where he was. They'd quarreled. Bird left soon after that."

He picked up one of the crusty slices of bread. His hands were covered with age spots, which stood out against his smooth, untanned skin. Whatever he had done with his life, it hadn't been outdoors. He broke the bread in half with studied care. Faith was torn between wanting him to eat and needing to hear the story.

"I came home and there was a note on the table. Said she had to get away. Find herself. That sort of thing. I guess I wasn't too surprised. There wasn't much in the town for her. I knew if I tried to go after her, she'd just leave again, so I waited. I didn't want to lose her."

Did that first step lead to this end? Faith wondered. Oh, why didn't Laura Sue stay at home, get married, and start a health food store! Was she looking for Roger?

"She'd phone every once in a while so I'd know she was all right, and she'd send funny postcards. They came from all over. She started calling herself Bird after living with some people in New Mexico. 'I feel free as a bird, Daddy,' she said, so Bird it was.

"Did you know she was going to have a baby? The police told me." His eyes filled, and he stopped speaking. Faith poured some hot coffee into his cup.

"I don't know why she didn't tell me—or about Zoë either. Maybe she was planning on surprising me, turning up with two babies. I'd never pushed her to come back to visit, but she always said she would. She knew how much I wanted to see her."

Would she have come if he had asked, sent her a ticket? Faith was sure money was never plentiful for Bird. But her father must have been afraid she would stop getting in touch if he made any demands. Maybe he had been right.

"I knew she was in Maine, because I got a postcard with a sea gull on it. It had been mailed from Camden. I looked it up on the map. I always did that. I knew Roger lived in Maine. His mother told me, and I planned to tell Bird the next time she called. But I never got another call." He broke down completely at this point and, putting his face in his hands, sobbed uncontrollably. Faith got a box of tissues from the bathroom and stood with her hand resting lightly on his shoulder. There was nothing she could say. All those years of longing and separation. It was the saddest story she'd ever heard. Why did people have children anyway? If Ben had any ideas of cutting out when he was seventeen, he could just forget it right now.

Mr. Warner lifted his head, wiped his eyes, and blew his nose. "I feel so foolish. Please forgive me. Since I got the news I don't seem to be able to stop."

"Please, don't apologize. This has been such a shock for you."

"I have to see the police again. I've made plans to leave tomorrow morning. I want to take Bird home. She'll be next to her mother."

A tiny cry drifted down to the kitchen. Faith smiled. "That's Zoë. She's a slow waker."

They went upstairs, and Mr. Warner took his granddaughter in his arms. She stopped crying immediately and burrowed down against his suit jacket with obvious pleasure.

"She's a sweetheart," Faith told him. "Your daughter must have been a very fine mother. Zoë has such a lovely disposition. We're going to miss her."

Mr. Warner was gently stroking Zoë's cheek. "Don't worry about her. I come from a big family, and she has more relatives than she'll know what to do with and they're all standing ready to give me all the advice I want and some I don't."

"What about tonight? Would you like to leave her here? You could stay too. There's plenty of room," Faith offered.

"Thank you for offering, but I think we'll stay at the Holiday Inn. I already ordered a crib, and it's nearer the police and the airport. I stopped at the Shop and Save on my way down, and the car is loaded with everything from diapers to toys, so we'll be fine."

Faith took Zoë and changed her, then put on a warm sleeper. Arlene had appeared on Saturday with a bag of baby clothes from her mother's stockpile. Faith added a sweater and handed the little girl over to Mr. Warner. Ben had been running around waving toys at her. When they got to the front door and it became apparent that this big man was taking Zoë away, Ben started to howl. Faith felt much the same way.

Mr. Warner looked upset.

"Don't worry, he'll be fine," Faith assured him.

He managed a smile. "How can I thank you for all you've done, Mrs. Fairchild?"

He looked out toward the cove. From there it wasn't possible to see the water, but the sound of the steady pulse of the waves was plain. "I don't know why she came to Maine. Bird hated cold weather and she never liked to be near the water. I couldn't even get her to learn to swim when she was a kid. She probably never did learn." He gazed into the fog again.

Faith gave Zoë a last kiss and picked up Ben, who had attached himself to her leg like a suction cup and was still crying. Mr. Warner shook her hand awkwardly, both of them encumbered. "We'll be in touch. I'll let you know how things are."

"That would be nice," Faith answered. She knew she would never hear from him again. She waved good-bye and bundled Ben back into the house for an intensive dose of quality time. He wasn't fooled and cried off and on for an hour for the baby to come back. Faith was exhausted and it was only two o'clock. It always seemed to be only two o'clock when she felt this way.

She dug out some homemade playdough and installed Ben at the kitchen table with a garlic press and a small rolling pin. Soon he was happily making "sketties" and she was thinking of food too. She had a few quarts of fresh tomatoes, and she ought to make sauce before they went bad.

She had just finished seeding and skinning them when Pix called.

"Are you feeling as out of sorts as I am? Whenever I think about Bill, I sit and cry. The poor Fraziers have completely broken down. Their daughter and her husband arrived from Boston, and I left them to it."

"My news is not going to make you—or the two nannies—feel any better. Bird's father just left with Zoë."

"Oh no! I was beginning to think you would keep her!"

"Maybe I was too. It was quite a wrench to see her go, but Mr. Warner is a lovely man and he was so happy to have her. He didn't even know he was a grandfather. You should have seen him, Pix—he was grieving terribly for Bird. She'll never be back, but he has a part of her in Zoë."

"Bill and Bird gave her an appropriate name."

"Yes, and by the way, Bird's real name was Laura Sue. I don't blame her for changing. It sounds as though 'Tips for Teens' or 'Original Recipe Brownies' should follow, but I would have picked something with fewer comedic possibilities to replace it."

"Like what?"

"Oh, I don't know. Portia or Deirdre. Something, anything."

"I disagree. Bird was Bird. It suited her."

"That's only because you were used to it being her name, and is this conversation going anywhere or are we just bored?"

"Just bored," Pix agreed.

"Well, I'm going to finish my spaghetti sauce,

then read a million stories to Ben. It's too foggy to take a walk. We'd tumble into the sea. But if it lifts later, we'll come your way if that's all right."

"Of course. And just be happy you don't live on Whitehead Island. It's the foggiest place in Maine. They have eleven weeks of it a year."

"How many do we have?" Faith was slightly startled by her own use of "we." Had she said good-bye to the Hamptons and civilized life as she knew it forever? She hoped not.

"About five weeks—and sometimes all in a row, or it seems that way."

"Don't worry, it will lift before Hope and Quentin arrive. There isn't a fog that creeps on little cat or any other feet that would dare to obscure their well-regulated horizons."

Pix laughed again. "While you're creating culinary masterpieces, I'll go to work on the quilt. We've *got* to find out what those last two squares are."

"Call me if you have any luck. It would be fun to take Hope and Quentin on a treasure hunt when they arrive on Wednesday. And Quentin could probably figure out how to write the whole thing off as a tax loss. I think that's what he does, although I've never been too certain. One of those legally illegal things anyway."

"Good cooking, Faith."

"Good hunting, Pix. Oh wait! I must be losing my mind. I almost forgot to tell you the rest about Bird! She and Roger were from the same town in Iowa. They grew up together and, from the sound of it, Bird had been in love with him since she was a little girl. And the police told Mr. Warner that she was pregnant at the time of her death."

"By Roger, do you think? Oh, Faith, it just gets sadder and sadder."

"I know. Roger does seem the likeliest—or it could have been Andy? Her father didn't say how far along she was."

"This is almost too much to take in. Do you think Bill knew?"

"There are lots of things I'm afraid we're never going to know and that's one."

"Well, I'll try to find these squares and at least we'll know something. Talk to you later."

"Okay, good-bye."

Faith hung up and turned back to her tomatoes. She decided to give Pix some of the sauce. The Millers definitely needed some real food. The quilt photos were being hidden in a half-empty can of bread crumbs with Italian seasoning. Pix had told Faith she used this convenience all the time and that they were particularly good on chicken. Faith had asked Pix if she ever thought about where those bread crumbs had been. She used the same tone her mother employed years ago when Faith picked up a penny from a New York City sidewalk. It was impossible to be too stern about fresh bread crumbs.

The fog did not lift, and as the afternoon wore on, Faith began to feel suffocated by it. She was tempted to jump in the car and drive to the Millers', but it would take too much energy. Besides, once there she'd have to come back again. Her sauce was made and she was contemplating an early dinner, long bath, and bed—Benjamin permitting—when the phone rang. It was Pix again. A very excited Pix.

"I've got number fifteen! It's White House Steps and that's got to be it. Somewhere on that road there must be a white house, and the treasure is under the steps!"

"Pix, that's fantastic! If only the fog would lift, we could go hunt! But if the treasure was under the steps, why would Matilda put all those other squares after it?"

Pix sighed. "You're right. I didn't think of that. I was so excited to have found it. But it must be another directional clue. Starting from the steps you look for some fern berries, then number seventeen and a shady pine. If we could find the steps, we could look for large pines. It must be buried under one of them."

"Let's go back to Prescott Point first thing in the morning," Faith proposed. "But now I have to finish reading *The Three Little Pigs* to Ben. I don't know why he likes it so much. I've always thought it was such a prissy book. And what do you suppose would have happened if the wolf had gone to the third little pig's house first? Before he was finished with all his brickwork? He'd have been singing a different tune."

"You've been cooped up too long, Faith. See you in the morning."

Faith hung up and felt happier than she had in days. At least one mystery was becoming clearer.

The weather was not, however. When she awoke the next morning, the fog was thicker, if that was possible. She called Pix and they commiserated, resolving to go exploring the moment it lifted.

"It'll burn off," Pix promised.

Faith, thinking of those five weeks, was less sanguine. "How much fog has there been to date? Maybe we can approach this scientifically."

"There's nothing scientific about fog and I prefer

to trust Arlene. When she called Samantha this morning, she told her it would burn off by tomorrow, so no doubt it will."

Faith faced another long, housebound day squarely in the face and found it wanting. She decided to get ahead in cooking some treats for Hope and Quentin; then even if she had to bring a stick to feel her way, she'd take Ben to the Millers', one step at a time.

The morning passed quickly, and after making more bread and a large Basque salad with shrimp, sausage, prosciutto, peppers, onions, and rice for Quentin and Hope's arrival, she called Pix to tell her she was bringing lunch. Pix, who had stoutly averred she welcomed a few foggy days, agreed with more than a suggestion of cabin fever in her voice.

Faith took the path through the woods. It was quite clear in patches, impenetrable in others. Ben ran ahead, undeterred by frequent falls over tree roots and happily scaling small stones. He was chanting to himself, "See Samantha, Ben see Samantha," until it all ran together like a name from *The Arabian Nights*.

Pix and Samantha welcomed them eagerly. The quilt books and magazines were strewn about the living room, and they had been ardently pursuing square number seventeen. They seemed happy for a break. Samantha took charge of Ben with an obvious display of bliss on both their parts—Ben's perhaps a bit more obvious since he jumped up and down and whooped.

"Why don't you stop and have lunch?" Faith suggested. "We won't fuss. I'll just put everything on the table. It's fresh curried pea soup—appropriate for a pea souper—and there's plenty to go with it. This weather has given me an enormous appetite. All I've done is eat."

She went into the kitchen and unpacked her basket. A moment later Pix was shaken from a last contemplation of four-patches by a shriek from the kitchen.

"Damn! I forgot to bring the bread." Faith emerged and grabbed her sweater. "I'll have to go back. It won't take me long without Ben. Keep an eye on the soup and make sure it doesn't boil."

"Why don't you take my car?"

"No, thanks. I'd rather feel terra firma directly under my feet. I'd be liable to end up making a left turn into the cove or something. The kids can start on the soup if they get hungry. You too."

And she ran out the front door. She was annoyed with herself. She didn't usually forget things, especially anything to do with food. Could it be the first harrowing harbinger of her dotage? She hurried on purposefully. Halfway back to her cottage she slowed down and began to appreciate the sensation of walking through the dense fog. Sound seemed magnified. She could hear an occasional bird's cry and the rustle of the light wind through the leaves and brush. The tide was out and there was no noise from the sea. It was very quiet.

Until she heard footsteps behind her.

At first she thought she must be mistaken, that it was an animal scurrying about. But these were slow and deliberate steps. A branch cracked when he or she stepped on it. Whoever it was couldn't be far behind.

"Hello?" she called, and the steps stopped abruptly. She kept walking, increasing her pace. She decided not to call out again. It couldn't be Pix or

Samantha, and who else would be coming from the direction of the Millers' cottage? It could be a clammer, but why would he be so far away from shore?

She must have imagined it, she told herself. Then the footsteps started again, faint and faintly closer.

"Who's there? Who are you?" She tried to inject irritation into her voice and keep the mounting fear out.

There was no reply. Absolute and total silence.

She walked on hurriedly and realized that she was now very frightened. Bird had been murdered not too far away or too long ago, and she had no intention of joining her. She started to run and tripped, falling flat on her face. She had cut her cheek on something sharp and started to cry out in pain. She scrambled to her feet and realized there was no way she could get away quickly. And where could she go?

There was only one thing to do. Climb a tree.

She crept as noiselessly as she could off the path and looked for the nearest tall spruce. A gigantic one rose out of the fog. She couldn't even see the top as she started up. The inner branches were like the rungs of a ladder, and she began to make headway slowly. She didn't dare to climb fast for fear of the noise the branches made as parts snapped off. She didn't hear anything below. Her pursuer had paused—or gone away. Twigs caught in her hair, and she was forced to take her sweater off when it caught in the needles. Her cheek was throbbing, and when she touched it she could see the blood on her palm. Fresh red blood. Not like Bird's had been when Faith found her, but like Bird's had been once. Without her sweater Faith was cold, and what she was thinking chilled her more than the cool air about her. She was shivering.

At last she was high up in the tree, clinging to the trunk and trying to keep her full weight from the fragile branch on which she stood.

She looked down. She couldn't see a thing.

And no one could see her.

Tears filled her eyes and her arms were already aching. She was afraid she was in for a long stay. She wanted to scream, but screaming was the last thing she should do. She clamped a hand over her mouth for a second to steady herself.

After what seemed like hours, she heard the footsteps again. He or she had not gone away. The steps came close to the tree and stopped. Then walked on. Then returned again. Softly, slowly, deliberately.

Whoever it was was not just passing by. He was looking for someone. Looking for Faith.

After several more forays the stalker moved down to the beach; filled with dread, Faith heard the footsteps squish into the sand. Her heart was beating fast and she felt sick. There was no way her hiding place could be discovered unless the fog lifted or blew away from the tree. Dread kept its steady grip on her. Please stay by the shore. Don't come back, she prayed.

The steps continued their slow, deliberate quest—systematically covering the beach. The sound echoed obscenely in her ears—squish, squash. Then the noise stopped. The hull of a boat scraped across the sand and rocks as it was pushed into the water; then came the steady lapping of oars. He or she was gone. Weak from relief, she started to climb down.

She had loosened her grip and put one foot on the next branch before she realized she was doing exactly what her pursuer wanted. What was to prevent the stalker from landing in another spot and waiting for her at the cottage, or along the path? She clung to the tree again and prepared to wait. Surely Pix would begin to worry.

She was so cold. She tried to concentrate on other things to keep her mind off the rapid loss of feeling in her fingers and toes. The fog felt like a blanket of snow on her bare arms. She cautiously loosened her grip to rub her left arm with her right. It helped a bit. She could catch glimpses of her sweater stuck several branches below when the fog moved. It had been a birthday present from Tom—a bulky Stewart Ross cardigan. She practically lived in it. Should she try to get it and climb back up? Lived in it, lived in it—the phrase had a reassuring sound as she repeated it to herself. She was safe so long as she didn't move. She would still live in it. Just don't move. She closed her eyes. She had no fear of falling asleep in her precarious position. She just wanted to get away for a moment.

There was no sound, except the sounds of the sea and forest. Nothing to threaten her, but nothing to save her either. Pix must have assumed Faith had gotten a phone call or held up some other way. But by now surely even unsuspicious Pix would have begun to wonder and come after her.

Faith leaned her uninjured cheek against the trunk of the tree, gave her arms a good rub, and settled down to wait.

But it wasn't Pix who rescued her.

"Mrs. Fairchild? Mrs. Fairchild? Are you all right? Faith? Where are you?" It was Nan Hamilton, and never had a voice sounded so welcome.

"I'm up here—in a tree."

If Nan thought that was odd, her voice did not betray it. "Well, deah, just keep talkin', and I'll follow your voice. We were afraid you were hurt in the fog."

Faith shuddered as she started to climb down, thinking of what Nan might have stumbled across if it hadn't been for the pine.

"Can you tell where I am?" she said loudly, and kept talking. "Someone was following me and wouldn't answer when I called out, so I climbed a tree until they went away."

Nan was close enough for Faith to see her now.

"Now I call that real smart," she said, and much to Faith's surprise folded her in an ample hug. "We'd better keep going to your house and call Pix. She was in quite a dither. Why, you're about frozen! Put this on and let's get you home." Nan wrapped Faith in a huge sweater that smelled pleasantly of pancakes, wood smoke, and balsam. She hadn't forgotten to retrieve her own sweater in her climb down, and she flung that on too. She was still cold.

Faith felt so relieved to be both alive and out of the tree that it didn't occur to her to ask what Nan was doing at the Millers' until they got to the porch. The door was shut, and if someone was waiting for them inside, he'd have to deal with both of them. It was a reassuring idea.

Nan spoke before Faith could ask.

"I came over here to give you some mushrooms I'd dried. Thought you might be a little restless with all the fog. I saw the car and knew you couldn't be far away, so I went over to Pix's. She was just starting to get nervous and about to call Earl, but I said I'd take a look."

"I hope you don't think I've imagined the whole thing," Faith told her, beginning to feel as if she might have.

"No, deah, I don't think you've dreamed it all up. Wish you had." She looked solemn. "I can't remember a time when the island has been like this. Everybody looking at everybody else like they don't know who they are. And you've got a nasty cut we'd better wash." Faith stood still while Nan gently bathed her cut. She was feeling like a five-year-old about to get a cookie after skinning a knee. It was a lovely feeling.

She went into the kitchen and picked up the offending loaves lying all ready on the counter.

"Why don't you come back to Pix's and have a late lunch with us?" Faith didn't want Nan to leave yet.

"I think I will, thank you. Nothing but Freeman at home, and all he wants to do in weather like this is mend his traps and sleep. Not terrible interestin' for me."

They took the car. There was no way Faith was going back into the woods except in the clear light of day, and maybe not even then.

Pix rushed out of the house. "Oh, Faith, thank God you're all right! You can't imagine what was going through my mind!"

Faith could and had.

Over lunch the three women speculated on who could possibly have been following Faith and why. After a quick exchange of glances and a slight nod toward the quilting books, they told Nan about Matilda's quilt and the map.

"It sounds like her. Mind you, she was a friend. Maybe because we weren't related and she couldn't boss me around. But she had a peculiar streak in her. Like leaving the house to those two boys. That was just orneriness. Same thing with the gold. If she had it, she should have given it to her nieces and nephews. Fine people, most of them, and they work hard for a living, every day. Would have been pretty glad of some extra money."

Faith tried not to picture the gold this way—a Prescott legacy. She pushed the image back toward her id and away from her usually high-minded super-ego.

Nan had stopped talking and appeared to be lost in thought. "I don't know who was following you, Faith, but I have a hunch if you find the gold or whatever it is Matilda hid, you'll be a lot safer."

"My sentiments exactly," agreed Pix. "You know the island so well, Nan. Why don't you have a look at the squares and see what you make of them?" She went to the closet and took down the bread crumbs. Fortunately she had taken the precaution of wrapping the photos in a Baggie, so Faith did not have to touch the crumbs. They spread them out on the table. Pix had labeled each one, and they told Nan how they had followed the map as indicated by the squares.

"She was a very smart woman," Nan commented admiringly. "But I didn't know she was this smart. She was spry until a few years ago, so she must have had a lot of fun running around the island and figuring out her clues."

She paused at number seventeen. "Why doesn't Rail Fence have a name to it?"

"Oh! You're wonderful! We couldn't find it," Pix exclaimed.

Nan pointed a finger at number fourteen. "I've never seen a Jacob's Ladder like this one, but they are different in other parts of the country."

"But Matilda would have used one she was familiar with. Oh, Pix, you don't think we've been wrong about these!" Faith turned a stricken face toward her friend. She had felt they were virtually at the end of their quest.

"Maybe Jacob's Ladder, but not the others. The

names have fit the clues. And anyway, we know White House Steps. That's the most important part, and I'm sure about it. Nan, can you think of a white house on that part of Prescott Point?"

"I know the very house she's thinking of. Only it's not there anymore."

Pix and Faith looked at each other, crestfallen.

"Which house was it? Did it burn or was it moved?" Pix asked. Houses were moved routinely on the island as fortunes rose and fell.

"Neither. It just fell down and most of the lumber got hauled away. Belonged to Clifford Prescott. It wasn't even a white house. It was gray, but it got that nickname in the forties. FDR was yachtin' up here and they hailed Clifford when he was out lobsterin'. Wanted to buy eighty pounds of lobster. Clifford was a friendly sort, and he got to chatting with them and gave the President some special lobsters as a gift and got a thank-you note from The White House. He was right proud of that letter. Had it framed on the wall. That was when people started calling Clifford's house the Prescott White House. He loved the joke, and Matilda must have too."

"That's a great story," Faith said. She was in the mood for a cheerful story or two.

"If the house caved in, it's possible that the steps are still there." Pix was thinking out loud.

"Of course," Faith agreed eagerly. Nan looked a bit wary.

"Just be careful," she said. "Now I'd better get home or Freeman will try to make his own supper, and there's no tellin' what the mess will be like." She looked at Faith. "I hear you don't think much of island cookin'. You have to come over and have a meal with us sometime. I'm not a bad cook, if I do say so. The two best cooks on the island are two sisters. Had a restaurant in their old farmhouse. You may remember it, Pix, South Beach Farm? It was too popular and they got worn out, had to close. But that was some good."

Faith blushed. Had her distaste at the casserole supper been so obvious? She remembered all the good smells in Nan's kitchen and didn't doubt her expertise.

"A lot of the food at the supper we went to was delicious—the baked beans, the biscuits, and the desserts. I don't care much for casseroles," Faith said apologetically. "I hope you don't think I don't appreciate the island."

"Well," Nan admitted, "some of those casseroles the girls got from magazine recipes, and I never did lean that way myself."

She turned at the door. "By the way, those were Freeman's beans."

Nan left, and Faith decided to spend the night. The idea of going back to the cottage alone was both terrifying and exhausting.

After supper they put Ben to bed, popped some corn, and played Trivial Pursuit, to Samantha's infinite delight. Faith reminded her that this was a once-in-a-blue-moon occasion and she would always detest all forms of board games. She also enjoined her to secrecy. If Tom discovered she had played Trivial Pursuit, then backgammon, Othello, parcheesi, Chutes and Ladders, whatever, would not be far behind. It was pleasant to sit and be beaten, basking in the ordinariness of the situation, but when she climbed into bed at last, she was aware that her arms still ached from being treed, her cheek was sore, and she was still afraid. Pix had suggested reporting it to Earl, but Faith wanted to forget the whole thing. She wasn't going to be alone anymore and she'd be leaving soon. She wasn't sure if she was happy or not at the prospect. So many loose ends remained, but today's intimate experience with a spruce had given her a longing for impersonal sidewalks and forests of skyscrapers of her childhood.

When Ben came in and jumped on her bed the next morning, thrilled with the novelty of sleeping in a different house, Faith noticed at once that the fog, as predicted, had gone wherever it goes. It was a perfect Maine day.

She got up and dressed hurriedly. She wanted to look for the White House steps, and she had a lot to do to get ready for Hope and Quentin. They had said late afternoon, but that could mean virtually anytime between two o'clock and midnight.

After bolting breakfast, Pix and Faith climbed into the Woody and set off on the trail. They drove straight to the area of Prescott Point where they had been on Saturday. After driving up and down the road searching fruitlessly, they finally admitted there was no indication of where the road to the White House was, or had been. Nothing suggested Jacob's Ladder either and they agreed the square could have been mistakenly identified.

They'd have to get in touch with Nan to find the old road and since she didn't have a phone, that meant going to her house. Pix volunteered to do it while Faith went back to the cottage. It was impossible to feel apprehensive with such a blue sky.

As Faith was dropping her off and fetching her son, she took a deliberately cheerful view. "The Hamiltons are bound to know where the road is, and it won't take me too long to get things in order. Quentin can always remake the bed if my hospital corners aren't taut enough. Call me and we can re-

sume the search. Ben shouldn't be a problem."
Samantha was with Arlene for a joyful reunion after
their fog-induced separation.

"Don't worry, I'll call the moment I have any
news. Oh Faith, isn't this exciting! Even if it's not
the gold, we've solved the puzzle."

Pix phoned a half hour later. "Nobody's home!
I'm so disappointed. I'll go back in an hour or so
and keep checking until I find them. They can't
have gone far. Freeman says the last time he went
off island was in 1979. Hasn't needed to since. Nan
does go up to Ellsworth to shop occasionally."

"Well, let's hope she didn't go today. Talk to you
later."

It was almost four o'clock when Pix called again.
"Still nobody home!" she cried. "Should I wait until
tomorrow?"

"Why don't you try once more at dinnertime, island dinnertime that is? And maybe by then Hope
and Quentin will be here and can help us hunt."

"All right, I'll let you know one way or the other."

At five o'clock Hope and Quentin pulled up to the
cottage in the Jeep Cherokee they had rented. Faith
grabbed Ben and rushed out to meet them. Hope
was getting out of the car in one swift motion. It was
the way she did most things. Like her mother. They
didn't look the same, but they moved the same way.
Women who knew where they were going.

Faith hugged her sister warmly and turned her
cheek to Quentin. It wasn't an air kiss, but it wasn't
a big smacker either and that pretty much summed
Quentin up. Nothing in excess. He and Hope
looked as if they had just stepped out of the J. Crew
catalogue. Faith knew for certain that everything
Hope was wearing was brand-new, but it could just

as well have been sailing in Newport for years. And Quentin's jacket was either an old favorite of his father's handed down or the equivalent at a price. Dressed for the part, they were delighted to be there.

"We've been having such fun, Fay. Maine is wonderful!"

"But the last few days were a bit foggy, don't you think?"

Hope and Quentin looked at each other in astonishment.

"Foggy? They've been the best of our trip. We were out sailing all day yesterday and the sun never stopped shining."

Of course.

"Are you hungry? Why don't we go in and get something to drink and sit on the porch? I have a nice 1987 Bertani Catullo white chilling and some tidbits to go with it," Faith proposed.

"I'm sure you do. We stopped for clams at Beal's, but I can eat again. How about you, honey?" Quentin said. He was very appreciative of Hope's sister's talents. Hope herself had firmly told him her own culinary expertise involved knowing which number to dial.

"We have been eating like pigs. Lobster, clams, all those biscuits and pies, but it's vacation, so lead me to the trough." She was on a permanent diet. The Sibley side of Faith and Hope's family were tall and also had what was referred to kindly as "big bones." Hope's skin had been stretched tightly, but not too tightly, over those bones so far, and with her dark hair and deep-green eyes—the only ones in the family, to Faith's chagrin—the hearts Hope Sibley did not cause to quicken in fear over her business acumen quickened for more pleasurable reasons. Quentin was tall too, although less exotic in appearance: light brown hair, brown eyes. Just your average, run of the mill, good-looking-enough-for-any-ad-campaign-from-Dior-to-Dewars kind of guy. They made a nice couple.

They settled onto the porch and took turns retrieving Benjamin from trying to climb onto the Jeep's hood. He had settled into car worship and Faith had to keep her car locked at all times after once discovering him at the wheel, steering away and screeching in imitation of squealing tires.

Quentin seemed to find it all very amusing, and Faith and Hope exchanged looks of relief. Quentin did not have a great deal of experience with children. None, in fact, and viewed the whole notion of parenthood with fear and loathing. There was no question of avoidance, he had told Faith once as she was cleaning spit up off his linen suit in Ben's earlier days. The line must continue, but preferably out of sight with a good nanny. Hope felt almost the same way, with moments of thaw when Ben was particularly winsome.

Faith raised an eyebrow in inquiry and glanced in the direction of her sister's ring finger. Hope shook her head slightly. She didn't seem worried about when and if Quentin would pop the question. He could do no wrong.

They began to eat the gravlax Faith had made with the salmon from Sonny Prescott and dill from the Millers' garden. There was dark-brown bread to go with it, and Faith had heated up some tiny chèvre tarts, in case anyone was still hungry.

"Delicious! And we certainly wouldn't need dinner after all this." Hope leaned back against Quentin, sitting on the stair above.

"Speak for yourself. I always need Faith's dinners," he protested.

"Me too," Faith said. "Besides, we'll eat later, after Ben is in bed. Anyway, it's a simple meal, a bourride, some salad—"

Hope sat up. "And now, sister dear," she said, fixing Faith with that gimlet eye usually employed in sizing up a building, or individual, in her capacity as a real estate appraiser for Citibank, "tell all, and I do mean all—not the edited-for-Mother-and-Father version."

Faith had sandwiched a brief mention of finding Roger's body between glorious descriptions of the flora and fauna of the Maine coast in a letter to her parents. After finding Bird's body, she had decided not to say anything more and confined herself to postcards of lighthouses and sunsets with brief messages about the weather.

"I know you found some poor drowned man's body on the beach, Fay, but knowing you I figured there had to be a whole lot more going on."

Her sister was smart. But where to begin and where to stop? She gave an only slightly edited version of the last few weeks, and had just gotten to Bill Fox's suicide when the phone rang.

"I hope that's Pix," Faith cried, and ran inside.

It was.

"Faith, I had just about given up. They weren't home again. Then on my way back, I passed them on Route 17 and waved them over to the side. They'd been at Nan's sister's house helping her pack. She's moving to her daughter's in Granville or maybe it's South Beach."

"Pix! Tell me about it later! Did they know where the road was?"

"Of course, and what's more we all drove over there and I know where it is now too. Is your sister there yet?"

"Yes, and there's just enough daylight to go and have a look. I haven't had a chance to tell them about it, but I'll fill them in on the way. Can you meet me there in ten minutes?"

"Of course. See you then."

Faith ran back to the porch and hastily told Quentin and Hope about the quilt.

"Are you making this all up to entertain us?" Quentin asked reasonably. "If so, it's very kind of you and a lot of fun—especially after the tale of horrors you've been relating."

"I swear it's true," Faith protested.

They were still claiming disbelief as they got into the Jeep while Faith threw some shovels, trowels, a pick, and a crowbar—all easily to hand in the Thorpe cottage's well-equipped barn—into the back. Soon they were headed off to Prescott Point. Ben chortled with joy at riding in the Jeep and made little *vroom-vroom* noises all the way there.

Pix was waiting by the side of the road.

"We have to walk in. A car can't get through anymore, but the Hamiltons said to follow the remnants of this stone wall and we'd end up where the house used to be. Maybe Jacob's Ladder was meant to look like a stone wall."

Quentin swung Benjamin up on his shoulders and they set off. It was easy going at first; then they had to pick their way through a dense mass of alders. They emerged into what had obviously once been a clearing and looked across to a heap of fallen boards in an old cellar hole. The stairs were almost intact and looked odd leading to the pile of dereliction behind them.

"That's it! Those are the stairs! Come on, let's look for ferns."

Quentin and Hope clearly believed Faith had gone mad and taken her neighbor and friend with her, but they decided to humor her. After all, there *could* be money involved. They walked purposively over to the steps and fanned out to look for ferns.

A few minutes later Quentin, with Ben, his adoring disciple, in tow, strolled over to Faith. "This is a fern, isn't it?" he asked, waving a giant frond at her.

"Yes! Where did you find it?"

"Over there"—he waved his hand—"by that fence."

"Faith!" Pix screamed. "Rail Fence!" This was no lighthearted scavenger hunt now.

They all raced over to the fence.

"Then," said Faith slowly, "the treasure must be buried under this pine." She looked up at the towering tree, starting to merge with the sky in the dusky twilight. She was developing quite an affection for the pines of the Pinetree State. "It's the only one standing alone." Matilda's clues had been perfect.

They circled the base of the tree. Quentin handed Ben over to Faith and began to dig in a few places. The earth was packed solid.

"I think we ought to come back with a metal detector," he suggested. "There's no telling how deep this thing is buried, if it's here at all."

"It's here," Faith and Pix chorused.

Hope had been looking at a piece of ground between two exposed roots. "Why don't you try this spot, darling? This would be where I would have hidden something; then I'd have these roots to guide me if I ever wanted to dig it up again."

Sensible, very sensible.

Quentin started to dig, and at two feet the tip of

the shovel hit something. He removed some more dirt, and Faith took the hand trowel and carefully scraped away the rest. After a long five minutes, she lifted a small tin box out of the hole.

They stood in silence and gazed at it before Pix said, "Workbox," and Faith nodded. Perhaps none of them, not even Faith and Pix, had ever been sure that there would be something there. And here it was—a small box, the black paint worn away in spots with some gold-painted trim still visible around the edge. It had a padlock that was intact.

"Prosperity," whispered Faith. It was all too much.

"Well, well," commented Quentin, "I guess we don't need the crowbar for this baby. I can probably pry it open with my hands. That lock must be pretty rusty."

"No," cried Faith. "We want to save it." She had the feeling that breaking open the box was somehow a desecration. "There are thousands of keys in a drawer at the cottage, and if those don't work, there's always the bobby-pin method. Come on, let's go."

"Oh my God." Pix put her hand to her mouth. "I forgot all about Samantha. She's waiting at the bridge. Arlene's mother took them to the Bangor Mall today and was going to drop her this side of the bridge to wait for me, since she had to pick up the other kids at six. I've got to go! Faith, would it be too much to ask if you could wait until I got there to open it? Yes, of course it is. Just open it, don't wait."

"Of course we'll wait. It's yours just as much as it's mine."

Hope and Quentin looked a bit disappointed. Quentin, ever gallant, reassured Pix, "Of course we can wait. We didn't even know about it until an hour ago, so we can certainly wait another few minutes. How long did you say it would take you to get your daughter?"

"I'll be back in a flash," promised Pix, and she was off.

Faith was feeling slightly dazed. They walked slowly back to the road and she gave the box a shake or two. No coins rattled, but it was heavy.

"That's an old cash box," Hope told her knowledgeably. "You wouldn't use it to keep your buttons in."

"You don't know New Englanders. It could just as well be string too short to be saved or something like that," Faith rejoined, but Hope's positive identification increased her already wildly spiralling expectations.

They got back to the cottage and Faith looked around for a place to put the box. She set it on the table in the living room, but immediately picked it up and put it in one of the desk drawers instead. Who knew how long Pix might be? It was more temptation than anyone should have to bear to have it in plain sight.

"I'm going to feed Benjamin, and why don't you two go through the keys from the junk drawer in the kitchen and sort out all the small ones? That's not opening the box. If we don't do something, we'll go crazy." She walked about snapping on lights. It was after seven o'clock and getting dark.

She went into the kitchen and put Ben in the high chair she'd found in the attic and sprinkled a few Cheerios kept for that purpose on the tray to keep him from screaming the place down, since his dinner had not instantly appeared. Hope followed her and took the whole drawer out to the other room to rummage through with Quentin.

"How about a drink?" Faith called to them.

"Fay," came Hope's voice—or some approximation of it; this was not her usual strident tone, more like a gasp. "Fay, you'd better come in here."

Faith dropped the zucchini she was cutting into strips onto Ben's tray and went into the living room. They must have found a key, she thought.

But they hadn't. What they had found was Eric—standing in the shadows by the huge fieldstone fireplace that filled up one end of the room. Standing with a gun pointed at them with unmistakable intent.

Eric. Of course, Eric.

The only possibility—and the most obvious. That part was now clear. What wasn't was why.

Speculation could come later. She had to do something. Anything was worth a try. "Eric, what on earth are you doing? Did you think these were intruders? This is my sister, Hope, and her friend, Quentin."

"Pleased to meet you," Eric drawled, suddenly reverting to his Texas youth. "But it's no mistake, Faith. Give me whatever it was you got at Prescott Point. Awful nice of you to go to so much trouble finding it for me."

Pix would be coming back, and the noise of the car might startle him enough so Faith could catch him off guard. She moved as close as she dared to the table, which had a large oil lamp on it. She could heave it at him, if he would only look away. She was damned if she was going to give him the box after all their work and especially before they even knew what was in it. There were three of them, after all. There must be some way of getting the gun. She had to stall. Keep him talking.

"Now, Eric, I'm sure you don't want to hurt any-

238

one. Not after all that has happened. Why don't we look inside the box together and decide what to do?" It was feeble, yet it might distract him.

"I *know* what to do. It's you folks who don't. Fetch the box, Faith dear, while junior here gets some rope from the barn. The Thorpes have a pile of it inside the door. Then I'll be on my way and you won't be tied up for long. Somebody is sure to come along one of these days." He laughed unpleasantly. "Now get going. Both of you and I'll keep sis here for company."

He walked over to Hope and grabbed her, placing the gun against her temple. Quentin took a step toward them and Eric cocked the gun.

"Don't think about any noble gestures. Hurting people doesn't particularly bother me."

Quentin gave Hope an anguished look and went out the front door toward the barn.

"Now you, Faith."

Faith took the box from the drawer and Eric uncocked the gun, but did not release his hold on Hope.

"Put it on the floor in front of me and then go back to where you were," he directed her.

There was still time. Quentin's return could divert him; meanwhile talk. Say anything, just keep him talking and off guard.

Faith stared Eric squarely in the face. "You did it, didn't you? Sabotaged the boat. Murdered Bird?"

"Shut up, Faith." His face clouded briefly. "Dumb-ass Roger. If he hadn't been so pure, he'd still be alive. And he was going to marry her, that cunt. He couldn't see what she was like. Anyone would have been better. But he just kept raving about finally finding each other. Made me puke."

The house. He was in love with the house.

"You're leaving your house? After all you said it meant?"

"Yeah, that's a bitch. But I can't take it with me and anyway I'm going to be able to buy any house I want with what's in this box."

Quentin was back and Eric immediately cocked the gun and tightened his grip on Hope.

"Tie Faith up and don't waste any time, then you can do your girlfriend here. You might even enjoy it," he leered.

Quentin started over toward Faith and just as he began to loop the rope around her wrists, the front door swung open.

Sonny Prescott walked in, not Pix. He must have come by boat, since they hadn't heard a car.

Sonny looked at Eric and the box on the floor, then at the rest of them frozen in various poses around the room.

Faith had never been so glad to see him in her life, not even the day he had called and said he had fresh salmon.

"Sonny!" she warned. "He's got a gun, be careful!"

Eric smiled slowly. "Oh, I don't think old Sonny here has to worry. You see, he's with me."

Ten

It was a nightmare. The kind where the steady ground under your feet turns out to be quicksand and you can't take a step. Sonny! Sonny and Eric!

And what made it worst of all was now there were two to deal with.

Faith frantically tried to figure out how she could do something. If only the light switch wasn't so far away—she could use the element of surprise to get the gun. It wasn't just the box now. The idea of Eric getting away free made her furious.

She was sure Eric didn't plan on killing them, but he might not mind an injury or two.

Ben's angry cries of starvation from the kitchen presented an unlikely solution.

"Go get your brat and shut him up—and don't think about leaving, unless you want to be Mommy and Daddy's only little girl."

Faith raced into the kitchen and grabbed Ben. She filled a bottle, left from Zoë's stay, with juice and grabbed a large handful of cookies. It was no time to be thinking of the four basic food groups. Then she quietly opened the back door and put Ben in the portable crib on the porch, zipping closed the mesh screening on top. Ben settled right down, charmed by vestigial memories of happy nursing days. She ran back in and took a large cast-iron frying pan from the pantry. Most New England kitchens were a veritable arsenal of utensils. She paused to lift the receiver on the ancient dial phone, found the phone dead, as she had suspected, stood behind the door, and started screaming.

Ben was safely out of the way for the moment and if she could manage to get rid of one of them, the other wouldn't be able to leave his post to search for the baby. Eric had obviously been watching a lot of B movies and Faith had no doubt he would use Ben as a hostage if he decided he needed one.

She thought of Roger and Bird and Bird's father and Zoë and Bill—all the sadness and horror of the past month. She screamed in real anguish. It felt wonderful.

The door swung open and Sonny stepped in. Before he had a chance to look around, Faith swung too—bringing the frying pan down on top of his head with all her strength. He crumpled to the floor with a resounding "thunk." She felt for a pulse, was reassured, and started to tie his wrists together with some clothesline from the pantry, which she was beginning to regard as King Midas's storeroom.

Eric's voice interrupted her.

"Faith, if you don't get in here right now, I'm going to shoot your sister."

He meant it. Faith could tell. He hadn't added any extraneous lines.

"Fay," implored Quentin. "Fay, please, hurry!"

The crisis rivaled the tragic benchmark of young Quentin's life to date—the time in October 1987 when the computer was down just before the market closed.

Faith hurried in. What did they think? She was

going to let her own sister die because of a nick-name and a few hundred other things that had happened in childhood?

Eric again had Hope in a stranglehold with the gun up against the side of her head. The box was under his arm. He waved Faith over to the table.

"I guess I have to assume I'm on my own now," he said in a matter-of-fact voice, which, to Faith's surprise, held no anger. That fight at the dance had been too real to be staged. Maybe he really did hate Sonny's guts. Maybe he just wasn't good at sharing.

He moved quickly toward the door. When he got there, he pushed Hope to one side and as he did so, the box slid to the floor and opened, spilling its contents all over—contents that appeared to be letters and some kind of currency.

Just then they heard a car pull up. Pix—and Samantha—ready for the end of a treasure hunt.

Eric grabbed Hope again and turned out the lights.

"Don't answer the door and keep quiet!" he hissed at them.

The door opened.

"Eric? Sonny? Anybody heah? I found the note and set off right away."

Eric turned the lights on. It was Margery Prescott.

Things were informal on Sanpere, but this was getting ridiculous, Faith thought. Did the Thorpes have this many unexpected guests when they inhabited the cottage? And who would be dropping by next? Jill? More Prescotts? Were they all in on this?

"Pick up the papers on the floor and let's get the hell out of here," Eric directed Margery. He let Hope go and she gave him a poisonous look, which had no effect whatsoever.

"Where's Sonny?" Margery asked as she stuffed everything back in the box.

Eric grinned nastily. How could she ever have liked him? Faith wondered.

"He's out cold in the kitchen. Maybe you'd better go make sure he stays that way."

"What!" exploded Faith. This was too much for her to keep her mouth shut.

"You just saved us the trouble of doing it off-shore."

Margery looked at Eric with adoration and nodded. Margery and Eric? Marjorie Main and Douglas Fairbanks?

"Margery, how can you trust him? He's killed three people. Now look what he's doing to Sonny. Just what do you think he's going to do to you once he's away and doesn't need your help?"

"That's where you're wrong, Faith. I'll never be finished with Margery. Never have. We go back a long way. Business partners who got friendly. And I didn't kill three people, did I, honey?"

Margery laughed. It was truly repulsive.

"No, Margery here took care of Bird. Took care of her very well."

Faith began to feel sick. She saw the scene in the cabin projected on the living room walls. All that blood and hate. It had been Margery who had hated that beauty so much.

It was beyond horror. Faith felt completely overwhelmed by the evil in the room.

"Margery and I are going to take our business to a new location. Maybe north. Maybe south."

Business. Did Margery have talent as a potter? Faith looked at her strong hands and stubby fingers. She certainly would be able to wedge a lot of clay.

"Can you really go back to making pots after all

this?" She was stunned. Did Eric actually think he could start production again, even under an assumed name? He must really be mad.

"Pots?" Eric laughed. "Not pots, but pot. Pot—and other things—in with the lobsters in those nice big trucks of Sonny's. Lobsterpot. Not floats—the real thing." He was enjoying himself. Showing off for Margery, who rewarded him with an affectionate grin.

The night noises, all that action in the cove. It finally made sense. Too late.

Margery stood up to go to the kitchen.

"Bring the baby back with you. He's out there somewhere, probably asleep, since he isn't yowling. We'll forget about tying anybody up. Instead, I think we'd better take him and his auntie for a short boat ride to make sure these folks don't decide to follow us too soon or do something else stupid like call the police."

"His auntie" directed her "this-is-just-about-enough" look at Ben's mother. The steady gaze was as plain as skywriting on a cloudless day.

As Margery walked by, Hope tripped her and delivered a forceful, lightning-swift chop to the back of her neck, at the same time grabbing her left arm and twisting it in a way it was never meant to go. Faith didn't stay still to watch. As soon as Hope moved, she threw the oil lamp at Eric, ran over and jumped on him, brought her right knee up sharply between his legs, and wrestled the gun from his surprised hand.

Only slightly flushed, and firmly astride Margery's lumpy, cursing body, Hope called out to Faith, "Aren't you glad I signed us up for those self-defense courses, Fay?"

It was a sister act nonpareil.

Eric was lying on the floor moaning and writhing in pain. Faith stood over him with the gun aimed at his chest. She was in no doubt about the location of his heart—only of its existence. Quentin, somewhat stunned, knelt beside Hope. "Darling," he said with a note of awe in his voice, "will you marry me? Soon?"

"Of course!" She beamed at him radiantly.

Faith hated to be a wet blanket, but they did have two murderers and a drug trafficker to attend to before any epithalamic toasts could be raised.

"Quentin, you go for the police, but first see how Sonny is. Oh, and Ben too. He's on the porch."

Quentin returned immediately with the news that both Sonny and Ben were oblivious. He tied Margery securely, then Hope helped him with Eric, lovingly clover-hitching him to one of the more uncomfortable chairs in the cottage. Faith kept a steady aim and hoped she didn't have to fire any shots. Goodness knows what that would do to their security deposit.

"If Margery took Sonny's truck, there's a CB in it and you can call for help. Do you know how to work one?"

Quentin, who despite his flush of joy was beginning to feel a tad inadequate, hastened to assure Faith that a CB was something he was capable of handling. Hope went out into the kitchen, finished tying Sonny up, and dragged him into the living room so they could keep an eye on him.

"I moved Ben inside, Faith. Do you want him in here?"

"No, he's fine where he is and this room is beginning to get badly overcrowded."

Quentin returned. "I reached your Sergeant Dickinson. He seemed pretty surprised. I had to repeat everything twice."

Eric and Margery, after some foul-mouthed moments, had subsided into bitter silence. Faith had placed a chair by the door and was sitting in it with the gun aimed and cocked. She felt like Annie Oakley.

Three deaths. Three shattered lives. For what? Money? In Margery's case, love? Money! Faith sat up straight.

"Hope, let's see what's in the box! I don't know what has happened to Pix and Samantha, but I'm sure they wouldn't blame us for looking after all this."

"And it *is* already open," her sister agreed.

She and Quentin sat as close as possible on the couch and sorted through the contents. Quentin was making a neat stack of the currency.

"Sorry, sister-in-law to be, it's a bundle, but it's Confederate money. Still, not completely without value."

"As wallpaper?" Faith proposed. She was trying hard not to be desperately disappointed.

"Here's a letter, Fay, from Matilda. I'll read it out loud to you:

To Whoever Finds This Box:

I hope you had a good time figuring out my quilt. I had a lot of happy hours planning it and don't intend to die until it's finished. You probably expected the gold, unless it's already been found, but that's someplace else fun. You have to forgive an old woman her amusements.

Please give the top two papers to my nephew,

Sonny Prescott, who is my executor. Tell him he's to call a family meeting and decide what to do with the land. I never wanted anyone to know I had it or I would have been pestered to death years ago by real estate agents and developers. If no one ever finds this box, that would be all right too. Maybe the Point would remain the way it is. I'd like to see it stay unspoiled, but I know this may not be possible. Anyway, I won't be around to know about it.

As a prize for figuring out an Old Maid's Puzzle, the rest of the contents of the box is yours. Sorry I can't be there to shake your hand.

Yours respectfully,
Matilda Louise Prescott

Hope scanned the two remaining papers.

"They're old deeds, all right. What is this 'Point' she refers to? Is it big? Because these seem to indicate a large property." And Hope should know, Faith reflected.

Before she could answer her sister, Margery broke in.

"Gorry, the Point! Deeds to the whole thing! We're rich!" She appeared to have forgotten that she was tied up, awaiting the police and charges of murder, attempted murder, and drug trafficking. Faith was also pretty sure that Sonny wouldn't be giving Margery so much as a green stamp once he found out about her passion for Eric.

The thought must have occurred to Eric, too.

"What do you mean *we're* rich?" he spat out. "Sonny and all the rest of those damn Prescotts are rich. And this is what I've been busting my ass to find—a bunch of papers for Sonny? That old witch! She swore she had the gold and was hiding it. I should have made her talk before I . . ." He stopped speaking abruptly and clamped his mouth shut.

"Before you what, Eric? Before you killed her too?" Faith was sure that was what he had intended to say.

Margery raised her head off the floor. Her cheek was imprinted with the mark of the braided rug she was lying on. It stood out against the rest of her face, which had paled.

"Eric! You killed Sonny's aunt?" It was one thing to murder strangers and off-islanders, but family?

As Faith was endeavoring to run this perverted morality through her mind, Sonny came around at last. Either the fact that he could be rich, his aunt's murder, or both had doused him like a faceful of cold water.

"What's going on? Why are we all tied up?"

Before Faith could get to the explanations, there was a loud knock on the door and Sergeant Earl Dickinson strode in. He moved his head slowly, taking in the full sweep of the room.

"Judas Priest, I heard it and I couldn't believe it. I'm seeing it and I still don't."

The giant Ferris wheel, crown jewel of Smokey's Greater Shows, rose high above the fairgrounds, silhouetted against Blue Hill. Ben had had several rides on the merry-go-round. Now it was Faith and Tom's turn for some fun.

People were still getting into the bottom car, and the Fairchilds were suspended at the top of the wheel. Below them, Pix, holding Ben, was waving and trying to direct his attention skyward. He was more interested in the gears of the machine that moved the wheel.

"I love Ferris wheels," Faith said, sitting as close as possible to Tom.

"Me, too. And I've never been on one with such a magnificent view before." He gestured toward the bay, which looked like another fairground, its flat expanse reflecting the moon in tiny spots of white light as the current changed.

The gondola swayed and the wheel began to turn. Down they swept past the Millers and Ben, past the midway, the animal barns, the 4-H Beef Show, the State of Maine Two-Crusted Blueberry Pie Contest goods lined up in the exhibition hall, the John Deere booth, and the grandstand where people were patiently waiting for Joie Chitwood's Auto Thrill Show to start.

Faith was content. Pix had sworn there was a concession run by a local grange that served up a perfect lobster stew, and after that there would be fireworks. That last night of the fair. The last night of summer.

The wheel began to slow and soon they were up at the top again, immobile for a brief moment as people got off.

"Hey, honey, wanna neck?" Tom breathed into her ear.

"Okay, but I'd better tell you right now. I go all the way."

"I'm a lucky guy. Do you want to go 'round again?"

"Absolutely, but I think we'd better relieve Pix and Sam. Maybe after we eat."

The wheel lowered them down and they stepped out. Ben began to squeal with delight as soon as he saw them.

"Daddee, Daddee!" Far from having forgotten

Tom, as was feared, Ben would barely let him out of his sight.

"Lead us to that lobster stew, Pix. I'm starving," Tom said as he hoisted Ben up on his shoulders.

"This way. The Fraziers are meeting us there, but I want to get some french fries first."

Pix had been steadily consuming french fries since they arrived. Faith succumbed as well when she saw the sacks of potatoes outside the stands and tasted one of Pix's fries—crisp, fresh, and with a bit of the skin still clinging to it. But douse it with vinegar, as was the local custom, adopted by the Millers, she would not.

The Fraziers were eating corn on the cob, near the French Fry Queen's stand. Louise's chin was shiny with butter and they looked as if they were having their first good time in a long time.

They all made their way together to the picnic tables set up by the grange under a tent. The night air was beginning to assume an autumnal character and it was pleasant to walk into the warm tent filled with the smells of fair food.

They sat down around a big table and ordered lobster stew, biscuits, and coffee. While they were waiting, Jill came in. Jill and Sergeant Dickinson. Faith wasn't surprised. She had expected the full cast of characters to appear—those that were not dead or in jail, that is. They had already seen the Hamiltons at the 3,200-pound six-foot oxen pull and Hope and Quentin were happily wandering the arcades, toting an enormous white bison Quentin had won pitching pennies. This was what "Meet Me at the Fair" was all about. Sooner or later you'd run into everyone you had met all summer.

Faith waved. "Come join us," she called.

"Thank you. We'd be glad to," answered Earl, putting a protective arm around Jill and steering her toward the table. So it was like that.

Jill was the first to bring up what was on everyone's mind.

"Don't think you have to avoid talking about what has happened because of me," she told them. "It's going to take a long time to sort it all out and talking is the only way to do it. To say that I didn't know what Eric was like is a major understatement."

Faith was relieved. She still had a question or two and the people who could supply some of the answers were sitting right there.

"I still can't believe I missed the whole thing," Pix said ruefully. "If Arlene's mother had taken proper care of her tires, she wouldn't have had a flat on the way back from Bangor. I spent all my time driving back and forth from the bridge to the Prescotts', sick with worry about Samantha. Of course, if they hadn't been delayed, I would have had her with me and that wouldn't have been good."

"Or good for you either, sweetheart," Sam said emphatically. "There's no telling what you might have taken it into your head to do."

Faith was afraid they were going to get hopelessly sidetracked on one of the famous Miller tangents. She interrupted.

"You're off duty, Earl, or so it seems." She smiled as she caught him dipping a spoon to taste Jill's chowder. He'd ordered a hamburger. "What were Eric and the Prescotts up to?"

"Well, I figure you have a better right than most to know, Mrs. Fairchild. Anyway, it's no secret now. Sonny Prescott has turned state's evidence and hasn't stopped talking since we got him to Ellsworth. He's pretty sore about Margery. Never knew she was carrying on like that. Come to mention it, quite a few of us were surprised."

"Matilda never liked Margery," Louise commented. "Said she used to poke around the house and attic at night. Looking for that gold, I suppose."

"I think we can forget about the gold. I know it was in that letter in the box you found, but I've been hearing about it since I was a kid, and nobody ever saw it or ever will."

"Don't forget, Earl, somebody over in Penobscot dug up a vase near the Bagaduce river with more than two thousand gold coins inside. It was believed to be pirate gold," Jill reminded him.

"Honey, that was more than a hundred years ago! Any gold around these parts has already been found or is just imagined. Anyway, a lot of people believed Matilda had the gold and I have an idea she liked them to. But that didn't get her killed. No, what got her killed was kindness or foolishness or both."

"What do you mean?" Tom asked. He had a lot of catching up to do and had barely gotten all the people straight. What he did have straight was that his wife had once more unaccountably landed herself and child in danger and been miraculously spared. He squeezed her hand as he fed Ben some stew.

"Matilda's people weren't paying a whole lot of mind to her, and those two young fellows were. She was flattered and got to care for them. Genuine niceness on Roger's part, more than likely, but Eric must have always had his eye on the main chance. I thought he might have burned his house down himself to convince her to leave them hers. But Sonny did that and he's been kicking himself ever since."

"Sonny? Why?" Faith realized she had missed something.

"He was trying to get Eric to leave the island. He tried other things too, but nothing worked."

"So that fight at the dance *was* real." Faith was beginning to put it all together. "He wanted out of the business, right?"

"Ayuh. I'm not saying what he did wasn't wrong, very wrong, especially when you see all the drugged-out kids around this area. Right here tonight—kids who would have been showing the sheep they raised or the jams they put up before all this hit. I blamed the bridge that they built to the mainland, but that's neither here nor there and it was bound to happen one of these days. Pretty hard getting across the reach by boat in the winter."

Now it was Earl who was off.

Faith felt like the lady they had seen at the sheepdog trials earlier. She resisted the impulse to say "come on, Laddie." "But you think Sonny did have some excuse for doing what he did?"

"Not excuse. Reason. He was in big trouble financially. Two summers ago was a bad one for lobsterin' and an especial bad one for Prescott's pound. They had just bought a new six-wheeler when they lost a boat in a storm and then there just weren't any lobsters. That was when Eric came along. Sonny was only going to do it until he got on his feet again, but it was easy money and after a lifetime of strain and struggle, which fishing is, I guess a little easy money like heaven. They landed the bales on some of the small islands offshore, then loaded them into the front of the trucks at the Old Ferry Cove dock, which hasn't been used for years. Then they'd go back to the lobster pool and fill the rest up with lobsters. If they did get stopped, an inspector looking for shorts would never make them unload the whole truck without a pretty good reason. And they were lucky. The drivers didn't know what they were driving and Eric had it all worked out on the New York end. Sonny didn't even see the stuff. He just provided the transport. Andy and his crew from Camden were doing the heavy work."

"But then Sonny wanted to stop," Jill picked up the story. "I was so stupid. I should have known what was going on. I heard them arguing one night. It didn't make any sense to me and when everything else began to happen, I forgot about it." Her voice lowered and she looked away. "I guess it was hard for me to believe Eric could be involved with anything illegal."

"I'm still confused. Why did Eric kill his friend Roger? And why did he have my wife at gunpoint?"

All the pieces had fallen into place and it was Faith who could answer him. "I think Eric was a very selfish person. Enough was never enough. He had a lucrative pottery business, but he started dealing drugs to make more money. Then Matilda left them the house. That would have been fine, so long as it was Roger, but when he found out about Bird and the baby, that was too much. There are so many sad stories here, but Bird's is the saddest. She had finally found Roger after all those years and was looking forward to marriage, motherhood. But Eric couldn't allow that. It also may be that Roger had found out about the drug dealing. Something Eric said the other night suggested that. And Bird probably knew because of Andy. So he sabotaged the boat, no doubt put something stronger in place of what Roger usually smoked, and took off for his friends. He returned grief stricken and oddly enough, I think he was."

"Roger was the only person Eric ever really cared about or let get close," Jill said softly. "Oh, I never fooled myself into thinking he loved me as much as I did him. There was always a distance between us. But he loved Roger, almost like a part of himself—a better part. I remember when Bird came to the island, he was upset. If she and Roger hadn't gotten together, I'm sure Eric would have given up the dealing rather than lose Roger. But since Roger was already lost to him, he just went ahead taking care of himself."

" 'Taking care of himself' is an apt expression," Faith continued. "It was going to be so easy too, before things began to go wrong. He had planned a nice tidy little murder."

No one seemed about to interrupt her and Faith kept a firm grip on center stage. "He'd get the house—which did obsess him—marry Jill, maybe see Margery on the side, maybe still run the drug business, but basically settle down. Then Bird didn't go out in the boat and he had to tie up that loose end. He may not have intended Margery to kill Bird, just find out what she knew. But the deed was done. He had to plant the evidence on Bill Fox, then Andy got picked up and things began to get even more complicated. At some point he must have decided to cut and run, but he wanted to take the gold with him and the key to the whole thing was in my hands. We know he tried to steal the quilt and did take my bracelet," Faith remembered indignantly before winding up her tour de force. "It looks like Margery was getting secondhand goods all the way around—not that I feel particularly sorry for her. She or Eric must have been the person following me in the woods to see if I was on the track of the gold. They were probably following us all week."

"I should never have asked you to bring the quilt over that night," Louise apologized. "Then they would never have known."

"How long have you lived on this island?" her husband demanded. "When does something like a treasure map in a quilt get hushed up?"

Pix shook her head. "I feel like I'm still on that Tilt-a-Whirl ride. The whole summer has been like that. Roger, then Bird, then Bill—and everything finally colliding in your living room, Faith."

"If he hadn't been afraid Andy would talk, he might have stayed, believing that the police thought Bill had killed Bird and Roger. You didn't, did you?" she asked Earl.

"No, we weren't too happy with that one, although it all made sense."

"Sense! Bill would never have killed Bird, never would have killed anybody. Besides, whoever killed Roger had planned to kill Bird at the same time. We were too dense to see what was in front of our faces. Remember? Samantha told us originally Bird was going out in the boat with Roger? And she didn't know how to swim, according to her father. That would have eliminated Bill right away if we had only thought of it."

"I think once Bird was gone, it was only a question of time for Bill," Elliot said. "We've known him for years and there was a dark side to his nature. You mustn't blame yourself."

Tom looked at Faith in annoyance. "You've got the perfect candidate for blame in Eric, and you and your sister, Bat-woman and Robinette, are responsible for his capture. Think about that instead."

"We all trusted him and liked him so much," Sam mused, "it's hard to understand how so many of us could have been taken in."

"He would have been some good as a con man—was in the case of Matilda, conned the house right out from under her and the rest of the Prescotts, then killed her once he was sure she had changed her will," Earl pointed out. "No scruples and a lot of self-importance."

"And what about Sonny? Think how we trusted him! I can't get over someone from the island being involved." Pix looked devastated.

Earl grinned, "You summer people are all alike. Somehow you've dreamed up this idea that Sanpere is like the Garden of Eden before Eve got hungry. Nobody lies, cheats, or steals. We just go along our blameless ways. Every carpenter is a master. Every fisherman gets a good catch. Every woman can make good pie crust and raise prizewinning tuberous begonias. Well, surprise—we're just like other people, good, bad, and mostly in between."

The sergeant was getting more interesting by the moment. Faith wondered whether the combination of boyish charm and good looks plus an interesting philosophy of life was working any magic on Jill. Goodness knew she needed some after Eric.

Sam looked at his watch. "I hate to break this up, but something tells me we're going to be repeating this conversation with some frequency and if we want a good spot for the fireworks, we've got to get going."

"I think I can find you a spot," Earl promised. Rank had its privileges.

Quentin and Hope were waiting by the information booth. Hope was eating cotton candy and feeding it to Quentin. The bison had been joined by a raccoon, or rather a mutant of the species three feet tall, wearing goggles and a vest. All four of them looked disgustingly smug and blissfully happy.

Samantha ran over. "Mom, we want to sit in the grandstand. Is it okay if we meet you after?" She pointed back at Arlene and two gangly boys who were stolidly munching fried dough.

"Why is it always 'Mom'?" Sam complained. "Don't I get a vote?"

"Oh, Daddy, just say yes. They're waiting for me!"

"Yes. But be here at ten-thirty on the dot."

She ran off and Sam looked at Pix. "By the time I get used to having a teenage girl, she'll be in college."

Pix took his arm. "Poor you. It's hard when Daddy's little girl takes her hair out of braids."

"I always liked those braids," Sam muttered.

The spot Earl found for them turned out to be away from the grandstand, across the track that circled the field where the fireworks would be launched. It was safe, but close to the action and away from the lights of the rest of the fair. Tom fetched blankets from the car and they spread them on the damp grass. Faith lay back and put Benjamin on her chest. The stars were beautiful.

"Should start seeing the Northern Lights soon. It's getting to be that time of year," came a familiar voice from the darkness. It was Freeman.

Faith sat up. "I'm glad you found us."

"No, deah, *you* found us," he replied.

"Hush, Freeman. They're staatin'."

They were the best fireworks Faith had ever seen. Even better than the Fourth of July in New York City, though she wasn't about to admit that to anyone.

Two large ships lobbed fiery shots at each other on the ground. Then, just as they were disappearing, the sky above was filled with tiers of brilliantly colored light. Huge chrysanthemums that looked as if they were made of gold dust exploded and drifted lazily down toward the sea.

The whole fair was frozen in intense light.

And every time he heard an explosion, Ben crowed with delight and clapped his hands.

Catherine wheels spun at eye level and an immense American flag rose and fell. Silvery fish darted across the sky accompanied by piercing whistles. Niagara Falls stretched from a trickle to full force across the field, the magnesium illuminating the workers who were darting from one side to another. There was something familiar about the tallest of them, Faith realized. In the intense light, his red hair and beard glowed like sparks from one of the aerial shells.

"Why, that's John," she exclaimed.

"It's a hobby of his. Told me once he'd been doing it since he was a boy. He works for the fireworks company when they need him," Elliot told her.

John Eggleston looked supremely happy, happier than Faith had ever seen him. Soon his image faded back into the night as the set pieces were extinguished and a hushed crowd waited an instant in total darkness for the end of the show.

The finale was orgasmic and a chorus of ohs echoed across the field as volley after volley rocketed into the sky, sending trails of red, gold, white, blue, and green light shimmering across the darkness. Just when everyone thought it was over, another series would begin. It was perfect.

Faith and Tom were nestled close together, Ben wedged between them.

"I love you, darling," Tom whispered.

"I love you, too."

The fireworks continued to tumble across the sky.

Tom gazed up, then put his hand on Faith's cheek and gently but firmly turned her face toward his.

"I've been so worried about you these last weeks. I had no idea what was going on. Please, please promise me you won't ever get involved like this again."

That was easy. Faith put her hand over his, looked him straight in the eye, and swore solemnly, "I promise you I will never find a body in the kelp again."

After all, how much kelp did one normally run across in a lifetime?

Epilogue

From *The Ellsworth American:*
Thursday, Sept. 14

MASSACHUSETTS MINISTER FINDS
KING'S RANSOM IN AUCTION BOX LOT

Aleford, Mass.—Monday night, the Rev. Thomas Fairchild of the Aleford First Parish Church was surprised to discover a cache of gold coins disguised as checkers in a box lot of old games his wife had purchased for him at the August 17th Matilda Prescott estate auction held in Sanpere Village.

The coins have been the object of much speculation for years. Said to have belonged to Darnell Prescott, who died in 1960, the coins also figured in the recent arrest and arraignment of Eric Ashley. Mr. Ashley is alleged to have held several people at gunpoint, Mrs. Fairchild included, in the belief that a different box in their possession held the coins. He is also charged in three separate murders.

The coins, uncirculated 1913 and 1920 Eagles and Double Eagles, had been painted black and red and mixed in with an odd assortment of old checkers pieces. The Rev. Fairchild came upon them as he was sorting out the games.

When reached for comment, the Rev. Fairchild said he was "completely stunned," especially as he had believed the story of the gold coins to be "a bit of island lore." When asked what he planned to do with the coins, valued at roughly half a million dollars, he answered, "That's no problem. My wife and I believe the money belongs to the island, and we are returning it by purchasing the Point for The Island Heritage Trust, saving a small part for a summer house of our own." "The Point" refers to a parcel of land on Sanpere recently offered for sale.

Faith stopped reading aloud and threw the paper down with a gesture of irritation. Who spotted the box? Who bought it? And what about all that work on the quilt? By all rights the coins were hers. And Pix's. Though of course Pix was delighted with Tom's plan.

"Now, Faith, you know you agree with me."

"So what if I do? It would have been nice to dream for a few days. You didn't have to be so definite. We could have let it run through our fingers a while."

The gold was in a safe deposit box at the Shawmut Bank, and Tom had breathed an enormous sigh of relief when it got there. It was volatile enough having Faith in the house.

Faith picked up the paper again, the bold headline stretched across four columns and even farther in her mind. She looked at Tom, who was obviously not enjoying the rain on his parade, and felt a twinge, a very small twinge, of guilt. "Well," she reluctantly conceded, "it's all turned out neatly. The Prescotts have their money, the island has its land, and we have a summer house in Maine. I suppose I'll get used to it, darling—just so long as we go to the Hamptons first for a vacation."

Enter the World of Katherine Hall Page

Katherine Hall Page, one of today's favorite authors, writes the well-loved, critically acclaimed and Agatha Award-winning mystery series featuring Faith Fairchild: transplanted New Yorker, minister's wife, mother of two, renowned caterer, and amateur sleuth. Faith has an uncomfortable habit of innocently entangling herself in murder, and a knack not just for puff pastry, but for unraveling a mystery. From Aleford, Massachusetts, to Boston to Maine to New York to France, Faith grapples with murder, kidnapping, blackmail, and arson, always managing to land on her feet. The pages that follow provide a quick glimpse into Faith's world.

*Faith Fairchild, late of New York City, currently of peaceful Aleford, Massachusetts, is ecstatically happy with her much-loved minister husband, Tom, and infant son, Benjamin. Ecstatically happy, but bored, bored, bored. In Katherine Hall Page's Agatha Award-winning debut, **The Body in the Belfry**, Faith hasn't the faintest suspicion that the dark undercurrents of village life are about to rise to the surface and disturb her dull but pleasant existence . . .*

When Faith announced she was dipping into the small but adequate trust fund set up by her grandfather, "and mine own" she reminded them, to start a catering business, they were amazed. However, nothing daunted, she went forward and *Have Faith* was born. The rest is history, culinary and cultural. As soon as the initial confusion over the name was straightened out—people thought she was a new cult, an escort service for the guilt ridden, or, worst of all, a food service specializing in lenten fare—New Yorkers were vying for her services and she was a year ahead in her bookings. The fact that she had been at their parties as a guest added to the image. Now she supplied not only her beautiful self, but her beautiful food.

By the time Faith met Tom at a wedding she was catering, she had been featured in *Gourmet*, *New York Magazine*, and the *Times*.

Thomas Fairchild was in town to perform the

ceremony for his college roommate. Tom had grown up in Massachusetts on the South Shore. His family was not particularly religious. They went to church every Sunday and the four little Fairchilds regarded it in much the same light as the invariable Sunday dinner that followed, or as playing baseball in the town league or doing well in school. This is what the Fairchilds did. Not with a lot of show, but solid and steady. This was what life was all about. The family had lived in the area for generations and Tom's father's business, Fairchild's Real Estate, had several counterparts: Fairchild's Ford in nearby Duxbury (Tom's uncle) and Fairchild's Market in town (Tom's grandfather and another uncle).

The wedding was a small one in an apartment overlooking Central Park, and if Faith had divined the past and present of the man hovering over the buffet when she went to check on the supply of *saucisson en brioche*, she might have approached with a little trepidation. As it was, all she saw was a terribly attractive, tall, handsome stranger. Always good qualifications. She liked his reddish-brown hair and figured she could get rid of the straggly mustache once she got to know him better. Nobody told her he was the minister and nobody told him she was the caterer. They started to talk.

They were still talking several hours later, huddled under blankets against the February cold, riding in one of those tacky, impossibly romantic horse-drawn carriages around Central Park. If Faith gave an embarrassed thought to what her friends would say if they could see her in one of these, it quickly vanished in the moonlight.

And there was a lot of moonlight.

The mustache came off the next day.

In the days that followed, the actual murder itself was almost eclipsed by the debate that raged within the town over whether Faith should have rung the bell or not. Leading the group that opposed the action was Millicent Revere McKinley, great-great-great-granddaughter of a distant cousin of Paul Revere. It was this progenitor, Ezekiel Revere, who had cast the original bell.

"I don't know what Grandfather would have said," Millicent remarked in a slightly sad but firm tone that went straight to the hearts of many of her listeners—in the post office, the library, the checkout line at the Shop and Save. Wherever she could gather a crowd. Faith grew accustomed to dead silence and slightly guilty smiles when she entered these places.

*In **The Body in the Kelp** ... Faith buys a lovely handmade quilt at an estate sale with her best friend, Pix Miller. But the quilt is not only patchwork; it's a map which leads Faith on a treasure hunt—toward her second taste of murder.*

Faith and Ben ate their sandwiches and wandered out to the receding water. This wasn't a clam flat and there was no mud. Faith held tight to Benjamin's chubby little paw. He was racing toward the water crying, "Swim! Swim!" Faith stuck her big toe in and promptly lost all feeling. She decided her shoes would fit better if she did not get frostbite and managed to steer Ben away from the beckoning deep, over to the tidal pools that had been left behind in the warm sun.

"Sweetheart, we'll go look for little fishes and shells in the pools, okay? We'll swim another day." And in another place, Faith added to herself.

She helped Ben climb up onto the flat ledges that stretched around the Point, and they began to explore the endlessly fascinating pools. At first Ben wanted to jump in or at least stick his hand in right away, but Faith was able to get him to pause and look first—to see the busy world of tiny fish darting among the sea anemones and starfish, small crabs making their way across the mussels and limpets clinging to the pink and orange algae that lined the bottoms of the pools. They went farther away from the beach, carefully avoiding the sharp remains of the sea urchins the gulls had dropped on the rocks and the lacelike barnacles that covered the granite.

"What's that, Ben?" Faith looked up from the life in the pool she had been studying. It looked so arranged, so deliberate, like the pine cones she had found in the woods placed on a mat of gray moss in a star shape with a feather in the middle.

"Wait, honey, I'm coming." She made her way across the flat rock and stood next to Ben, who was crouched and gazing intently at something in a lower pool.

"Man swimming," he said. "Ben wanna swim."

"What man?" Faith started to say before she looked and the question was answered for her.

It was Roger Barnett, draped over the rocks and secured with thick ropes of brown kelp. Small waves were systematically covering and uncovering his head, filling his slackly opened mouth with sea water, fanning his long brown hair against the rockweed. His shirt was gone, and the dark kelp stood out against the unnatural whiteness of his bare arms and chest. His eyes were open and staring straight into the sun. Roger wasn't swimming.

Roger was dead.

*The crème de la crème of Massachusetts elderly go to Hubbard House. In **The Body in the Bouillon,** when a friend of Faith's favorite aunt dies there after hinting to her of scandal, Faith is duty-bound by family affection to investigate. If it means volunteering as a Pink Lady and trying her hand at standard New England cuisine (not her favorite), so be it . . .*

Faith moved behind the desk, which was bare except for a crystal bud vase with a stalk of white freesia in it, and knocked at the door. It was instantly flung open by a small woman of a certain age with pinky-red curls, a navy-blue suit, and a kitty-cat-bowed, fuchsia blouse.

She grabbed Faith by the arm. "Thank goodness you're here! I've been out of my mind trying to get someone. What with Mrs. Pendergast ringing me every other minute from the kitchen and Muriel from the annex, I haven't been able to call my soul my own all morning. Now, come straight along."

It took only two seconds for Faith to decide to keep her mouth shut and follow this woman. She couldn't have asked for a better entry to the workings of Hubbard House than to be mistaken for a worker, and it appeared the job was in the kitchen, so there wouldn't be any bedpans.

She trotted along obediently as the woman sped through the halls and down a flight of stairs, observing that the decor of the living room had been continued throughout, augmented by rows of hunting and botanical prints. It was almost too predictable. She also observed that the place was completely devoid of the smells Faith associated with nursing homes—Lysol, rubber sheets, iso-propyl alcohol, yesterday's cabbage.

Her guide darted through a swinging door and Faith found herself in a cavernous kitchen, not fit-ted out as she would have arranged, but not bad. Presiding over the cuisine was a middle-aged woman of greater than average proportions on any scale. She was stirring something in a huge marmite on the top of the stove, and when she turned around to greet them, Faith was sure the "Mrs." was an honorary title. Faith had never seen a mud fence and had always thought it would be hard to construct one, but "homely as" immediately sprang to mind. Mrs. Pendergast had perhaps tried to compensate for the dun hue of all her features by choosing incongruous black eyeglass frames with rhinestones on the corners, which served only to emphasize the drabness of the rest of her appearance. Still, it suggested a lurking sense of humor—or something. They should get along all right. Two women with the same interest, although at the moment Faith was thinking more of plots than pans.

*In **The Body in the Vestibule,** the Fairchild family (soon to be increased by one) is spending a month in France, where Faith can indulge her passion for French culture, language, and most of all, cuisine. They're having a glorious time . . . until Faith finds a body in the entryway of the apartment. What's even more upsetting is that when she calls in the gendarmes, the body's gone. And no one, not even Tom, believes her . . .*

Faith stood contemplating the group for a moment, then asked, "What is it? What's happening?" No one seemed to be rushing forward to tell her anything.

"Why don't we sit down, sweetheart," Tom said, and led her to one of the chairs left in the living room after the party. The police glanced around in some surprise at the lack of furniture and remained standing.

"Faith, honey," Tom said gently, "there wasn't anything except trash in either of the *poubelles.*"

"What!"

"This is not to say you didn't see the *clochard,*" Tom started to explain, but then the younger of the two policemen interrupted.

"If I may, Monsieur Fairsheeld? I have some English, madame," he explained, and pulled a chair next to hers and sat down, but not before glancing over his shoulder toward his partner. Madame was in a fetching white *chemise de nuit* insufficiently covered by a robe of the same material, her blond hair was delightfully disarranged, and her blue eyes, perhaps even larger than usual at the odd events of the evening, were striking. Madame Fairsheeld had been in bed no doubt and would soon return—it was a prospect with much appeal.

He pulled his chair a bit closer. "First permit me to introduce myself. I am Sergeant Louis Martin and this is Sergeant Didier Pollet." He paused for emphasis. "Madame, what we believe has occurred is of course deeply upsetting. Occasionally, one of these men of the street—we call them *clochards*—will wander into a building and sleep there. Yes, even in the dustbins," he added as she seemed to protest. "Your presence most certainly awakened him, but he was afraid you would berate him, or worse, so he pretended to be asleep and as soon as you left, *phhtt*"—he made one of those French noises impossible to reproduce, accompanied by appropriate gestures with his hands—"out the door. So when we arrive, we find nothing."

*Faith's back in business in **The Body in the Cast**, with a brand-new daughter and a brand-new start in Aleford for her famous New York catering company, Have Faith. She's well on the road to success when she's hired by a movie company to cater their production of* The Scarlet Letter, *to be filmed in quiet little Aleford. But someone's playing nasty tricks, and when it affects Faith's cooking, she just has to get involved . . .*

When more than a minute had passed, Faith tentatively asked the question that had been on her mind since he'd told her what had happened.

"Are you going to have to close me down?"

"I'm supposed to. You know the law as well as I do, probably better."

"Yes, except this was not a result of the caterer in question's actions. I mean, we're not talking salmonella chicken or spoiled mayonnaise here."

"Sort of what I said to the Department of Health."

"And they said?"

"They agreed—after a while. But whether the movie people still want you . . ."

"It would be perfectly understandable if they didn't. I just don't want to be shut down. You can't imagine how grateful I am to you, Charley." Faith would have thrown her arms around the chief, but he wasn't the hugging kind.

Charley still had the notebook out. He was

thinking out loud. "A fire and food poisoning—all within the same hour. Could be one of those movie people is some sort of lunatic. You ever notice any of them behaving more strangely than the rest?" Charley took it for granted all of them were demented in some respect—otherwise, they wouldn't live in California. Faith had observed this regional chauvinism in Charley, and other Alefordians, on numerous occasions. New York City was the worst. Make no mistake about that, but L.A. was definitely in the running.

"No, I can't say I've seen anyone wandering around talking to lampposts. The only slightly maniacal outburst was an eight-year-old girl's, and she's merely spoiled." Faith then gave Charley an account of Caresse's temper tantrum, which was accompanied by noises from Amy's room, indicating she was up and ready for company. The first soft babbles became increasingly puzzled syllables, then finally insistent crying as Faith ignored her—hoping to finish the story before tending to her child.

"Get the baby, Faith, before she blows a gasket. I have to check in at the station and see what's going on there before I head over to the Marriott."

Amy's cries had become one long antiphony.

"But I still have so many questions. At least tell me if the fire was set or an accident."

"You have questions! Some things never change."

*In **The Body in the Basement,** Faith's best friend, Pix, is irritated when she checks on the Fairchilds' new summer home and realizes the contractors haven't even begun—there's nothing there but a foundation! And there's something wrong with the foundation . . . something very dead . . .*

Pix called to the dogs. Dusty and Henry came running from the woods, barking happy doggy greetings as if they had been crossing the country for months, desperately trying to find their people. But the third dog did not emerge from the greenery.

"Artie! Artie! Arthur Miller! Come now! Do you see him, Samantha?"

"No, but he can't be far. He never strays from the others."

Pix found him immediately. "Oh, naughty, naughty dog!"

Artie was down in the cellar hole, digging furiously. He glanced up at the sound of his mistress's voice, then went back to his work.

"What is he doing? He must have found an animal bone."

Pix jumped in, landing on the soft earth. She went over to the dog and grabbed his collar. "Stop it this instant!" As she pulled the dog away, she noticed that what he had unearthed was not a bone, but a piece of fabric.

"Samantha, look what Artie's found. I think it's part of an old quilt."

"I'll get something to dig with."

"It's probably in tatters. Remember the beautiful Dresden Plate quilt I saw in the back of Sonny Prescott's pickup? He was using it to pile logs on, to keep the truck clean!"

"Here's a stick. It was all I could find."

Pix took it from her and scraped away the dirt. So far, the quilt seemed to be in good shape.

"It looks like a nice one. I love the red-and-white quilts," Sam said excitedly.

"Me, too." Pix crouched down and tugged at the cloth. "It's Drunkard's Path. I've always meant to do one, but sewing all those curves seems much harder than straight lines."

"Artie, sit!" The dog had come to her side, about to resume his labors. The other two were looking over the edge of the excavation, puzzled expressions on their faces. At least this was how Pix interpreted them, and she prided herself on knowing her dogs' moods.

"Look at Dusty and Henry. They're all confused. People aren't supposed to dig like this." Dirt was flying out behind her as she dug deeper. "You pull while I dig."

Samantha gave a yank and a large chunk of earth flew up, revealing more of the quilt. And as it unfolded, something else was exposed.

That something else was a human hand.

Something's rotten in the town of Aleford. In
The Body in the Bog, *the village's peace is
disturbed by the ubiquitous nemesis of rural
tranquillity—land development. Tensions run
high, culminating in a highly unpleasant death.
Faith wanted to campaign against the development, but she's even more eager to work against
murder . . .*

Faith loved to feed people, especially her family.
She sat close to him at the big round table that
was the gravitational center of the house—the
place where they ate most meals, the kids drew
pictures, and friends automatically headed. Faith
had religiously avoided anything suggesting either Colonial New England or neocountry in her
kitchen, opting instead for the sunny colors of the
south of France and bright Souleido cotton prints
on the chairs and at the windows, with nary a
cow or pewter charger in sight.

"Now tell me everything," she demanded.

Tom's mouth was full and she waited impa-
tiently. Maybe she should have grilled him before
the sandwich.

"There's not a lot to tell," he said finally, and
seeing the look on her face, he put the sandwich
down for a moment. "Person or persons unknown killed her and left her in the fire. There's
no way of finding out whether she was setting the
fire or whether the fire was set to cover up the
murder."

"And nobody heard or saw anything?"

"Ed Ferguson, who lives next door, thinks he heard a car around eleven. He'd gotten up to pee, but he's not too sure about the time. It couldn't have been Margaret's car, because she didn't take it. She was on foot."

"Which seems to eliminate her as the arsonist. Surely she couldn't walk all the way from her house to Whipple Hill Road lugging a can of gas without attracting some notice. Plus, it's quite a distance."

"Not if you cut through the woods, which of course she probably did. And even if she walked down Main Street at that time of night, nobody would have been around to notice."

This was true. The woman could have been naked and on horseback without a single observer. And if she came through the woods, might she have hidden the gas in some thicket on one of her previous maneuvers?

"So whoever killed Margaret decided to pick up a brick and heave it through Lora's window for the hell of it on his or her way home?"

"It's not impossible. It's certainly complicated things, and if I were a murderer, that's what I would want to do."

"Any victims in mind?" her husband asked, scraping the last of the soup from his bowl.

"Well, you know what they say," Faith replied.

"What *do* they say?"

"You're much more likely to be done in by your spouse than by a random stranger."

"I've already been done in by mine. Now let's go to bed. The dishes can wait."

The decision was made even easier. Outside,

there was a sharp crack of thunder and the wind howled. All the lights went out and the parsonage fell silent. Hand in hand, they groped their way out of the kitchen, up the stairs, and didn't even bother with the flashlight prudently placed by the side of the bed.

*In **The Body in the Fjord,** Faith's best friend, Pix, and her mother, Ursula, are off to see the natural wonders of Norway—or at least that's their cover. In fact, Pix is undercover, joining the tour group from which an old family friend has disappeared without a trace ...*

"Why don't you wait here," Pix told her mother. "There's a bench by the door and you can keep an eye on Jan so he doesn't leave without me."

"What are you going to do?" her mother asked.

"Never mind. Just hurry. You can tell me later."

Pix went inside. It was crowded, but since everything was conveniently translated, she soon found the information booth.

She was about to approach the genial-looking man behind the counter when she realized she didn't have a plan, or much time. She'd simply have to bluster her way through.

"Excuse me, but isn't this the place where that poor young man was last seen? You know, the boy who drowned and has been in all the newspapers? They're saying his girlfriend had something to do with it. She was here, too, right?"

The man looked startled. Maybe he recognized Pix's attempt at a complete personality change for the phony one it was. Or perhaps it was the southern accent she'd unaccountably found herself assuming.

"Seen? No, no one saw them here."

"But I thought the papers said something about

282

Voss. This is Voss, isn't it?" she said with the unsure air of a tourist about to find out she might have joined the wrong group and should be in Stockholm instead.

"Yes, this is Voss," he told her patiently. Then, aware that she wasn't going to leave until she'd heard some detail about the sad case that she could use to impress her friends back home, he added, "They left a message here saying they were running away together to get married."

"How on earth could they leave a message if no one saw them?" Pix asked plaintively. Could this possibly work?

It did. "We got the message by phone. They were already someplace on the road."

Pix feigned excitement, which wasn't hard. Her first actual clue!

"And were you the one who spoke to the girl? What's her name? Karen? Something like that."

For a moment, the man seemed to succumb to Pix's blandishments. He would be quoted someplace in the United States. He wondered if she lived near Minnesota and knew his cousin. "It wasn't Kari—that's her name. It was the man, Erik. He just told me to write the message down for the Scandie Sights tour guides who would be arriving by bus to take the train to Bergen."

"I never dreamed that things like this could happen in Norway." Pix as Blanche DuBois continued: "It's such a calm and happy place. People are so kind."

"Sad things can happen anywhere," he told her solemnly. He was so nice, Pix felt a twinge of guilt as she thanked him, said good-bye, and raced for the door. She didn't want to miss the bus. Or dinner.

*In **The Body in the Bookcase**, Faith pays a parish call on the town's librarian and finds the gentle old lady's house ransacked. A burglary ring has targeted peaceful Aleford, and no one is safe, especially when the crime spree turns deadly . . .*

There was still no answer. She must be out for a walk, Faith thought, feeling glad that Sarah had recovered. She'd probably gone to the library or down the street to Castle Park, a small green area kept trimmed and tidy, where children sledded in the winter and people brought their lunches at other times of the year. Faith was tempted to keep walking in that direction and see if Sarah was there, sitting in the sun at one of the picnic tables. But she might have taken another direction. Faith let the knocker fall one last time, then decided to go around to the rear and leave the basket in the kitchen. The jam had her HAVE FAITH labels, so Sarah would know who had been there. She'd know anyway. Faith had left similar offerings in the past—in the same basket, which Sarah always conscientiously returned.

A path, faintly brushed with moss like the herringbone brick one in front, wound around the small house to the backyard. Several fruit trees were blooming and an ancient willow's long yellow-green branches drooped toward the ground.

No one in Aleford ever locked their back doors, and they often neglected the front entrances, as well. Faith knocked again at the rear for form's sake. Sarah would certainly have heard the front knocker from her kitchen. A discreet starched white curtain covered the door's window. Faith turned the knob, pushed the door open, and stepped in.

Stepped in and gasped.

The room had been completely ransacked. All the cupboards were open and the floor was strewn with broken crockery, as well as pots and pans. Drawers of utensils had been emptied. The pantry door was ajar and canisters of flour and sugar had been overturned, a sudden snowstorm on the well-scrubbed old linoleum. A kitchen chair lay on its side. Another stood below a high cabinet, its contents—roasting pans and cookie tins—in a jumble below.

Faith dropped the basket and started shouting, "Sarah! Sarah! It's Faith! Answer me! *Where are you?*"

*For her tenth Faith Fairchild mystery, Katherine
Hall Page goes back to Faith's beginnings. In **The
Body in the Big Apple**, it's the 1980's, and
young Faith Sibley is the up-and-coming caterer
at a party where she runs into an old school
friend, socialite Emma Stanstead. Hidden secrets
have come back to haunt Emma, and she begs her
friend Faith for help . . .*

Emma seemed to be having trouble beginning.
She sighed heavily, opened her purse, took out a
handkerchief, and blew her nose. After her tirade
about meetings, she hadn't said much as they
walked through the museum. Her steps did slow
as they passed the famous Christmas tree deco-
rated each year with the Met's collection of intri-
cately carved eighteenth-century Neapolitan
crèche figures. She'd murmured, "Remember?"
And Faith did. As little girls, the appearance of
the tree had marked the beginning of the holiday
season for them and they haunted the museum
until it appeared like magic. Each had a favorite
ornament. Emma's was an angel with rainbow
wings and trailing silken gold robes; Faith's one
of the three kings, in royal robes astride a magnificent white horse. Emma's single word had reminded Faith how much time they had spent
together and how much they had shared.

It was time for Emma to start sharing now.
With one job tonight and two on Saturday, Faith

couldn't sit around watching her friend get a cold.

"Okay, what's going on? Much as I love seeing you—and it's ridiculous that we've been so out of touch—I do have—"

"I'm being blackmailed, Faith," Emma said quietly, handing her an envelope. It looked like the one she'd been holding at the party. "One of the other guests found this in the hall last night and gave it to me. He must have thought I'd dropped it. Of course, I'd never seen it before."

Emma being blackmailed! Faith had rehearsed a number of scenarios for this tell-all rendezvous, most of them involving a philandering husband or Emma herself in love with another, but blackmail! This didn't happen to people Faith knew. This didn't happen to people her age, for that matter. Blackmail was old guys caught with their pants down or hands in the till or whatever.

Faith took the card gingerly. She had some notion that they should be preserving prints for the police. She also felt a primal repulsion—who knew where it has been?